Ana fr

She heard Ian's unspoken message—the potential that there were things she might want him to do. His eyes told her as much, seeing her absorb the meaning, confirming it—smiling just there at the corner of his mouth.

Run away. Run fast.

Run to safety, where the flush of her awareness wouldn't expand into a flush of wanting—of wondering what it would be like to be touched by such strength and consideration. As if this man might just give back as much as he received.

Ana took a sharp breath, using it to slap herself back to reality. There would be no running, no matter how smart it would be.

Doranna Durgin spent her childhood filling notebooks first with stories and art, and then with novels. She now has over fifteen novels spanning an array of eclectic genres, including paranormal romance, on the shelves. When she's not writing, Doranna builds web pages, enjoys photography and works with horses and dogs. You can find a complete list of her titles at doranna.net.

Books by Doranna Durgin

Harlequin Nocturne

Sentinels Series

Sentinels: Leopard Enchanted
Sentinels: Alpha Rising
Sentinels: Lynx Destiny
Sentinels: Kodiak Chained
Sentinels: Tiger Bound
Sentinels: Wolf Hunt
Sentinels: Lion Heart
Sentinels: Jaguar Night

Claimed by the Demon
Taming the Demon

Visit the Author Profile page
at Harlequin.com for more titles

SENTINELS: LEOPARD ENCHANTED

DORANNA DURGIN

If you purchased this book without a cover you should be aware that this book is stolen property. It was reported as "unsold and destroyed" to the publisher, and neither the author nor the publisher has received any payment for this "stripped book."

Recycling programs for this product may not exist in your area.

ISBN-13: 978-0-373-00950-3

Sentinels: Leopard Enchanted

Copyright © 2015 by Doranna Durgin

All rights reserved. Except for use in any review, the reproduction or utilization of this work in whole or in part in any form by any electronic, mechanical or other means, now known or hereinafter invented, including xerography, photocopying and recording, or in any information storage or retrieval system, is forbidden without the written permission of the publisher, Harlequin Enterprises Limited, 225 Duncan Mill Road, Don Mills, Ontario M3B 3K9, Canada.

This is a work of fiction. Names, characters, places and incidents are either the product of the author's imagination or are used fictitiously, and any resemblance to actual persons, living or dead, business establishments, events or locales is entirely coincidental.

This edition published by arrangement with Harlequin Books S.A.

For questions and comments about the quality of this book, please contact us at CustomerService@Harlequin.com.

® and TM are trademarks of Harlequin Enterprises Limited or its corporate affiliates. Trademarks indicated with ® are registered in the United States Patent and Trademark Office, the Canadian Intellectual Property Office and in other countries.

Printed in U.S.A.

Dear Reader,

So often, our lives have a kind of unacknowledged duality about them. We're complicated beings. We can love someone and still be furious at them; we can struggle to understand someone else and still want the best for them. We quietly juggle these small conflicts in the privacy of our own thoughts, sometimes not even acknowledging that they exist—or that even while in conflict, both things can still be perfectly true.

Ana Dikau doesn't have the option of struggling privately with her dualities. She's an Atrum Core operative who finds herself irrevocably in love with a Sentinel she's been taught to fear—and she's still deeply committed to her life's work even as she learns that the Core might just be a worse enemy than those the organization reviles. Ian Scott finds himself equally attracted to the woman who ultimately betrays him. Together, theirs is a journey of acceptance and unflinching honesty...and a love that prevails. I hope you enjoy it!

Happy reading!

Doranna

The Sentinels

Long ago and far away, in Roman/Gaulish days, one woman had a tumultuous life—she fell in love with a druid, by whom she had a son. The man was killed by Romans. She was subsequently taken into the household of a Roman, who fathered her second son. The druid's son turned out to be a man of many talents, including the occasional ability to shape-shift into a wild boar, albeit at great cost.

The woman's younger son, who considered himself superior in all ways, had none of these earthly powers and went hunting to find ways to be impressive and acquire power. He justified his various activities by claiming he needed to protect the area from his brother, who had too much power to go unchecked...but in the end, it was his brother's family who grew into the Vigilia, now known as the Sentinels, while the younger son founded what turned into the vile Atrum Core...

Prologue

Ana Dikau saw him before anyone else did.

The rest of the Atrum Core team crouched behind a camo blind in the pines uphill of the narrow, rocky trail, watching the camera feeds on a laptop encased in a rugged military shell. The wireless cameras pointed down along the trail, one of the less popular tracts of New Mexico's high, looming Sangre de Cristo mountains.

But Ana watched the trail itself, and she saw Ian Scott first—a shock of bright silvered hair, long and spiky and pretty much unreal in the perfection of its fall across his forehead. Crazy lean features and cheekbones to match his jaw, a rangy body to match his face, and a way of moving that made her feel quiet and small and very much like prey—a flush of warmth and awareness.

Then again, she had practice at feeling like prey. And she was far too aware of this man's Sentinel nature. The fact that he was so much more than human.

Snow leopard.

Walking into an Atrum Core trap.

Not to capture him—they knew better than that. There were far too many strictures between the Core septs prince and the Sentinel consul, between their factions as a whole. Direct action meant trouble. Even indirect action such as that they were about to undertake…

It was risky.

So they were hedging their bets. Filming this staged encounter to justify their need for action.

Ana's new assignment.

She'd long begged for this opportunity, a mission that would prove her worthy of more than her usual personal assistant work for Hollender Lerche, her supervisor since she'd been transferred to active Core duty at the tender age of thirteen.

Ian Scott bounded a few effortless steps uphill to clear a scattering of hard-edged rocks embedded in the trail, and she drew a deep, sharp breath—holding it, all unaware, until her lungs ached. He was beautiful in an uncivilized way, muscle and lean form perfectly evident under a casual shirt and the dark gray cargo pants riding low on his hips, shaping the strong curve of his bottom.

He was the enemy.

The team leader murmured into his field mike, "You're on." She didn't know his name. It didn't matter; she hadn't expected the courtesy of an introduction. All that mattered was what came next.

The mountain lion, barely caged just down the trail from their position.

The animal had been caged for days, starved and prodded into a frenzy. The hiker was one of their own, a man familiar to Ana who was working off a disgraceful failure—and he was already scented with blood and mountain lion urine.

Ana wasn't sure he knew it, though.

The mountain lion knew.

Freed, the beast didn't hesitate. It charged onto the trail in a snarling blur of tawny motion, claws already reaching to bat the man down.

The big cat screamed and the man screamed with it—a bloodcurdling thing with all the authenticity the team could have wanted. Convincing, because the man hadn't known these details of his work.

"Here we go," murmured the team leader. "Watch the bastard."

Ana watched, all right. Scott didn't hesitate. He sprinted forward as man, all coiled strength and energy, and then leaped—a dive, as if he intended to take cover in the scrub of the pine-shaded mountainside.

Instead he dove into a blinding roil of lightning and sharded energy, and when he emerged from the thick of it he landed on the two massive front paws of a snow leopard. Lush white fur splashed with black spots, staggering blue eyes, a thick length of tail—Ana held her breath again. He leaped forward almost before he'd fully found his feet in that form—smaller than the mountain lion but never hesitating.

Ana's handlers had said that the Sentinels looked for any excuse to unleash their violent natures.

He blindsided the mountain lion, latching on with claws and teeth so the two animals rolled off the hiker and right down the steep slope, spitting and snarling and breaking brush along the way. Fierce growls rose from below, and the mountain lion's angry scream split the air.

Ana strained forward as if she'd be able to see; the

team leader's hand closed around her arm in a harsh and warning grip. She wanted to tell him she wasn't so stupid as to risk their cover, but she bit her lip and kept her words inside. She couldn't afford to be blamed for anything that went wrong, even an errant whisper—no matter that this man had already broken their silence.

The hiker rolled to his feet, stunned and unsteady—and marked with fresh blood, but remarkably unharmed in the wake of Scott's swift reaction. He staggered on up the trail to rendezvous with the other half of the Core team, where they'd dig in out of sight until Ian Scott had moved on, protected with the same silent amulets that hid this camo blind.

The conflict below broke away into a few hissing spits, and then the sound of running retreat—and the quieter sounds of one of the animals returning, his footfalls more deliberate and almost silent. Ana watched the trail, waiting to see which of the big cats would emerge.

Not that there was any doubt. The mountain lion had been weakened, and Ian Scott was more than animal and more than human. Utterly beast, too dangerous to live unfettered.

The leader's hand closed more tightly around Ana's arm. "The team will finish recording. He'll be looking for trouble when he gets back up here."

She resisted his pull. "This is why I'm here," she said. "To see this. To see *him*. So I know what I'm up against." It was, in fact, the purpose behind this entire operation, although the footage would also be used to study the enemy in a way they'd never accomplished before. "I'm safe, as long as we're quiet." None of the Sentinels could detect the perfected silent amulets—not even Ian Scott, the Sentinel bane of many an amulet working.

The man made no effort to soften his derision—at

her, at the Sentinel. "You've seen enough to know he's not human—he's nowhere near human. And we can't risk you. We don't have the time to start over with this op."

Because they didn't have another woman in place to fill her role. Not because she mattered, personally. It shouldn't still sting, after all these years.

But it did.

So Ana allowed herself to be led away, doglegging back to pick up the trail in the direction from which the Sentinel had come. Eventually the team leader released her arm, and she forbore to rub away the marks his fingers had made.

She'd wanted to see Ian Scott again. She'd wanted to see more closely the look in his eye when he took himself back to human—to get a glimpse of what lay beneath. Without it, her mind's eye showed only his instant understanding of the mountain lion's attack, and his instant response to it. *Efficient ferocity.* And somehow, she could think only of the warm flush of her reaction, and the fact that if she'd been that hiker, she would have wanted someone coming to her rescue, too.

But then the team took her back to the Santa Fe mansion that served as the local Core installation, and she learned that Ian Scott had returned to the trail and bounded after the Core hiker with only one thing in mind.

To finish what the mountain lion had started.

Chapter 1

"*'Take a vacation,'* he said," Ian Scott grumbled, lifting free weights as he sat out in the gorgeous landscaping of the gorgeous Santa Fe property under the gorgeous blue skies in the gorgeous fall weather. "*'You'll like it,'* he said."

"You *could* like it." The woman's voice from the patio sounded anything but repentant for her eavesdropping.

Ian found her standing on the porch with her arms folded over her motherly shape, her expression a mix of affection and exasperation.

His own face held nothing but exasperation, he was certain of it. "He took away my team. My *computer*. My *tablet*. My *lab*!"

"Pfft." She made the noise with no sympathy at all. Her name was Fernie, and she ruled this retreat with nothing so overt as an iron fist. An iron spoon, perhaps.

With cookie batter on it. "That's what happens when you work yourself sick."

Ian's grumble grew closer to a growl. "Field Sentinels," he said distinctly, "don't get sick. And I wasn't." He hefted the dumbbell for a quick set of curls, proving the point.

"You," she said, just as pointedly, "were injured. And Nick Carter knows better than to let his people wear themselves down."

"Right," Ian said, switching the weights to his other arm. "Can't have that. Can't have people getting *tired* when there are lives to be saved."

His angry sarcasm was meant to drive her away. Instead she came down the three porch steps, past the towering, bloom-heavy hollyhocks and into the yard, her body language neither aggressive nor submissive—a woman with an extra touch of empathy who well knew the full-blooded Sentinels with whom she often worked.

Especially the cranky ones.

"Ian," she said, and the soft lines of her face held understanding, "you can't do it all. Maybe you can do most of it, but not *all*."

Something in his temper snapped; he felt the hard coil of it in his chest. "I don't have to do it *all*. I just have to do this one thing! *One* thing, to keep my friends safe!"

The best amulet tech in Brevis Southwest, and he still hadn't devised a defense against the Atrum Core's rarely detectable silent amulets—a failure that had cost them all dearly. Repeatedly. And which had given the Core time to devise other new deadly workings—while also leaving them vulnerable to new third-party interlopers, as of yet undefined in spite of their recent activity in the Southwest.

Fernie stood her ground. "That working is a fearful thing, no doubt. But the man who made it is dead now. You have time. And you've only been here a week."

He glared. "They have stockpiles of silent blanks. Sooner or later, they'll reproduce his work. And then the rest of us will die."

"Let it go for this moment," she said, quite steadily. "Don't you think that's why you're here?"

That hard spring coiled tighter. Ian left the weights on the ground and gave way to his leopard, letting the prowl of it come out in his movement—pacing away to the tall latilla coyote fence and back again, feeling the strength of four legs and solid big cat muscle lurking beneath his skin. Out and back again, thinking that although he could detect any normal amulet within a mile, identify its nature, even *trigger* it if he wanted, he still didn't have a thing on the silents.

Until Fernie said, in understanding admonishment, "Ian."

He snapped a look at her. Her eyes widened; she took a sharp breath. But she held her ground, because that's what she was here for. *"Ian."*

His snarl was as much acquiescence as temper. He paced onward…but tucked the leopard away.

Mostly.

"All right, Fernanda," he said, pausing by the fence. He found his fingers tapping against the rough, pinto bean bark of the hand-peeled latillas; he stilled them.

Maybe a run. Better than a hike up in the Sangre de Cristo trails, at least until he was certain the previous week's activity hadn't roused any interest. Strange that an aggressive mountain lion hadn't been reported.

The narrow Santa Fe River Park ran east-west before them, a riverbed greenway full of cottonwoods and trails. He drifted to the front of the compact yard, through the groomed pines to the thick old adobe wall—four feet near the open gate, stepped up to five feet and then six to meet the tall latilla poles at the corner; another group of stout blooming hollyhocks festooned the transition from adobe to the old fashioned poles. The rest of the fencing was just as idiosyncratic, done in stages to include a high adobe corner in the back and token rail fencing along the property line. Typical of these old Santa Fe properties, where bits and pieces had been added over time.

A dirt road stretched out before them, defining this barely developed privacy in the middle of Santa Fe. The Sangre de Cristo mountains loomed to the east, marching northward to Taos and Colorado—over fourteen thousand feet high, full of bear and cougar and pristine air, tall pines and craggy outcrops. Perfect for a snow leopard.

That had pretty much been the whole point. Nick Carter, Southwest Brevis Consul and definitely the boss of Ian, could have sent him to any one of the Sentinel retreats, from oceanside to low desert scrub. Instead he'd sent Ian from their Tucson base of operations into the high cool mountains for his snow leopard to love.

Ian had simply been too preoccupied with what he'd left behind to truly walk away from it.

Atrum Core bastards.

Two thousand years earlier, the strictures of their cold war with the Core hadn't been so important—not when druids held sway and Romans were trying to beat them down. Then, the Sentinels hadn't tried too terribly hard to hide their developing nature, their mandate to protect the Earth—and the Core hadn't even considered hiding their intent to gather power, ostensibly to make sure the Sentinels didn't get out of hand.

Mostly it had been seen as a power struggle between two half brothers—and maybe, mostly at the start it was.

But the Core turned to dark ways and corrupted energies to achieve its goal, and the Sentinels honed their skills—and the world changed around them until both factions were in agreement over the need to remain undetected. Their conflict went underground, a worldwide détente with certain understandings: no direct offensives, no breaking cover. Theirs would be a cold war.

Until the Core's most recent Southwest *drozhar* had gone rogue. Thanks to his silent amulets, too many Sentinels had been killed or wounded—especially the full-blooded field Sentinels. Those who took the shape of the other within.

Like Ian.

Atrum Core bastards.

"Go take a run," Fernie said, startling him. "You think I can't tell that you've gone off inside your head again?"

He growled at her.

She waved it away. "Go," she said. "Run. Think about something else." And she left him in the yard, returning to tend the cause of the yeasty sweetness wafting out into the yard.

What good was it to have a great growl when people ignored it? Ian propped his foot against the wall and retied his laces. *All right, Fernie. A run.*

But if he was distracted, he wasn't oblivious. He saw well enough that he was no longer quite alone. Never mind the male cyclist at the end of the road…the woman coming his way deserved plenty of attention.

She walked along the edge of the dirt and gravel with

a green cloth shopping bag tucked over one shoulder and a small leather shoulder bag over the other, wearing a lightweight blazer over a creamy shirt that shimmered with her movement and set off the olive tones of her skin. Her tidy jeans were more smart than casual, and they highlighted her every move. Even from here, he found his gaze drawn to the delicate set of Eurasian features, from the distinct tilt of her eyes to the defined elegance of her nose.

She hesitated several properties away, eyeing the typical adobe wall, gravel driveway and gate—and then, rejecting it, looked ahead to the next property. And finally to this one, where Ian leaned against the wall, watching her. She picked up her pace, walking with more purpose—no longer looking at house numbers, but at him.

All right, Fernie. First her, *then a run.*

Ana knew better than to assume anything about this man. She'd seen what he could do. She'd heard what he'd *done.*

The Core soldier playing the part of a hapless hiker on the mountain hadn't deserved to die. She'd known him. He'd been only moderately skilled and not as hard-edged as most, taking his punishments without complaint. He hadn't been nice to her, but he hadn't been cruel, either.

She approached Ian Scott with one hand hooked into the grocery bag strap and the other in her purse and on her pepper spray—and even so, she hesitated.

She thought she'd known what to expect. Not just from the week before, but because she'd seen head shots—the faintly lengthened nature of his canines in that often rueful smile, the pale and unruly nature of his hair, silver by nature and smudged with faint streaks of black. She should have been prepared for the impact of those pale gray eyes rimmed with black, and for the striking contrast of dark brows and dark lashes. *The snow leopard, coming through.* Not all of the Sentinels showed their other so strongly, but this man…

Even standing there, he had a physical grace. Even not as tall as some of the Core posse members, even not as brawny.

She thought she'd known.

But she hadn't been this close to him on the trail. So she hadn't really known at all.

It took everything she had to offer him a steady smile. "Hi," she said, taking advantage of an opportunity she hadn't expected when she'd set out to survey this Sentinel retreat in person. "I'm so embarrassed, but when I left my rental this morning I didn't realize how similar these yards are—"

"And they aren't well numbered," he finished for her, as polite as any man should be, but his eyes…never to be mistaken for anything but a predator's eyes. His muscles ran strong and well-defined beneath a bright red sport shirt, his shoulders wide and body lean. Just as it had the week before, her body flushed with the awareness of what he was.

She swallowed her reaction, nodding to the drive beyond this one. "It might be that one. I'd recognize it if I went back for a look. But I don't want to intrude."

"I'll come with you, if you'd like," he said. "As long as you don't taze me." Those eyes flicked to her purse.

She lifted her hand from it. "Pepper spray," she said without apology.

"Of course, pepper spray." He said it amiably enough. "I wouldn't worry too much about intruding. That driveway goes to a cluster of rentals. You won't be the first person to look around."

It was, she realized with surprise, his way of politely giving her space to move along on her own. For that instant, it flummoxed her; she was unused to such courtesy. Something fluttered in her chest, and she thought it might have been regret.

But in the next moment she jerked back, stumbling as his expression changed entirely—turning feral and predatory and triggering the fear that not only came of knowing what he was, but of *seeing* it in him. *Oh, God he's going to—*

And he did, planting his hands on the wall to leap over it in one smooth—

The blow came from behind, so suddenly she had no warning—just the impact, the wrenching twist of her shoulder, and her instinctive grab at her purse. She scraped against the adobe, losing the purse after all—and only then seeing the cyclist behind her.

Ian came over the wall feet first. The cyclist went flying, the bike went flying, the purse went flying…

Ian landed on his feet.

The cyclist scrambled up and away and somehow thought he would make it. Even Ana knew better, dazed and clinging to the wall—and stunned all over again by Ian's speed as he pounced. She winced in anticipation as he landed on the man, poised for a fierce blow—and then slowly relaxed as he drew himself up short, one knee on the man's chest, his knuckles resting at the man's throat in an aborted strike that would have been fatal.

"Bad move," he told the man. If he was breathing hard, Ana couldn't see it.

But she could see the man's face. And she knew him.

The shock of it piled on to the shock of the attack and kept her pinned to the wall, struggling to understand.

He was Core, she was sure of it. She couldn't fathom it. Why would Lerche seek to sabotage the assignment he'd given her?

She came back to her wits as Ian Scott scooped her purse from the ground. Her attacker pedaled wildly away, not quite steady on the bike.

"What—?" she said, far too nonsensically.

"You okay?" Ian said, and held out the purse.

"Yes, I—" She rubbed her arm, taking the purse to fumble for her phone. "I should call the police—" Not because she truly thought it best, but because she thought it was the thing to say.

He sidestepped the matter—no surprise. Sentinels eschewed official notice as much as the Core. "I'd rather offer to see you home again. You have any idea why that guy would be targeting you?"

For the moment, she forgot her script. "What do you mean, *targeting* me?"

"He's been lurking at the end of the street, watching you."

Ah. She understood now. Someone hadn't trusted her to get this job done on her own…and then hadn't trusted her enough to let her in on the plan. She groped for words that would ring true. "I can't imagine it was personal."

"Didn't smell like coincidence," he said, his fingers tapping lightly against the wall. Surely the man sat still every once in a while. "It smelled like—" He stopped himself.

She had the sudden understanding that he spoke literally, and she remembered again who this man was—no matter his charismatic presence or his beautiful eyes.

He was Sentinel, and he was the Southwest's best amulet specialist. If the Core had sent out a posse member who carried amulets…

Even Ana could sometimes perceive the regular amulets, like a stain in the air. Many Core members couldn't, and it wasn't considered a necessary skill. But of course he'd know, and far better than she would. And of course he'd want to avoid the cops. The Sentinels and the Core kept their encounters off the books.

"You're probably right," he said, making an obvious choice to relinquish control of the conversation. "Coincidence." He bent to pick up her groceries, scattered as they were from the encounter, and appropriated the bag so he could reload them. "You're all scraped up. Come on inside, we'll get you fixed up."

She hesitated a moment too long. He added, "Fernie is inside, too. She'll slap my hands if I do anything you don't want me to."

For that moment, she froze. She heard the unspoken message there—the potential that there were things she might *want* him to do. His eyes told her as much, seeing her absorb the meaning, confirming it—smiling just there at the corner of his mouth.

Run away. Run fast.

Run to safety, where the flush of her awareness wouldn't expand into a flush of wanting—of wondering what it would be like to be touched by such strength and consideration. As if this man might just give back as much as he received.

She took a sharp breath, using it to slap herself back to reality. There would be no running, no matter how smart it would be. Because getting inside the house had been part of her assignment all along.

Get inside the house. Plant the silent amulet.

And maybe, finally, she would gain not only the respect and belonging she longed for, but also the safety that came with it.

Chapter 2

Hollender Lerche hated adobe.

He hated flat roofs and stucco and chunky viga pine columns and pretentious entry arches, and he hated a high altitude climate that thought it could be desert and yet still had far too much snow in the winter.

Still, he should be grateful. Many from Tucson had died during the illicit attack on the Sentinels; others had acted too publicly and paid the price at the hands of the worldwide septs prince.

In the wake of that attack, Lerche had merely been assigned to this small city—an annoyingly artsy place that had persistently remained the region's capital city. He didn't have to be told that his future rested on his quiet success. The septs prince would turn a blind eye to certain events as long as they brought results—but not for an instant if they brought more embarrassment.

For now, results meant taking out Ian Scott.

A man who had so conveniently ambled into Lerche's new territory, leading him straight to the quaint little retreat property—and to opportunity.

Lerche looked out onto the rolling piñon and juniper foothills of the Sangre de Cristo mountains and narrowed his eyes as if that spearing glare could blast the high grasslands into something more palatable. When someone rapped politely on the sliding glass door behind him, he ignored them. This second-story patio was his *Do Not Disturb* zone.

But eventually he left the squintingly bright sunshine of the morning and returned to the oppressive gloom of thick textured walls. The man inside greeted him with an unusual combination of resentment and defiance.

"Mr. Budian," Lerche said, which meant many things at once—a greeting, a demand for a report…a demand for explanation.

David Budian stood before him not in the neat suit of an active posse member or the dark slacks and shirt also allowed those working strenuous field positions. Nor was he the usual stature of such field agents—the classic deep olive skin and black hair, set off by silver studs and rings. Budian was a man of middling complexion, middling height, middling features.

None of that came as a surprise—the man's appearance was why Lerche assigned him to particular activities with particular anonymity. Even Ana, as naive as she was, would spot a man of brawn and classic full-blooded complexion.

But it surprised him to see Budian in torn clothes and bruises.

Lerche said, "Have you compromised us, Mr. Budian?"

Budian looked as alarmed as he should. *"Drozhar—"*

"Don't suck up." *Drozhar* was a term held by regional princes, as well as the world septs Prince. Not a posse leader. Not even when the posse was as large as the one Lerche now commanded here in Santa Fe. "I want to know what's happened!"

"I observed Ana as ordered. She was dawdling, so I provided an opportunity for her." Budian's self-satisfaction made it to his face in a way he likely didn't realize. "You know how those Sentinels are, sir. If they see a chance to meddle, they'll take it."

Lerche sat at his massive desk, relaxing into the padded chair. He brushed his hand across the black gleam of the surface, displacing invisible dust motes. "True enough. Did you achieve results?"

"I gave him a chance to play the hero and he took it. If that little dirt-bred bitch can't make something of it, then she's as hopeless as I think she is."

"Mind your tongue, Mr. Budian." Lerche's words held no heat; it went against everyone's instincts to use a woman in an important field operation. But Ana was everything they needed—petite, beautiful with an elegant delicacy and utterly determined to prove her worth to them…without the faintest idea that she never could. "She knows nothing of that thin Sentinel heritage, and I want it to stay that way."

"Until it's too late, you mean," Budian suggested.

Lerche smiled. "Exactly so, Mr. Budian." And then he would be free of her. "Just exactly so."

Ana found herself sitting in cool Santa Fe comfort—saltillo floors and kitchen counters, hand-painted Talavera tiles set in the walls around the light switches and along the counter backsplash, gauzy curtains under shaded windows. The air was redolent of spices and oils and the scent of something baking. Something *good.*

Ian had introduced himself, and Fernie—Fernanda—and had handed her a damp washcloth, disappearing with "Be right back."

Ana waited on a spindle-backed stool at the breakfast bar and patted the cool cloth against the road rash beneath her elbow, near to dizzy with the conflicting experiences of being in such a homey welcoming atmosphere while within the grasp of the enemy.

Especially an enemy who kept her on edge in every way.

Ian—the enemy—returned to the kitchen in a billow of what seemed to be his usual energy, dropping a tub of salve on the counter. "This stuff will speed the healing."

Fernie put a hot tray of muffins on the sideboard and sent Ian a disapproving frown. "A gentleman would help her take care of such awkward injuries."

"Oh," Ana protested. "You can hardly call them *injuries.* A few scrapes and bruises—fewer than that cyclist had, I'm sure."

Ian stepped back. "A gentleman respects the boundaries a lady sets." But his gaze met hers with amusement, as if they were somehow in this together.

She understood why. Fernie obviously ruled this house—a so-called *corporate retreat*—with an iron pot holder. Of medium stature, with a plump figure and shining strands of gray in her black hair, Fernie's Latina and Native heritage came through in both her features and the gentle roll of her words. Given Fernie's position here in the house, Ana guessed that she wasn't a full-blooded field Sentinel—one of those with roots deep enough to reach to their lurking *other* within.

Looking at Ian, Ana would never doubt it of him.

Even if she hadn't actually seen his snow leopard the week before.

But field Sentinel or not, Fernie was obviously formidable and just as obviously possessed of an uncanny ability to read beneath the emotional surface of those around her. She cleared her throat at Ian as she tapped the previous tray of muffins loose from the cups.

Ana pressed her lips together in a smile. "Well," she said, and offered Ian the washcloth, "maybe under the circumstances..."

"All right, then." He stopped tapping to whatever rhythm ran in his head to take the cloth. The same hands that had taken down the cyclist became surprisingly gentle as he turned her arm to see the scrape.

"Don't you ever sit still?" she asked, not truly having meant to say it.

Fernie laughed, placing a selection of muffins on a plate and sliding it within reach along with butter, a knife and napkins. "Not that anyone's observed so far. What brings you to Santa Fe, Ana?"

Oh, nothing of importance. Just spying on you.

"A quiet vacation," she said, in spite of the fact that she'd lived here for months now, along with the rest of Lerche's posse. They'd had no idea the retreat existed until Lerche had tracked Ian to it. "The Georgia O'Keeffe museum, the plaza, the pueblos, the Indian Market... I meant to come with a friend, but family issues cropped up." She shrugged, comfortable with the amiable cover story Lerche had given her. "It's a little strange to be here without a travel companion, I admit."

Fernie sent Ian a pointed glance. "You see? You *could* be doing something other than fretting. See the sights with this woman!"

Ian glared at Fernie, not Ana. "I do not *fret*," he said,

even as he dabbed her arm. "And I don't need mothering."

Fernie ran a trickle of water into the sink, briskly rinsing dishes before stashing them in the dishwasher. Ana only got a glimpse, but she was pretty sure the other woman smiled behind her noncommittal noise of response. And Ian, with his mix of annoyance and affection…

He wasn't what she'd expected. Even beyond what she'd seen and what she'd read.

She knew he'd been badly hurt in early spring but had healed well and quickly, as Sentinels did. She knew he'd had several skirmishes with the Core before that. She knew, most of all, that the Sentinels counted on him to solve the mystery of the silent amulets, and the Core therefore needed to find out everything they could about his progress—here, away from protected Southwest Brevis headquarters.

That was her job. To plant the spy amulet—to connect with him and absorb what she could of him in person.

"You're staring," he said, keeping his voice low—although Fernie had left to clatter around in the dining room, laying out silverware and dishes. He held her arm as he dipped into the herbal unguent and spread it lightly over her skin.

She shivered at the touch, bemused at her own sensitivity—at her sudden extreme awareness of his fingers against her skin. "I was thinking," she said—but stopped, caught by his eyes—the contrast of those pale irises with the dark rims, the dark lashes and glinting silver hair, mussed with the casual authority of a bad boy model even though she doubted he paid much attention to it at all. "Your eyes—"

His brows shot up; she looked away, profoundly embarrassed. She wasn't cut out for deception. *The Core should have known better.*

She'd never understood why they'd chosen her for this—she knew only that she was desperate for acceptance and that this had seemed like her chance. She decided on the truth, after all. For the moment. "They're striking," she said. "I'm sorry. I didn't mean to embarrass you. Or me. Maybe I hit that wall harder than I thought."

"Maybe," he said, applying a transparent film bandage of a size that few households would carry as a matter of course. "Or maybe it would just be nice to see this city with a companion." He smoothed the bandage into place, stroking her arm with a confident touch.

Maybe I should *run.*

She was in so far over her head.

She should plant the amulet under the counter edge, make her excuses and run. She should tell Lerche that Ian was so much more than she'd expected—much more than she could handle, a Sentinel force of nature. They expected her to fail; they'd always expected her to fail. It would come as no surprise to them if she did. She'd simply be sent back to the personal assistant work she found so very stifling.

But she hesitated there at the breakfast bar with his hand still closed over her arm, full of warmth and a very personal touch—and she noticed, to her surprise, that he stood perfectly still. He didn't vibrate; he didn't shift his weight or bump his knuckles against the granite counter.

He only watched her.

And she didn't want to run from that.

He grinned, an unrepentant expression on an irrepressible face. "Georgia O'Keeffe. Tomorrow, if you'd like. Now. How about we go figure out where you're staying?"

Ana smiled back at him. And when he turned away to toss the bandage wrappings and rinse the washcloth, she pressed the tiny silent spy amulet into place, activated it with the faintest twist of will, and told herself she was only doing what she had to do.

Ian paced the yard perimeter, rubbing a restless thumb across the sample amulet in his hand—a simple thing of rough making, and a thing with which he was already deeply familiar, even if he hadn't cracked the secrets of its silence.

That breakthrough wasn't likely to happen now, with his thoughts so scattered. Ana might have left the retreat the day before, but she'd definitely lingered in his thoughts.

Soft skin beneath his fingers, the gleam of honey beneath the brown of her eyes when she'd been caught staring, the faintest of blushes over cheek and neck when she'd realized it. The way she'd owned up to it, seeming surprised at herself while she was at it.

There was something about her matter-of-fact acceptance of her injuries that bothered him; he hadn't quite put his finger on it. They weren't serious, but they must have stung like the dickens. A little *ow!* wouldn't have been out of place.

Ian glanced down the road and decided he wasn't *quite* as bad as a kid with a schoolyard crush, no matter what Fernie had said. He'd dressed in the best of the casual clothes he'd brought, been glad for the lightweight hiking boots, and wandered out to the yard thirty minutes early for his meeting with Ana.

He'd figured it would take that long to settle his mind

over the working he thought he'd detected that morning. Now he knew himself to have been optimistic, and he paced the yard perimeter with impatience.

Just as well that he wasn't one of those Sentinels who could reach out to mind-tap Annorah, their brevis-wide communication hub. Or to anyone, for that matter, though he could hear well enough if someone else initiated a tap on his shoulder. No doubt he'd be driving her just as crazy as he was driving himself, checking in to see how things were going with his AmTech assistants—if they had what they needed, if they'd stumbled over any faint clue he might build on…

No doubt she'd be ignoring him by now.

The working on this crude amulet was innocuous enough—easily identified as such by the lanyard. Simple identifying knots, rough leather…nothing worth the silence that had been stamped on it. But this particular amulet had been recovered at Fabron Gausto's evil little hideout in Tucson, where Nick Carter had almost died in the attempt to stop *Core D'oíche*.

The thing's value lay not in its function but in its silent nature. Only the rare Sentinel tracker had any chance of perceiving this one.

Ian couldn't. In spite of his expertise, his ability to find and identify amulets at a distance, it was nothing but a disk of crudely inscribed bronze. No matter how tightly he focused his attention, nor how finely he sliced the bands of his perception.

He prowled back over into the shade. This morning in the house he'd thought he'd felt something from this amulet, but he wasn't the only one in occupancy, and that meant interruptions and noise. He shared the retreat and its half-dozen cozy little rooms with a light-blood couple from Kachina Valley, Arizona, a strong-blood courier from Senoita who quite obviously took the cheetah, a tech of some sort from Tucson Brevis and a midteen youth who couldn't more obviously be in retreat from the mundane world while he grew accustomed to his burgeoning Sentinel gifts.

The accumulated effect left him far, far from the buffered and isolated conditions of his lab. Trying to pin down the subtleties of what he'd felt had only served to trigger a headache, driving him outside to wait while he ignored Fernie's reminder that the whole point of his presence here was to take a break from such things.

The faintest sound of a footfall on sandy grit lifted his head from those inner thoughts. When Ana appeared over the wall some moments later, he was waiting, his mood lifted by an anticipation he hadn't expected. She caught sight of him and turned to rest her elbows on the wall. "Surely I'm not that late?"

"Not late at all," he told her, resolutely stuffing the amulet away. "But I'm not much good at sitting still."

"I got that impression." Her smile softened those dry words, lighting features that had seemed just a little too somber before she'd seen him. A delicately angular jaw, a sweet curve of a mouth, dark eyes that dominated her face…they lent her an air of mystery, the impression of strength and vulnerability that wasn't the least offset by the way the breeze teased her hair—short enough to reveal the peek of earlobe and the graceful sweep of her neck, long enough to tousle and beguile.

But he'd looked too long, for the smile faltered. Not so much uncertain as just a little too serious. "You know, I never asked. I thought at first this place was your home, and Fernie your housekeeper. But as I was leaving yesterday—"

"Jack came out." Lured by Fernie's muffins, no doubt, given how much the kid could eat.

"And I heard laughter from the lower level, so I gather you're not alone. Family?"

"In a manner of speaking." Ian told her the truth easily enough, if not the entirety of it. "This place is a retreat. Sometimes it's a think tank, and sometimes it's just a place our people come when they want the same thing you're here for—a quiet vacation."

She looked at the house a moment longer, a faint furrow between her brows. "Your people?"

"The group I work for." It was close enough. He laced his fingers between hers over the top of the wall and his thoughts stumbled, his equilibrium lost. For an instant he knew the stunning peace of having one focus and one focus only. *Ana.*

"Are you all right?" She let him keep her hand, but not without concern. "You look...distracted. Something's wrong?"

"The opposite," he told her, and captured that hand, too—did it without second thought, as though he had every right. Even the headache had lifted. "You ready to take in some Georgia O'Keeffe? It's a twenty-minute walk from here."

She didn't hide her bemusement. "Something tells me you'll enjoy that twenty minutes of motion more than the museum itself."

"I'll enjoy the company," he said, surprising himself by just how much he meant it. And she surprised him back, squeezing his hands in an unspoken response.

She might just have surprised herself, to judge by the look on her face—a little bit uncertain, a little bit amused. She glanced down the greenway path. "Would you like to just...walk?"

"I've got a better idea." He looked east toward the mountains—not thinking of the trail where he'd encountered the mountain lion, but a little south of it, where the scenic byway wound upward to Vista Grande through splashes of aspen gold. "If you don't mind a motorcycle, that is."

Her eyes widened faintly, pleasure behind them. Ian grinned at her, for the moment, not thinking of the silent amulets at all.

"I've never been on one," she warned him.

"It's a touring bike," he assured her, and then laughed when she only looked blankly in response. "It's comfortable. You'll feel secure. Though the retreat has a car—we can take that, if you'd prefer."

She lifted a brow. "What kind of car?"

He nodded at the side of the house, where the bright blue Smart car just barely peeked out. She eyed it and then leaned over the wall to also ostentatiously eye the length of his leg. "Maybe not."

Ian laughed. "Maybe not," he agreed. "Come on around. We've got a jacket you can use. It'll be cool up on the mountain."

The retreat had plenty of such little extras, and if the leather jacket was a little big on her, the sleeves shoved back well enough—and the biking gloves fit perfectly. He showed her how to secure the motorcycle helmet, threading the double-D rings and snapping the trailing strap, then stowed her purse in the saddlebags. A quick primer on mounting, the foot pegs, the muffler placement and how to be a neutral passenger, and they were ready to go.

By then Fernie had emerged from the kitchen, an unusual flush to her features and her smile looking a bit determined. She proffered a packed lunch, and while

Ian tucked it away and grabbed his own jacket, all black leather and zippers and snaps, Fernie leaned close to Ana as if Ian didn't have the ears of a Sentinel to hear every word. "You hang on tight, now."

Ana laughed—a faint uncertainty to it, but a low musical note, too, and one that tickled his ears.

Only once, after he'd mounted the bike and held it steady for her to settle in behind him, did she hesitate—and then, only just for a moment. Long enough to touch the pocket of her dark slacks, and he guessed she had her phone there—although reception on the mountain road would be touch and go at best. Then she climbed on, placing herself precisely on the seat and her feet on the passenger pegs, her legs barely brushing the outside of his hips and her hands resting loosely just above them.

"The trick is not to think too hard about it," he told her, briefly resting a hand on the side of her lower leg. "And just nudge my shoulder if you need anything. I'll pull over."

"What are you waiting for?" she demanded.

He laughed and started the bike—and if she clutched tightly at him on the first turn and made him fight to keep the bike on line at the second turn, by the time they eased out of town and through the expensive foothills real estate, she'd started to relax. By the time they'd climbed through the piñon-juniper to the ponderosa, swooping gently through the curves and ever climbing upward, her hands rested around his waist as though they'd always been there, her knees snug at his hips without tension.

She shifted only slightly, never interfering with their balance, as he pointed out the things he spotted along the ride—the ferruginous hawk perched off the side of the road, the amazing tower of an ancient pine. He slowed down for the scatter of elk in the trees, giving her a good look and grinning when her hands tightened in the thrill of spotting them.

And along the way, he found himself just as relaxed as she was—just as willing to go along with the moment, without the constant nag of activity in his mind.

Huh.

Sixteen miles later he pulled over at the Vista Grande overlook, bracing the bike while she dismounted, her hands suddenly self-conscious as she steadied herself on his shoulder. He felt the distance like a cold chill, the descent of cares and the weighty awareness of…

Everything.

She fumbled at the helmet strap but managed it, pulling the helmet off to fluff up her hair. Then she got a good look at the view and faltered, her eyes widening.

"The Jemez Mountains," he said, hooking his helmet over a handlebar as he dismounted and moving up behind her to point out the distant range, his arm over her shoulder where it felt like it belonged. "The Rio Grande Valley. Albuquerque, if you squint." Not to mention the swatches of golden aspen against the dark green of the predominant ponderosa pines, Sangre de Cristo fall drama in all its glory.

She leaned back into him; maybe she didn't even realize it.

Ian realized it. Boy, did he realize it. He cleared his throat. "There are a handful of trails leading out from this overlook—including one that goes into the Pecos wilderness." He nodded eastward, and her hair tickled his chin. "If you'd like—if you have some hiking shoes—we can come again, and hike out into the aspens."

A car drove past, slowing for the overlook…not stopping. When the sound of its motor no longer hummed among the trees, Ana pulled away from him—turning to face him, her hand touching her pocket as if it steadied her…her expression a little wary.

"Why?" she said.

He grew still inside, understanding the danger of taking this question lightly. "Because it's beautiful, and I'd like to share it with you."

She turned away, looking out over the sprawling vista of forest and valley and distant ranges rising anew.

Ian tapped a pattern against his thigh. "Hey," he said, resisting the impulse to close the space between them. "If I misread the situation, no worries. We drive back down the mountain, you head off to the rest of your vacation, and we still had a good ride together in amazing country."

He could hardly believe himself. Not when he wanted to—

Except it didn't matter what he wanted, if she *didn't*. And it wasn't as if he didn't have work to do, no matter his orders and Fernie looking over his shoulder. Until he cracked the secret of the silents, they were all at risk. *High* risk.

He hadn't come near to convincing himself when she said it again. *"Why?"*

This time, he realized what she was asking—but not before she turned to look at him, searching his expression as she added, "You don't even know me."

He suddenly felt off balance. "That's how it usually starts," he said. "By meeting. And liking. And wanting more." Who could *not*? And not just because of her delicate beauty, or the natural color of her lips against the glow of her complexion, or the way she wore that ill-fitting jacket that made it perfectly clear what curves lurked beneath—although his body responded to those things readily enough.

No, it was more about the complexity waiting behind her eyes, calling out the puzzle lover in Ian. One moment laughing, the next turned inward, and always—always—a shine of vulnerability. As if she simply waited for someone who could figure her out.

It was the way she made him feel. Moments of peace and inner quiet.

She must have seen something on his face. Her expression turned suddenly fierce. "I don't need saving from being alone, if that's what you think."

Ian made an impatient sound. "That's not what this is about." He closed the distance between them then, reaching out to cradle her head and thread his fingers through her hair—holding but not constraining, and watching her eyes go wide while her body stiffened inside the ridiculously large jacket.

But then she relaxed, those eyes still huge and not so much wary as uncertain—waiting. *Learning*, he would have said, as he leaned down to her. Her hands rose to brush against his forearms as if they didn't know what else to do, but her mouth…it rose to meet his. And when he kissed her, she kissed him back—a gentle thing, as uncertain as the rest of her could be.

He wooed her with that kiss, making it light and teasing, just a touch of tongue along her lips and a touch of nibbling tooth. Keeping it light in spite of the instant fire licking along his skin and settling heavily in his groin.

Maybe he trembled faintly—maybe it was just the breeze stirring her hair. Either way, Ian knew his limits, no matter how it surprised him to hit them so soon. He stroked the fine line of her cheekbones with his thumbs and lifted his mouth from hers, unbending himself into his full height.

Another car drove past, slowing dramatically until it moved past the vista. Ana closed her hands around his wrists, holding his hands where they cupped her head, and lifted her gaze to his—luminescent brown eyes that caught him as securely as the warmth of her fingers. "But how do you know this is what you want?"

He instantly sensed this wasn't about fishing for compliments. He hunted for truth.

"For sure?" he said. "You don't. You just believe. You feel, and you follow it. The rest either comes or it doesn't." He slid one hand around to the back of her neck and lifted slightly, changing her balance just enough so she stepped forward, bringing them together in the most unmistakable way. His other hand slid down to the small of her back, absorbing every inch of the curves along the way and stopping just above the round swell of her bottom.

No way would she miss all the evidence of his response to her, from the tension in his body to the distinct erection so uncomfortably trapped by his jeans.

She drew a sharp breath, and her hands tightened on his arms—at least until he laughed, just a short huff of amusement. "Breathe," he advised her, and brushed his cheek against hers. "If you faint, I'll never figure this out."

At that, she stepped back, brushing her hand over the pocket he'd decided held her phone. "Figure what out?"

"Whether you want me, too," he said as matter-of-factly as anyone could. "Because I don't want *yes.* I want *hell, yes.*"

Finally, she laughed. "Either way, we're not getting

back on that motorcycle until you're a little more *relaxed*, are we?"

"No," he said, and grinned. "We certainly are not."

She scraped windblown hair from her face. "You don't doubt yourself much, do you?"

He shrugged, his peripheral vision catching yet another car on approach. "All the time," he told her. "But I don't fear the doubt."

Failure was another story. He could sell her nightmares about failure.

"You know," she said, "you're right. You knew it, didn't you? Meeting. Liking. Wanting more. Yes, I'd love to go on a hike with you while I'm here. Yes, I *feel*...and I want to follow it."

This grin came along with a slow burn of warmth—a spot inside himself that made itself quiet long enough for him to feel the simple pleasure of the moment.

But damn, it didn't do a thing for his ability to hop back on that bike.

The approaching car slowed enough so he thought it might stop, then moved on. Gawkers, he decided, fully aware of the moment they'd interrupted.

At least, he thought it right up until he felt the unmistakable taint of a Core working. He turned sharply from Ana, eyes narrowing, body readying—for attack, for defense, for the challenge of identifying the working just as quickly as he could even if he had very little means to protect from it. His shields were only moderate and, without laboratory conditions and warding to enhance them, of only minimal use against a direct working.

Ana whirled to follow his attention, cuing from his body language—shrinking back, but also readying herself—a shift of balance, a grab for the jacket pocket where he'd be damned if she hadn't probably stashed that pepper spray. "What—?"

Late model midsize SUV, a dark metallic green. Driver, passenger and enough tint to the windows so he couldn't say anything else of them.

And then it was gone, and the car accelerated away just as any other sightseer might have done.

"Ian?"

He tried to stand down; he tried to convince himself he hadn't felt the working—a thing that had passed too quickly to identify it as anything other than a detection amulet. His fingers drummed a pattern against the side of his leg. He hadn't quite found the right words, his mind too full of their vulnerable position here on the mountainside, the ramifications of Core presence, the phone calls he should be making—when she rested a hand on his arm.

Silence.

He turned to her, startled by it—not quite able to respond to it.

"Are you all right?" Nothing uncertain in those brown eyes now, just concern, her arching eyebrows raised in question.

"I'm—" he said, and shook his head. "It's nothing." And maybe it wasn't. Maybe it was just as simple as sightseeing posse members with an alert working—one that would warn against Sentinel presence simply because some Core members were no more prepared to deal with Sentinels than a light-blood support tech wanted to deal directly with Core.

No wonder they had sped away, if that had been the case.

"Nothing," he told her again. "And I've got an idea. You, me, takeout of your choice and a movie at your place tonight." Not that he wouldn't gladly spend the whole day with her, hitting the Railyard artisans or Old Town or even the O'Keeffe museum—but he had the sudden impulse to check in with the lab and see if they'd made any progress without him, and to check in on Fernie, who in spite of her cheerful send-off, hadn't seemed quite herself today.

"Me, you, takeout and a movie at my place," she agreed. "And then… I guess we see."

Dammit. It was going to take forever before he could get on that motorcycle again.

Chapter 3

Ana closed the door behind Ian Scott and leaned against it with a sigh, still fully feeling the movement of his mouth over hers and the way it woke everything inside her. Pounding heart, warmth pooling in intimate places, the frisson of those faintly pointed canine teeth on her skin, her breath coming just a little bit fast.

Until reality hit, a blow that momentarily took her breath away altogether.

She wasn't here to *feel*. She was here to plant two amulets and gather information. Tonight, when he came back with takeout and his unsuspecting, habitually wry hint of a smile.

He is snow leopard, Ana Dikau. He is beast.

She slipped a hand into her front pocket, running her fingers over the tiny listening amulet she hadn't yet planted.

Because I'm doing well so far. Because I don't want

to risk blowing the operation if he finds it. Because he's more sensitive to such things than his dossier indicated he would be. The amulet-tainted car along the overlook road had told her that much.

It was all true. But she didn't know if such reasons would convince Hollender Lerche, a man with little patience for underperformance. And she *did* know that this was her one and only chance to prove herself to the organization that had never quite found her of value. Certainly never treated her as though she was of value.

If she could just do this one thing for them…

"Ana."

She jerked her hand out of her pocket with a guilty start. "Mr. Lerche! What are you doing here? Ian might have come inside—"

He emerged not from the great room of this modest vacation rental, but from her bedroom—dressed in his usual suit, heavy silver flashing at his ear and wrist and fingers, his skin a darker shade than hers and his features heavier. She flushed, a furious heat on her cheeks, but the look on his face silenced her, and then so did his words. "Surely not into the bedroom, Ana. *Woo* him, dearest. Don't *fuck* him."

She knew better than to respond. He didn't want her; he wanted only to claim and control her. To distress her, because it made him feel more than he was.

The problem was, knowing those things didn't change his status with regard to hers—and it didn't change his effect on her. The dread in her stomach, cold and hard and a little bit sick. The way she felt smaller and weaker. And the way just *once*, she wanted to feel as though she belonged in this society to which she'd been born.

Maybe if she tried harder. Maybe if she was stronger. Maybe if she didn't let her sentimental tendencies get in the way, as they always had. Then again, few women rose in the ranks, preferring the anonymity and protection of an early marriage. No man in the Atrum Core would touch another's spouse.

Now and then it occurred to Ana that it should be enough that a woman simply didn't want to be touched. But experience proved otherwise.

Certainly Hollender Lerche felt free enough to touch her—as he did now, grasping her jaw in a hard grip and then tightening his blunt fingers even further, bringing a sting of involuntary tears to Ana's eyes. "We need to talk, Ana."

"He'll be back in this evening for dinner." Desperate words, barely intelligible. And that's all she said, because suggesting that he not leave a mark would only invite him to hurt her in ways that wouldn't.

His grip didn't ease. "I'm not concerned about an hour from now. I'm concerned about *now.* And why you haven't activated the second amulet. The one that should be planted on your friend Ian Scott."

"How—" But Ana didn't finish the question. She squeezed her eyes closed in understanding. "The car. The working Ian felt. That was someone checking up on me?"

"An entirely necessary precaution, it would seem," he said, and gave her a little shake before releasing her with a disdainful flick of his fingers. He turned away, withdrawing a folded handkerchief from his pocket to wipe his fingers.

"But he's an AmTech. He *felt* it. He knows we're here—"

"That was always a risk." Lerche snapped the words. The modicum of security she'd gained at his distance evaporated. "Entirely on your shoulders, Ana dear. If you were trustworthy, we wouldn't have risked exposure. As it is, it seems we had good reason."

"I just need a little more time!" she cried, trying and failing to soften the resentment threading her plea. She scrambled to find the right words, hoping to distract him. "He's more sensitive about amulets than we thought—and besides, if I plant it on the wrong item of clothing, the amulet could sit in a closet for *days*."

"You're cozy enough with him," Lerche said, tucking the handkerchief away and squaring the lapels of his suit. "Carry the activated amulet on your person until you can make that decision."

But I—

This time she managed to keep the words to herself—a protest at her loss of privacy would not be well received. It might even make him realize that such concern had caused her to delay in the first place.

She'd wanted to talk to Ian Scott without being overheard. She'd wanted to connect with him her own way.

Although she'd never expected to *connect* with him at all. Or to relax behind him on the motorcycle, clasping his hips as if such closeness was a familiar thing, or to respond so strongly to his presence.

To his touch.

Snow leopard.

Surely she should have been frightened. More than just nervous and unfamiliar, but downright terrified of what he was and of what she'd seen him do.

Snow leopard.

And yet he'd been gentle with her. He'd been respectful. He'd been *careful.* And he'd allowed every decision to be hers.

Not that she'd truly had a choice. The Core demanded

of her to do this thing—to get close to him, to plant spy amulets on him, to learn of him what she could.

You could have said no. In her heart, she knew that. *No, don't kiss me. No, don't touch me that way.*

If she'd wanted.

Lerche's voice was a silky thing, all the more dangerous for it. "What are you thinking, my little Ana?"

"About the best way to do what you've asked." As if there was any other answer.

His hand flashed out to pat her cheek—nigh on close to a slap, and enough to rock her head, jarring her vision. "You betray yourself, Ana. I haven't *asked* you to do anything. I've *told* you what you'll do."

She covered her burning cheek. "Of course," she said, and hated that her voice wasn't quite steady. "I misspoke."

He eyed her coldly enough so she knew she wouldn't be forgiven that easily. "It's fortunate for you that we don't have the time to bring someone else up to speed on this operation. See that you do better this evening. Wear the amulet yourself until you have the opportunity to plant it to our advantage."

"Yes," she said, forcing herself to drop her hand and stand straight but not facing him directly. Not a hint of confrontational body language. "Of course I will."

He smiled in tight satisfaction. The kind of smile that said he knew he was better than she was, that he was entitled to more respect than she was, that he was in control of his own destiny in ways she would never be. "I'll be watching."

Only after he'd gone did she allow herself to explore her hot cheek and tender jaw, and wonder whether he'd gone so far that bruises would bloom beyond what she could hide with casual makeup.

First step, an ice pack. She dumped ice into a zipper storage bag and wrapped it in a thin towel, curling up on the couch while she did the things that would calm her—thinking only of the cool relief of the ice and soft cushions of the couch and the quiet of this place. Reminding herself what the Sentinels were and why she did this—and of how much of that Sentinel *other* she could see in Ian at any given time.

Of how easily he'd killed a man the week before.

But somehow, as she dozed off, her thoughts wandered back to the forest that week earlier when Ian had heard the hiker's peril. The way he'd bounded forward without hesitation. The way he'd flowed from one form to another, surrounded by a cloud of stunningly beautiful energies. How he'd done it for a *stranger*—and what would he do for one of his own?

What would it be like to be with someone who cared that much?

She didn't heed Lerche's voice in her head, so scornful that she'd already forgotten Ian's true reasons for what hadn't been a rescue at all—the excuse to turn loose his beast, a thing so fearsome that it had turned on the man he should have been saving.

She thought instead of being allowed choices, and of respect, and of how deeply he'd responded to her without the hint of a harsh touch.

She didn't mean to fall so completely asleep with Ian on her thoughts, but she did. She woke an hour later with her jaw stiff and her body humming in memory of gentle hands and skillful mouth. She froze, making sure of herself—*am I still alone?*

Silence. A clock ticking. A brief flurry of birds outside.

No, Lerche hadn't returned. Nor had anyone else

made themselves at home here. Slowly, she unwound from her dreams, from the sensations.

From the fantasy of being loved.

And then she drew herself up and headed to the kitchen, dumping the bag of melted ice in the sink and heading to the bathroom to freshen up. Her cheek was no longer red, and she thought it wouldn't bruise at all. Her jaw was a different story—pale impressions from Lerche's fingers with the bruising coming up between them.

She pulled out her makeup bag.

Ana had an hour before Ian arrived. It was long enough to ply her skills with powder and brush, and to dim the bright reflected sunshine of a late afternoon in the fall—angling the blinds, drawing the shades. She set the table so the remaining light would fall on his face and not hers, placing a half-full glass of iced tea as a casual claim to the correct seat.

She might not have worried at all. When she opened the door to him, take-out bags in hand, she found an entirely different man than the one with whom she'd spent the morning. This one looked worn and pale and pained, and just a little bit baffled. She instantly forgot her concerns about hiding her bruises. She even forgot her mixed feelings about putting herself in the hands of a Sentinel for the evening—one who had been perfectly appropriate during their very public afternoon ride, but who might now reveal another side of himself.

"Ian!" she said. "You look—" and then stopped herself. She'd learned that mentioning someone else's condition tended to draw scrutiny to herself, and she didn't want that.

Besides, "You look terrible" didn't seem like a great opening for the evening.

But Ian just laughed, low as it was. "I do look terrible," he said. "I'm not one for headaches, but—" He shook his head, most gingerly.

She relieved him of the sandwiches. "Are you sure you want to do this? We can do lunch tomorrow, if you'd like. Or dinner tomorrow evening."

"You're kidding, right?" Distracted as he was, his gaze still pinned her—an intense stare peering out from beneath a civilized veneer. "I can forget about the headache if you can."

She gestured him into the little rental house. "I'll draw the blinds—maybe we can find an old movie."

"Bogart?" Ian said, head tipped with interest. Even not at the top of his game, he exuded intelligent energy and restlessness—at least until he tripped over the threshold as he entered the house. "Whoa," he said. "Smooth."

"You're sure—"

"I'm sure," he told her. "Let's eat that food while it's fresh."

She took the bag to the table, pulling out cartons and filling the room with the yeasty scent of fresh bread and savory herbals. He wandered in after her as she set ice water before his place and closed the blinds a bit more, feeling more secure about her ability to hide the bruises as they settled in for the meal, full of the small talk of such moments. Plain old normal small talk from a man who wasn't quite normal at all, while Ana thought about the amulet in her pocket. The one she'd been commanded to invoke.

Ian clearly wasn't quite focused. He fumbled his fork in the salad, nearly knocked over the salad dressing, and seemed to find his thick, layered deli sandwich as much by feel as by sight.

"Have you considered seeing a doctor?" Only in retrospect did she realize that of course he wouldn't, because Sentinels never did go to mundane doctors—not the strong-blooded Sentinels, at any rate. They wouldn't be able to hide enough of their true nature.

"If things don't get better." Ian ran a thumb up and down the ice water as if, even now, he couldn't find a way to be still. "I don't get sick often. I'm probably not much of a patient."

Compared to the Core posse members who demanded that she wait on their every need even when they weren't sick, she thought he was doing just fine. But it interested her to see how close he skirted to telling her the full truth of his nature—that, in fact, he'd not come right out and lied to her. Of course a strong-blooded Sentinel wasn't used to being sick. Given the unnatural rate at which they healed, it would be a wonder if they ever were.

Ana herself had been blessed with a naturally quick rate of healing—or cursed with it, rather. It was one reason Lerche felt free to leave his mark on her. But she got sick as often as anyone else, with the same clusters of cold and flu and a stomach that could be touchy. She made sure she was always a very good patient, requiring as little from the Core physicians as she could. But she said merely, "If things don't get better, you probably should."

Ian caught himself rubbing his temple and gave a rueful laugh, if not much of one. "It's probably something going around." He didn't look convinced, and she wasn't surprised. Field Sentinels like Ian Scott didn't catch such things, even if the light-bloods did. "Fernie wasn't looking well this afternoon, either. I spent the afternoon in the kitchen, helping her clean up after one of her bake-fests."

Her fork hovered in midair as she tried to imagine it…and found that she could. Found that she could easily see this sharp-edged man putting aside his work to help the retreat manager on a tough afternoon.

She couldn't say the same for Hollender Lerche.

"Maybe I shouldn't have come," he said, mistaking her hesitation. "If it's catching—"

She laughed and speared the fork into her salad. If he noticed how carefully she'd been chewing, he didn't mention it. "If it's catching, then I think I've already got it, don't you?"

He grinned. "There's something to that." And then they talked quietly of favorite old movies while she pulled her laptop open and rented them a Bogart flick—*Key Largo*, of course—and Ian demonstrated that whatever the state of his headache, his casual mastery of tech also included hooking a laptop up to the house TV so they could watch on the larger screen. By the time they finished the last forkful of their cheesecake dessert, they shared the couch as if they'd always done so.

Only when Ana was fully nestled in under Ian's arm, her legs curled beneath her while he stretched the length of his out on to the kitchen chair he'd appropriated for that purpose, did she realize she hadn't yet invoked the second amulet—and that she didn't dare do it now, for fear he would sense it, no matter its silent nature.

It didn't matter. Surely Hollander Lerche wasn't interested in murmured chitchat over a classic movie. Surely he couldn't expect her to delve into a conversation of more substance until Ian was more comfortable with her—more confident with her.

Although he was, most obviously, comfortable and confident enough to fall asleep on her couch.

She realized it as the film credits began to roll. She drew back from beneath his arm to consider him in the flickering light of the television, pulling her feet up on the couch to wrap her arms around her legs and rest her chin on her knees. Knowing that she ought to be curled up on the other end of this couch, trembling in fear. And that she ought to trigger the amulet, shortening the time she was exposed to Ian and his entitled, arrogant ways.

He was, after all, a man who represented everything about a race of people who considered themselves *more than* and *better than* and quite evidently above the law altogether.

But Ian's touch had given her choice. Brought her pleasure. Inspired her napping dreams. Protected her from a mugger.

It startled her to realize that Lerche's man had known Ian would leap to her side when the cyclist grabbed at her—that he'd counted on it. She frowned, thinking that one through—or trying to. Instead, she found herself distracted by the way dark lashes swept a shadow across Ian's high, strong cheek. And by the way his mouth, in repose, relaxed to show the definition of lips that pleased her—their shape, the little hint of a curve at one side that revealed his habitual dry humor. The faint cleft in his chin, the unlikely perfection of the way silvered bangs scattered across his forehead, the equally unlikely short, dark hairs that defined his hairline at sideburns, nape and even buried beneath the lighter strands.

The movie credits ended and the sudden silence alerted him; she saw the glimmer of his awakening gaze and smiled. She felt the promise of that look and of his interest in her. She felt her body warming to awareness—not of the Sentinel, but of the man.

Then again, the Core had always considered her to be weak of heart and mind, hadn't they?

"Hey," she said, and even her quiet voice seemed loud in the house. "Feel better?"

He stretched—an indulgent thing, right down to his fingers—and relaxed utterly again. "Hey," he said. "Much better." But then his eyes narrowed, and for an instant she felt pinned by his gaze—she felt all the fluttering uncertainty she'd told herself she ought to. "Ana…are those bruises?"

"Bruises?" she said, sounding as stupid as she felt. How could he…darkness had fallen, and she hadn't turned on any lights. Only what came from the TV, where the bubbles from her laptop screen saver drifted over the surface. Between the makeup and the darkness, she should have been safe from questions about the marks Lerche had left.

"You didn't have those this morning." He no longer reclined, relaxed, but now sat straighter, tension filling his shoulders. He tapped a quick pattern against his leg and nodded at her jaw. "I should have seen them earlier, but that headache…"

Of course. Right. Because Sentinels had that vaunted night vision—a spillover from the beast they carried within. What had Lerche been thinking?

But Ana knew the answer to that question. He hadn't cared.

"Are they that bad?" She touched her jaw, and a wince gave her the answer. Still, she addressed the bigger elephant in the room. "I can't believe you can see them in this light."

"Just one of those things," he said, making no attempt to explain it—but not making anything up, either. "Ana, *who—*"

"I'm here alone," she told him, and realized with those words that she was the one who lied to him, who had lied to him from the moment they'd crossed paths. "It was just one of those stupid things."

He searched her face as if he might find the truth there.

Well, it *was* one of those stupid things. She knew better than to show disrespect to Hollender Lerche. That was on her, that she'd done so. But she also knew that sometimes Lerche's mood meant there was no avoiding his temper. That was on him.

Ian let it pass, in a way she thought meant he wasn't actually going to forget it. He rose to his feet, so fluidly she couldn't believe he'd been deeply ensconced in the couch an instant earlier, and prowled to the window—looking out into the darkness and seeing who knew what.

"You *are* feeling better," she said. "And I guess I have the answer to my question."

He turned his head just enough to offer a puzzled frown. "Which question is that?"

"The one where I wondered if you ever sat still," she said drily.

He laughed, short as it was. "No," he said. "Not often. When I sleep. And..." He gave her a thoughtful look, and quite obviously didn't finish the sentence.

"Oh, come on," she said, unclasping her hands from around her legs and letting her feet slide to the floor. "Now you've got to tell me. Even if it's embarrassing. *Especially* if."

He padded back to the couch; somewhere along the

way he'd lost his shoes, and the barefoot movement only added to the prowl in his walk.

He killed a man. I should be frightened.

But she wasn't.

She was *alive.*

Her fingers tingled as he reached down to offer his hand. She took it; her body pulsed as he drew her to her feet. Warmth suffused her, instilling just a hint of weakness in her knees—a delightfully liquid sensation.

"And now," he said, pulling her closer—not with so much strength she couldn't hold her own, but with enough ease to demonstrate the strength still lurking. He touched her face; he skimmed his fingers along her jaw so lightly that she felt only their presence and not the pain of the bruises beneath. "Now," he said, and kissed one eyelid, and then the next. *"Now,"* he added, and brought his mouth down on hers, kissing her with a gentle assertion—and kissing her, and *kissing* her, until she threaded her fingers through his hair and stood on her tiptoes to kiss him back, so caught up in the firm sensation of his lips, the tease of tongue and teeth, the impression of being…not taken, but *worshiped.*

He bent over her and she trusted. He dipped her as if they were in a dance, and she gave herself up to his strength. He settled her perfectly over the cushions of the couch, and she never stopped reaching for him.

She had no idea how much time passed before he groaned and drew back—and said, with no little wonder, "*Now.* I can't explain it… I never—"

She silenced him with boldness, slipping her hand inside his shirt to caress skin and feel it flutter beneath her fingertips, a sensitive flinch that came with a grin. She suggested, "Just feel…and follow it?"

He searched her eyes. For once she didn't feel like

the vulnerable one—not with the uncertainty she saw there, or his eyes gone so dark with what she'd done to him. Or *for* him. Definitely not with the hard tremble of his arms and body—a tremble that in no way came from weakness. "Is that what you want?"

Yes. Because what she felt right now was safe and enclosed and *accepted.* As if, in that moment, she was everything she needed to be.

How could she do anything other than follow that feeling?

"Yes," she said, surprised by the husky sound of her own voice. "Yes, please. Let's."

"Let's," he agreed, and laughed just a little—in relief, she thought. Not that she had much time to think about it. He lowered himself over her only enough so she could wrap her legs around him, ruing the impediment of clothing—and then surprised her when he slipped his hands more firmly beneath her and pivoted to sit, putting her squarely in his lap. Squarely against him and his quite obviously already straining erection.

Pleasure speared through her, startling her into a cry—one she'd not heard herself make before. And then when he moved against her, another, this one echoed by the faint snarl of Ian's expression—just as surprised as she was, his fingers clamping down on her hips.

Such a pure, hot lightning, striking so deeply within… Her fingers dug into his shoulders, gathering the material of his shirt—but only briefly, because the more she *felt,* the more she wanted to touch him. Fumbling at buttons, pushing the shirt back to expose the planes of his chest—a lean man's muscled body, layered in strength without bulk, crisp pale hair scattered to tease her fingers and fade across his abs to reappear in a narrow line above his belt.

As it had before, his skin twitched, more sensitive than she'd imagined. When she spread her fingers across his belly and went seeking beneath the belt, he made a disbelieving sort of sound, half laugh and half gasp, and rolled them over again. The soft couch cushions enveloped her just as he found her mouth. He kissed her with fiercely thorough attention, his fingers at her blouse buttons and then tangling with hers. He moved his mouth to her neck, nipping, as she reached for his belt, and he reached for her slacks button. She tugged his pants over his hips; he deftly yanked hers out from beneath her, his mouth still on her neck, on her collarbones, dipping lower to ignore her bra and find one nipple right through the soft material.

She bucked up against him and reveled in it—reveled in watching herself and her response to him. No man had evoked such response in her…no man had ever tried.

Ian laughed again, this time with a growl in the background. He lifted his head to capture her gaze, and she stilled under the impact of it—bright intensity, heated desire…

"Please," she told him, understanding the question behind that look. "Yes. Most definitely *yes*."

He drew a sharp breath—relief or fettered passion, she wasn't sure. But then she didn't want to wait any longer. She kicked her pants aside, shoving her panties off with them, and then went after his boxers. In a moment they were both free, both already warm and wet with the wanting, and she didn't think twice. She wrapped her legs around his hips and reveled in his unrestrained grunt of pleasure as flesh met flesh.

And then Ian surprised her all over again, flattening himself on her, muttering—grasping for his pants while the couch all but swallowed them both. He made a sound of triumph and emerged with a condom. She shared his breathless victory with a grin, and between the two of them they got the thing unwrapped and in place, and then *he* was in place again, and with a single nudge of adjustment, they slipped together.

Ana stopping thinking. She stopped being able to think. She barely realized it when Ian swung her upright again, thrusting upward as her knees sank into the couch cushions. *Pure hot lightning...* Ana reached for more of it, finding a rhythm with him, barely aware of her own cries. She shot straight through that pleasure to sensations she'd never even imagined, and found herself with a sudden new awareness.

His response to her. His gasps and his expression, cords of muscle straining in his neck and his face flushed, his eyes widening with the same sort of startled recognition that suffused her own body. An utter vulnerability that he seemed to fight against and lose to with every thrust, with every breath.

"Ian," she breathed, and it was a kind of plea, an understanding that she was in an unfamiliar place and didn't know where to go from there. His hand slid from her waist to cover her pubic hair, thumb sliding downward to touch her *just so.*

Lightning struck. She cried out in abandon and lost herself to it, a flood of sensation that tugged at her toes and filled her from the inside out, every muscle clenched or throbbing in the best possible way. She dimly heard Ian's shout, feeling the pulse of his release in a way that had never mattered before but now suddenly did. She opened her eyes just soon enough to see it on his face—ecstasy ripping right through him, laying him as bare as it had laid her.

That's when she understood, even as the final throb of pleasure ebbed through her body, leaving her limp in its wake.

Being with Ian wasn't just about seeing where things went or following along in an adventure or *feeling*, even pulling the most possible pleasure from it all.

It was about doing those things *together*.

Chapter 4

Ian gulped for air, reveling in the sensation of Ana's body draped over his. Not to mention the pulses of lingering pleasure and the distinct memory of her expression as orgasm had washed over her. His breathing steadied; his mind steadied.

Quiet. Replete.

A completely unfamiliar inner silence.

He floundered in it, uncertain—looking for some mental handhold, even if it brought him back to the plague of internal noise he couldn't remember being without.

She stirred, pushing off his chest to look at him with her face still flushed and now blushing on top of it, her hair a delightful disarray. "Oh, my God," she said, putting a hand over her mouth. "I… I *screamed*."

He smiled, finding his anchor in her expression. "Yeah," he said. "You did."

"I never—" She stopped herself. "I...*never*..."

It caught his attention. There was more here than the aftermath of great sex. *Stupendously great sex.* Even he knew that much, still floating in the physical satisfaction and silence. "What?"

"No, I—" She shook her head, looking around—bringing herself back to the details of what had happened. He knew what she'd see—scattered clothes, scattered couch cushions and a man she hadn't known all that long still lying beneath her.

He stopped her just before she would have removed herself from it all, his hands over her thighs—enough to encompass, not enough to force compliance—and asked it again. "What?"

She covered her face, only briefly, and then flipped her hair back. "I've never come with anyone before."

He frowned. "At the same time? Because technically, you beat me to that finish line."

She laughed, but it sounded sad. "No, I mean...when I've been *with* someone. Ever." She took a breath as he tried to absorb this. "I'm 'too hard to please.'"

He half sat, his hold on her legs keeping them just as together as they'd been. "*Who* said that? Because—" Then he stopped, suddenly aware of the depth of his reaction, his protective response. "Never mind. That's not what I want to say. But just so you know, whoever said that is obviously fucking nuts. Pardon me."

She laughed again, this time sounding as if, just possibly, she'd been freed from something. But she quickly turned uncertain. "Ian," she said. "Seriously. Is this how it should always be?"

"Babe," he told her, still awash in the aftermath of silence within himself, "*this* is how we always *wish* it would be. But it should always be good. A man makes certain of that."

Blessed, blessed silence...

She said, "I'll have to think about that."

"Don't," he said, and was a little hard pressed to explain when she raised a brow at him. "Think, I mean. Just stay here with me a little while longer. *Not thinking.*"

"Look who's talking. I got the impression that you never actually do stop thinking. I bet you run calculations in your sleep." But she smiled, relaxing the fraction that told him she'd stay. She made another attempt to tame her hair back and gave up on it, instead turning her attention to his chest—chasing whorls of hair with her fingertips and the edges of short, practical nails painted something faintly pink. His skin pebbled in response, all the way down to his balls; he twitched faintly inside her. She laughed, disbelief at the edge of it.

"Hey," he said, though he couldn't help but grin back at her. "It is what it is." Then, as she scraped the outside edge of a nipple, he shifted with a less lighthearted purpose. "But be merciful, if you would. I only brought the one condom."

She withdrew her hands entirely. "Oh. Well. In that case—" and then she laughed again at his dramatic groan. "Not everything requires a condom, I hear. And there are some things I've always wanted to try—"

Of course his body fairly leaped to attention, squirming here and stiffening there, and this time she laughed right out loud—and then laughed again at his ruefully self-aware expression. "That felt to me like you might just be interested."

"C'mere, babe," he growled, an exaggerated version of manly prowess. "I'll show you *interested.*"

And she had the audacity to *stretch*—right there, still sitting on top of him and surrounding him, the faint light painting the lines and curves of her body, all beauty and delicate grace. "Okay," she said, and her tone had changed. More than confident. *Eager.*

He could do eager. With this woman? God, yes, he could do eager. And in that moment, and in the next, and the one to follow, he barely even noticed the silence in his mind at all.

Morning brought bright sunshine and the faintest taste of a hangover.

Or what Ian thought a hangover might be. Given the speed at which a strong-blooded Sentinel metabolized alcohol, it took a concerted effort to feel the effects—both during and after. Ian had done the usual youthful experiment and then ceased to bother.

But he was pretty sure this would be it. The underlying throb encompassing his eyes, the uncertainty in his stomach. Leftovers from whatever had struck him the day before.

And that deserved some thought. Ian wasn't good at being sick because Sentinels generally *weren't.* So what had he gotten into, or what had gotten into him?

He stared at the back of his eyelids a moment longer, taking in the unfamiliar sounds and scents of his surroundings, and especially the unfamiliar light. A different window, east-facing, than the one he'd taken here at the retreat. And Fernie's kitchen smelled of sausage and egg in the morning, not just tea and toast.

Because this is Ana's place.

Whoa.

Since when did he fall asleep so soundly in a strange place? Since when did he actually sleep the night through in *any* place? He finished waking in a burst of motion, rolling up to his knees, tangling in covers, and altogether ready for anything.

A cup of tea awaited him by the side of the bed, still steaming. He scowled at it, instantly aware of the significance—that Ana had not only left without waking him, she'd come and gone again with the tea.

And here she was again—padding out from the bathroom in a minuscule robe, scrubbing a towel over her hair. Damp and fresh and smelling… He inhaled deeply in spite of himself. *Smelling like woman. Smelling like...*

His.

"Not a morning person?" she asked, draping the towel over one shoulder. Her hair was mussed in a way he wished he'd done, her cheeks flushed with the shower and her eyes bright with…amusement?

He realized he'd frozen in that ready-to-pounce yet totally hungover fashion, and looked down at himself. Wearing his boxers, tangled in her sheets, thoroughly unable to get his thoughts together. Nothing to do but shrug. "Generally I'm an everything person," he said. "Clearly that doesn't apply to today." With effort, he clambered out of the bed, straightening himself joint by joint, and reached for the tea. *Irish black, oh, thank you.*

The first sip finished waking him. When he lifted his head and caught a glimpse of the bathrobe hitting the floor, he went beyond awake and straight to alert. *Attentive.*

Ana reached into a drawer to extract a bra—faintly pink, like her nails, an underwire thing that would support the beauty he'd seen the night before. Modest in size but perfectly shaped, just ready for his hand or mouth. She gave a meaningful glance at his groin, where the boxers hid nothing. "I'd wondered if I wore you out, but I'm not sure that's possible."

"Not when I'm with you," he said, somewhat fervently. Another Sentinel blessing, that recovery time—but he couldn't talk to her about Sentinels. Only the think tank aspect of his work.

"Leftovers from whatever got into you last night, then," she suggested, stepping into panties with faint pink stripes.

Oh, hell. Yes. Exactly so. And not just him. No one had been feeling quite right at the retreat when he'd left. Ian floundered, caught completely behind in his own thoughts. Thoughts he would normally have worked on in pieces through the night, rising to wakefulness long enough to chew on them and then, if he was lucky, falling back to sleep. Either way, awakening in the morning with his thoughts spread out before him, ready for the day.

Not *this* day.

"I've got to go," he said, gulping half the remaining tea in one swallow and setting the mug aside. His pants must be here somewhere, right? "I need to check on Fernie. And the others."

She cocked her head, a stretchy bit of ribbed camisole in hand and her expression gone careful. Very, very careful. "Is this you running away?"

Because of course, he could call the retreat. Or he could assume that a house full of adults could manage minor illness without panic. She had no way of knowing that these particular adults were, like him, not used to managing illness at all. Or that anyone with even modestly strong blood did better with a Sentinel healer than they ever would with the average urgent care clinic.

"This is me taking care of my people," he assured

her, spotting the neat stack of his shirt and pants where she'd smoothed and folded them. He scooped them up, pulling them on in record time—and then stopped to regard her, scrubbing one hand through his thoroughly disheveled hair, across the scrape of his beard.

She'd tugged the camisole into place and now looked back at him with evident doubt, and he had to face the brutal truth of his off-balance morning. "Yeah," he said. "I can use some space while I'm at it. But not because I'm running away. Because..."

Because I wasn't expecting this. To be affected.

Oh, face it. To be reeling in the wake of her.

She'd put on a mask—the same face she'd worn when he'd first seen her. Unapproachable. Distant.

And, he now understood, self-protective.

She held her ground when he stepped up to her, and when he put a finger under her chin—lifting it slightly so the bruises along her jaw were beyond evident, and careful of them—careful of her. Biting back on fury to see them and knowing he'd find out what they were about when all was said and done, but that this moment wasn't the right one.

"Because," he said, "sometimes when you follow the feeling, you get far more than you ever expected. And if you want to do right by that, it takes a little space."

Something in that stiff expression eased, allowing him back in. "Yes," she said. "Okay. I can see that. I guess I can even feel some of it, this morning." She caught his gaze, held it—a hint of honey in the brown of her eye. "Just promise this—when it's time for you to walk away from us, be straight with me. Tell me you're going. Don't leave me wondering. Don't leave me *hopeful*."

The anger bubbled up again on her behalf. "Someone,

somewhere, has done very badly by you." He rested his hands on her shoulders. "Look, I may not always know what I'm doing. I might mess up. But I'll do it *honestly.* And we'll figure this out. By which I mean—" and he couldn't help but grin as he bent to kiss her *"—this."*

Her mouth was just as soft as it had been the night before, just as responsive. And so was he, immediately slipping into a possessive, claiming frame of mind, the strength of which only swelled once he noticed it.

She put a hand on his chest—not pushing, but enough to remind him what they'd been about. What *he'd* been about. When he pulled back, she'd regained the hint of a smile he'd already learned to look for. "Okay," she said. "Check in with your mother ship. And today, the museum."

"Come at noon and I'll feed you first." Ian held her chin a moment longer, bringing his thumb up to run along her lower lip where it shone damp with the attention he'd just given it.

Feed you, and find out who put their hands on you, and make sure it never happens again.

But first he had to make sure his people were all right.

Hollender Lerche found himself annoyingly aware of intrusion. He barely needed to glance at his office doorway to know that David Budian hesitated—no, *hovered*, in a most irritating way—outside his domain. But glance he did, looking up from the two receiver amulets on the otherwise empty desk, his very attention a demand for explanation.

This day, Budian dressed in natty slacks and short-sleeved dress shirt, a touring cap on his head and glasses he didn't need over his nose. From this Lerche surmised that the man intended to again trail Ana Dikau. It was a precaution made necessary because she had only recently invoked the second amulet—and it, unlike the first, remained silent.

Not that the first had provided any useful information—although the primary working was as successful as they could have hoped, and the occupants of the house had definitely sickened.

Unfortunately, Ian Scott didn't seem to be one of them.

Budian asked, "Anything?"

"Not of import," Lerche told him. "The feeble-blooded Sentinels at the retreat are sickening, but Scott didn't spend the night there." Anger flickered to life at Ana's defiance—her delay in invoking the second amulet, her whorish behavior with the Sentinel.

"So my man reported," Budian said. "Scott left her rental a few moments ago—she wore him out, no doubt about that. I'll pick her up if she leaves—or let you know if he returns. I've also planted a tracker on his motorcycle." He took a breath on new words, hesitating there.

"What is it?" Lerche snapped.

Budian found the necessary mix of cautious respect. "Her face," he said. "She came outside to say her good-byes, and the bruises were visible. I must counsel caution when it comes to disciplining her, no matter that she deserves it."

The anger flickered higher. "She should take better care with her makeup."

"Agreed. But these Sentinels are notoriously possessive—that's been the problem with them all along, hasn't it? Possessive of the earth, possessive of whatever they deem to be theirs. It will complicate our task if this one goes looking for whoever left those bruises."

"She knows better than to talk. And she heals more quickly than most." Not that she knew it, or had any understanding of the taint her blood carried. She puzzled over her lack of acceptance within the Core ranks, but that was her problem. Lerche shook his head. "She is mine to discipline as necessary. But I'll take your words into consideration."

"Thank you," Budian said, as well he might. "I'll keep you apprised."

Lerche nodded in dismissal, turning his attention back to the spy amulets. One still offered a mutter of occasional conversation and clattering kitchen noises, and the other briefly provided a muffled and unidentified sound.

Ana Dikau was a problem. Had always *been* a problem. Too eager for acceptance, never seeing that she wasn't worthy, never understanding why—and yet constantly defying even the simplest edict. Never understanding that how little her value to him, she was still *his*.

She'd slept with the Sentinel.

Anger surged—and then slowly ebbed into satisfaction.

After all, she *had* invoked the amulet. She *was* spending time with Scott. He might sicken first, but ultimately she faced death right along with him. And she had no idea it would come at her own hand.

"Aspirin, yes. Ibuprofen or acetaminophen, no." Ruger's deep voice rumbled over Ian's phone. Southwest Brevis's skilled, no-nonsense healer was a man who took the bear in his other form—bigger than most, rumblier than most. "Keep 'em drinking—and put a drop of lemon oil in their water. *Not* the stuff under the sink for the furniture."

"Not the furniture polish," Ian repeated, amused in spite of the circumstances. He rounded the breakfast bar where he'd been taking notes, and opened Fernie's remedy cabinet.

"You'd be surprised," Ruger muttered. "Look, every once in a while something like this comes along—it sweeps through a bunch of us and goes on its way, showing up mainly in the light-bloods. Stick with common sense, and in a few days it'll be history. Besides, it'll take your mind off those silent amulets."

"Does *everyone* know I've been sent up here to turn my brain off?"

Ruger made a rumbling noise of amusement. "Who do you suppose talked to Nick about prying you out of that laboratory for a while, little leopard?"

Ian made his own throat noise, and it wasn't amusement.

Ruger laughed outright. "Never mind. We'll talk about that later. Meanwhile, you're not affected by this thing?"

Ian hesitated, thinking of the previous evening, not quite ready to admit vulnerability when he'd spent so much effort of late telling everyone he was *fine, dammit.* But then he'd hesitated too long, so he shrugged as he reached into the cabinet for the lemon oil. "Last night," he said, tapping the little bottle against the counter in a clinking percussive accompaniment. "Helluva headache. Today, a little…yeah, hungover. Nothing more."

"Sounds about right," Ruger said. "Take the aspirin. Drink the fluids. Don't get in over your head with activities."

Ian snorted. "Now you sound like Fernie."

"And," Ruger said as if Ian hadn't spoken, "call me if things don't get better over the next day."

Ian heard the serious note behind that directive. "Got it."

"In fact, just call me. Tomorrow. I want to know how this thing is going, in case you're not the only ones." When Ian hesitated again, Ruger offered no leeway. "You're not up there to get distracted by your work. *Call me.*"

Ian didn't quite mean to mutter, "It's not *work* that's distracting me."

Ruger laughed again. "Well, then," he said. "Tell her hello, and look no further for the source of your little virus."

"I only met her two days ago," Ian grumbled. "Hardly even that."

"That's all it takes, with the right virus." Ruger sounded altogether too cheerful. "It happens, you know. Even with us." He gave Ian a quick list of other remedies they might find useful and that Fernie was likely to have on hand, including a recent batch of Ruger's own tonic. "But don't pull that one out unless things are getting bad. You'll have the whole house bouncing off the walls. Of course," he added, humor back in his voice, "you do that as a matter of course, so who's to tell the difference."

"Ha," Ian said. "And *ha*." And managed to mutter a promise to make that update call before he hung up.

But when he turned to face the kitchen, he couldn't be quite as sanguine as Ruger—a man who had good reason to be cheerful, with his love Mariska newly pregnant. Another reason not to draw him up here. Mariska was also bear, small and fierce, and floundering a little in her new role as pending mother.

But Ian had arrived to find the place cluttered with an unprecedented number of dishes and no other evidence of the other retreat residents. A quick look around had revealed them all to be sleeping, and he'd left them that way, choosing to clean up and call Ruger before he disturbed Fernie.

Now he brewed her a quick cup of her favorite soother tea and added the lemon to it…and then hesitated and made one for himself, gulping an aspirin before he rummaged up one of yesterday's muffins to add to her tray.

Unlike Ian's room—a bedroom off the back of this quirky, open air home with its half-basement warren of little rooms and its common spaces—Fernie lived in a tiny little casita attached to the home but separate of it, just barely within the enclosed courtyard. Her own tiny kitchen, bathroom and bedroom—and a place into which Ian had never ventured, because it was quite obviously Fernie's territory. Full of Southwest color and wrought iron and photos of a family grown and scattered across three brevis regions.

But he'd stood in the doorway, and that's what he did now—knocking on the door until he heard the rustle of sheets and a sound of quiet dismay through a window that habitually remained cracked during the cold nights and warming days.

"It's me, Fernie," he said, cracking the door open. "I brought some tea. And one of your muffins. And I've talked to Ruger. So that means either I come in there with this tea or you come out, because…you know. Ruger said."

"Come in," she said, her voice a little ragged but perfectly alert. And then, practically before he'd crossed the threshold, "How are you? What about the others?"

He entered the bedroom bearing the tray like an offering, relieved to see that although he'd clearly woken her, her gaze was sharp enough and her expression alert. "I haven't checked yet. I'm triaging, and you're the important one."

"And you?" she said, tucking the covers around her plump waist so he could settle the tray into place. Her graying hair hung over her shoulder in a long, simple braid, and age had settled into her plain, welcoming features overnight. "You didn't look good last night, and you don't look good now—and of all of us, you must stay well."

"I'm—" He started to say he was fine, but didn't finish. He wasn't. The headache had returned, settling in behind his eyes. "Ruger says this should pass quickly—just some atypical virus. He didn't sound concerned. I took notes about the remedies that might help."

She'd taken a sip of her tea, and nodded. "The lemon is always good. But I need to know that you heard me. We're counting on you."

A stab of pain caught him behind one eye, and he winced, rubbing it. Fernie didn't fail to note it. "And if this isn't *just some virus*?"

He stared at her as if he'd suddenly forgotten how to think. Maybe he had.

"Ian," she said, buttering her muffin with quick, impatient movement, "I've been managing this retreat since my Manny passed. He had no Sentinel blood at all, you know. So I know what a virus looks like, and I also know what it looks like when we light-bloods get hit with one. You think this would be the first time?"

Ian pulled her robe off the back of a wooden chair and draped it over her footboard so he could flip the chair around and straddle it. "And this doesn't look right to you?"

She lifted one shoulder, sipping tea. "It doesn't look familiar. Even here, we don't take things for granted."

He thought about the working he'd felt at the overlook, the mere ripple of corruption in the air. It hadn't been a thing of significance—a passive detection spell, unless he missed his mark, and he wasn't *that* far off his game. And members of the Core were everywhere, just as the Sentinels were. Clustered, yes, but always with plenty of individuals moving freely between.

"I see I've got you considering it, at least."

"I'll take a look around," he said, tapping absently on the back of the chair. Slowly, to reflect the speed of his thoughts. "Once I've checked on the rest of us."

"Leave that to me." She pushed a strand of graying hair from her face. "I feel much better. If the others are anything like me, they simply went to bed last night and decided against getting up. It's more of a tiresome thing than anything else."

Ian rubbed the spot between his eyes. "Damned headache," he said. But the aspirin must have been kicking in, because it seemed to be easing. "Okay. I'll check outside. If I find anything...well, I don't have my gear, but we can improvise. A kitchen isn't so much different from a lab, when all is said and done." He gave her a meaningful look. "But you'll call me if you need help."

"If it makes you feel better about going out there, then, yes." She reached for another piece of the muffin. "But you, Ian—I hope you felt well enough to enjoy your time with Ana yesterday evening."

He grinned. "Now you're just prying," he said, standing back from the chair. "Let's just say I felt better when

I was with her. And," he added, before she could ask, "she's coming over around lunchtime."

"Because if this is a virus, she's been well and exposed to it." Fernie looked decidedly better now, that twinkle back in her eye.

"Now you *are* prying," Ian said. He put the chair back where it had been and bent over to kiss her cheek, ignoring her surprise. "You're right. We won't take it for granted. I'll check in after I take a quick look around, and then go back out for a second sweep."

"Good," she said. "Thank you."

But what Ian didn't say, and what they both knew, was that if the Core had targeted the grounds with a silent amulet working, Ian had no more chance of finding it than any of them—and that was no chance at all.

Chapter 5

Ana arrived at the retreat to find Ian prowling the grounds—a lean, sunlit figure in constant motion. He'd clearly showered and shaved, and now wore a pale, lightweight shirt over faded jeans. The jeans fit perfectly, hanging off his hips and snug over the strong curve of his butt, but the shirt had only received haphazard attention to the buttons—as if he'd been interrupted when he'd barely just started.

She had the feeling that the interruption had come in the form of his restless nature, but a second glance at the intensity of his expression made her think twice.

He wasn't just prowling. He was *searching.*

She stood back and watched for a long moment. Considering him. Still able to feel his hands on her skin, to see the care in his eyes. And to see so clearly his expression when she'd touched him back, and how it had affected her.

It had made her realize that until Ian, she'd never made love. She'd made sex. She'd had sex made with her…and to her. Her previous partners, limited as they were, had been Core. Had been expected of her. And after so many similar experiences, she'd thought the fault, if there was one, to be hers. Or she'd thought simply *this is the way it is.*

She'd been wrong. Ian had shown her that. He'd given her more of himself in one evening than all of her previous partners put together. And he'd shown her that it wasn't about what one could take…it was about what one could give.

Surely, if this man—who offered such clear care to her, and to the woman named Fernie, and even to Ana when she'd still been only a stranger under attack by a mugger—was a Sentinel, then it should be possible for the Core and the Sentinels to find common ground. To work together. No matter what she'd always been told.

But she'd need time to prove that. She'd need Ian's trust. And she'd need space from Lerche's interference.

He won't bother me if I'm with Ian.

The thought came out of nowhere, striking her as true as anything could. Lerche wouldn't bother her if she was with Ian—he wouldn't bruise her or intimidate her or push her. Because he knew as well as Ana that Ian wouldn't allow any of that.

Ian hadn't seen her yet, which startled her—it seemed to her as if he generally saw everything in his world. But this intensity, she suspected, was also uniquely Ian. So focused, so immersed in his work that he'd closed out everything else.

Though what *was* he doing?

Prowling.

And doing it with an expression that should have

alarmed her, dark brows drawn over piercing eyes—shadowing them. Utter concentration on his face as he paced the latilla fencing, gaze sweeping every inch of uneven vertical poles. Once he crouched, a stunningly simple display of the graceful leopard hidden within, and Ana found herself holding her breath—appreciating not just the beauty of it, but anticipating the outcome.

After a moment he merely stood and went on, his head cocked slightly as if he was listening for some inner voice.

Ana resumed breathing, her pulse still rocketing. How well she understood this man after only two days. How well she understood what his presence could do to her.

She swallowed hard against sudden fear in her throat, caught in fragile crystalline understanding. *Lerche would kill her.*

He would call her weak and corrupted and traitorous; he would call her a failure. And wouldn't tolerate those things, on top of years of barely accepting her in the first place. *He would eliminate them.*

But Lerche wasn't here. And he wasn't the entire Core. If Ana could prove to them that Ian's respectful nature was representative of the Sentinels, if she could broker a breakthrough in communication…

She'd be more than accepted. She'd be safe.

She released a deep and steady breath, settling her mind to it all. Putting herself back in the moment, where reaching her goal and simply spending time with Ian amounted to the same thing. Especially now that she'd put the second spy amulet into the pocket of her light blazer…and activated it.

That time, he heard her. Lifted his head and saw her.

For an instant, he looked stunned—and she immediately understood.

He'd forgotten all about their date.

She ought to feel hurt. She ought to feel resentful. Instead she blurted out, "What's wrong?"

Relief crossed his features, but only briefly. "Fernie," he said. "The others…not so much. But Fernie."

"Hey," she said. "I'm outside your brain. I need more words."

At that, he laughed and seemed to shake something off. "I think I should be frightened," he said, and stretched in a way that made her ache to touch him. "Do you know how long it takes some people to deal when I get stuck inside my head?"

"Then they aren't paying attention." She said it haughtily, deliberately lightening the moment. "But seriously, Ian. What's going on?"

He glanced back at the house. "Probably just a weird virus. The others aren't doing too badly—they stayed in bed—but Fernie is pretty sick." He frowned. "She seemed better this morning, but it didn't last."

She put hands on hips, tapped her foot a couple of times. "So Fernie is sick and you're worried, but you're not taking her to a clinic…you're out combing the yard?"

"Ah," he said, straightening a little. "Right. Actually, the company has a medic on call, so we've talked. This is just a precaution. Sometimes people throw things over fences."

It took her a moment, and then she understood. *"Poison?"*

He shrugged. "People get frustrated with the neighborhood cats."

She nearly laughed out loud, full of the double meaning of that sentence. But Ian had no idea she knew he was actually one of the neighborhood cats, so instead she said, "That's awful. Do you want some help looking? Do you need any help inside? We don't have to do the museum today—"

He shook his head—looking down at himself as if to check for dirt or grass stains. "We'll go. If our guy thought there was a real problem, he'd have come up to check things out himself." He rotated his shoulders, stretching again—completely unselfconscious, and completely unaware of the impressive display of lithe strength. "Besides, I'm doing okay. You?"

"A bit of a headache," she admitted, realizing it for the first time. "If you have an aspirin, I'd take it. And then we can be on our way, if you really still want to go." She glanced in the direction of the museum without thinking about it and caught sight of a figure hovering at the tree line of the greenway. Lingering.

Ian followed her gaze.

If the man hadn't frozen—hadn't so visibly thought about ducking to hide—nothing would have come of it.

But he did.

And Ian muttered, "What the hell—?" and hopped over the fence, striding toward the man.

Who took off.

Posse. It had to be. And Ana wanted to kick the man. What was he thinking, to lurk where a Sentinel could see? What was Lerche thinking, to send him out to watch after he'd already put Ian on alert with that drive-by at the overlook? He'd blow her cover if he wasn't more careful, and she knew exactly who'd get the blame for that.

There was no way Ian wasn't going to catch the guy. He ran full out, his strides long and swift, his movement effortless—

Except even as he closed in on the man, he stumbled. His movement grew choppy, his strides uneven. The man pulled cleanly away as Ian came to an abrupt stop, his hands braced on his knees. Staggering.

Ana ran to him, feeling not relief that the posse member had gotten away, but concern for Ian. Knowing exactly how lucky the fugitive had been. "Ian!" she said, reaching him just lightly out of breath, because the Core made sure she was as fit as anyone could be. "Are you all right?"

He straightened, his expression full of puzzlement—and something more. A wounded look, as though his body had betrayed him. "I'm okay," he said—and at her sound of disbelief, flashed her a wry look. "I guess I'm not quite back to myself."

"No kidding. And just what did you plan to do if you caught that guy?"

"Ask him questions," Ian said, more grimly than he probably meant to.

"What? Like why he thought he could get away with relieving himself on that tree?" Another lie, another misdirection. But she couldn't afford for him to suspect the man as Core. She *couldn't.*

"He was what?" Ian said in surprise, looking off after the man—long gone now. Ana held her silence, letting him work it through. "I'm sorry. I thought—" He shook his head. "I guess I'm on edge." He bounced on his toes a time or two, recovered from whatever instant of weakness had caught him—more like the man she'd seen upon her very first glimpse of him. "I'm still working out this *relaxation* thing."

"So I see." She offered her hand. "Let's grab an aspirin and a snack, and see what the walk to the museum does for you. We can take the greenway almost all the way there."

He took her hand, but the faint gathering frown at his brows didn't fade as they returned to the retreat porch, both of them warm in the wake of exertion and the beat of the midday sun. She pulled off her blazer when he went inside to grab them some water, dropping the coat over the back of a wrought-iron porch chair without a second thought—at least, not until they were walking away.

Only then did she realize that the second amulet had been left behind in her blazer and how Lerche would respond to her error. But amazingly, with her hand back in the warm and careful grip of the Sentinel who had trusted his body to her the night before, she couldn't bring herself to care.

She was, at the moment, right where she needed to be.

Ian's feet moved of their own accord, taking him through the beautifully spare hallways of the O'Keeffe museum; he only vaguely heard Ana's voice. His eyes were full of beauty under the museum spotlights in this stark adobe hallway, gaze drawn by paintings of sublime and subtle color and sweeping lines. And his mind was full of…

Frustration.

Ana moved in beside him, nudging his shoulder. "Where are you?" she asked. "I'm not sure you're quite here."

He pulled himself out of his thoughts to look down at her—there, where she'd so expertly covered the evidence of someone's damned fingers.

He was well aware that her whole story hadn't been

told. Not with the not-so-random mugging, or the man he'd scared off that morning. But he was beginning to fill in the blanks.

This was not, he thought, so much of a vacation as it was an escape.

He'd find out. But not now—here, in this museum, with her concern looking up at him. So he told her the truth, without much thinking about it. "I can't make sense of it."

"Your people? Are you still worried?" She took his hand—just enough hesitation to let him know she wasn't used to reaching out, and just enough confidence to reflect the startling nature of their fast-solidifying connection.

Quiet floated over his thoughts like a blanket, leaving him room to think. "More than that." He hesitated over just how much to say, O'Keeffe's winter cottonwoods drawing his eye back to the hazy brown sweep of branches emerging from misty beige and muted ochre. "The pattern of things just doesn't make sense. We feel fine…we feel terrible. And then we're fine again."

"Like you last night," she observed, rubbing a thumb lightly across his knuckles in a fashion that focused his thoughts in an entirely different way, thank you very much.

"And Fernie this morning." He didn't mention how badly he'd felt before he'd gone to the yard to hunt amulets; he didn't mention that it seemed to be harder to shake the illness off today than it had been yesterday. To clear his thoughts, which had blundered around in their usual overactive state—only now they seemed just as blurred as O'Keeffe's winter trees.

Abruptly, he turned away from the painting, moving along the stark adobe hallway to the exit and out from under the track lighting to the tight, unpretentious grounds where the building rose like an assortment of adobe blocks behind them.

She kept her hold on his hand, following without hurry. "Are you all right now?"

"When you touch me?" he said. "Never better." He made a quick, wry face, without explanation. "You give me a peace I haven't felt before."

She presented him with a dubious look, and he laughed. "That wasn't supposed to sound corny. It was supposed to sound…" He hesitated. *"Real."*

She looked away, her face dappled by the shade of the trees lining the street and sidewalk, groomed landscaping sand and gravel crunching under their feet. "There's a lot going on with me. You should know that."

"I already know it."

She flicked a glance at him and then away. As if she couldn't quite deal with meeting his gaze. "It's not anything I expected to get into with such a short time together. It's not anything I *want* to get into."

"Then, don't. You don't owe me anything." Why that brought a sheen of tears to her eyes, he didn't know. "Look. I came here because I was ordered to. Things at work have been intense, and I don't know how to slow down at the best of times."

Now she did look at him, intrigued—and guessing. "And it hasn't been the best of times."

Understatement. So many dead, so many attacks barely thwarted. Unless the Sentinels could detect the silent amulets, their field agents would continue to die, and their families would always be under the threat of another *Core D'oíche.*

Unless *Ian* could detect the silent amulets.

"No," he said. "It hasn't been the best of times. The

only time I've been able to take a mental breath..." *Is with you.* He didn't say the words out loud but wrapped his arms around her, resting his cheek on the sun-warmed tousle of her hair.

His mind settled. His thoughts quieted. He took a deep breath and absorbed her—how she felt sturdy and delicate at the same time, how her breathing synced with his, how she enveloped him not with strength but with caring. The warmth of his response rose not like the previous evening's lightning but as a gentler thing. A more lasting thing.

In that quiet clarity of his mind, his thoughts settled—a brilliant clarity of overlapping understandings.

Like the fact that he had no intention of letting this woman just *go*. Of walking away from this week—of walking away from *him*. That he wanted to scoop her up right here, let her wrap her legs around his waist as he carried her back to the retreat, back to his bed—to claim her, and let himself be claimed.

He stepped back from her just enough to tip her head up and hesitate the instant it took to see permission in her eyes. More than permission—request for the kiss he wanted to share. And he would have kissed her longer and deeper but he felt himself falling into her and knew better. Not here.

Even so, they made a mutual sound of regret when they parted, and Ana's face was flushed, her eyes bright. At least, until she stiffened, looking past him—

Ian jerked around, seeing nothing but the back of a well-dressed man as he walked away. He'd barely turned back to Ana before she grabbed his hand, tugging slightly as she angled in the direction of the retreat. "Let's go check on your friends," she said, taking a step or two before Ian responded, when it was clear she meant to drop his hand and keep walking.

He stopped her, closing his fingers around hers so she swung around to face him. "Look," he said. "We all have our secrets. And there's a lot we don't know about each other. But you should know that I want to follow the hell out of what's happening with us. And you should also know that if you need help—" he glanced back to where the man had disappeared around the corner "—*any* kind of help…then I'm here for that."

Her expression softened, not in the least hiding the distress in her eyes. "I knew that," she said. "I think I knew it from the moment we met." She gave his hand a gentle squeeze. "Let's go check on your friends."

The house greeted Ian with quiet…everyone sleeping again, with another round of dishes in the sink. Ian gave Ana a quick tour of the retreat's common areas, from the sunny sitting room to the courtyard, an area of flagstone, fountains and tasteful native plantings enclosed in the front with a privacy fence and the back with tall wrought iron, leaving a full view of the mountains rising up behind them. Afterward Ana pulled out the dish soap while Ian went to peek in on everyone and left a voice mail with Ruger that amounted to *call me*.

And then they tumbled into bed, where they didn't talk about illness or enemies or bruises, but explored each other with a thoroughness that left them both limp and panting. She had a mole in the dimple over her left butt cheek. Her voice grew breathless when he kissed the hollow of collarbone and neck, and she giggled when he licked the outside curve of her ear. And from him she evoked new sensations—her tongue down his spine, the clamp of her thighs around his hips, the way she could move herself just so and just when and wring yet another shout from his throat.

For a while they lay together, listening to the quiet of the house. No sound effects from the game room, no clinking from the kitchen, no laughter from the covered open-air dining area—not even to Sentinel ears. Then Ana rolled over to trap Ian's leg under hers, brushing a hand over his brow. "It's back, isn't it?"

The underlying ache in his head, the muddle of his mind. He didn't have to nod to confirm it; he felt the tension of it in his face and knew she'd seen it just as clearly.

"Me, too. Just a little." She scraped her fingers lightly through the disarray of his hair, massaging his scalp until he wanted to groan. Or purr. Or both. "But maybe we just got dehydrated—it's a warm day, and a dry one. Or maybe these things just come and go because that's the way illness is."

"Maybe," he said, not pretending to be convinced but fully immersed in her touch. Wanting not just to purr, but to show her the rest of himself.

Because she wouldn't run screaming to find a snow leopard in her bed, oh, no.

She touched his mouth, tracing a fingertip along his lower lip. "What's so funny?"

"I am," he said. "Because I don't think a couple days of this will be nearly enough."

Her breath caught; her fingers stilled. "It's not the real world, Ian. It's vacation. It's *indulgence*." But she sounded wistful.

He rolled over quite suddenly, pinning her, kissing her soundly, and rolling right off her again. "Doesn't mean it's *not* real."

She lay silent—tangled in his sheets, her hand trembling where it touched her mouth—so very well kissed, that mouth, even before his impulsive attention.

Delicate. In more than one way. *Don't push.*

"Tomorrow," he said, changing the subject just as abruptly as he ever did, "how about those trails?"

"Which ones?" She still sounded a little breathless—and maybe a little reticent. "Are they even open, after that man was killed last week?"

Ian stilled. "After what?"

She didn't respond immediately, and when she spoke he heard an unexpected caution. "That man on the trails. They said he got between two mountain lions in a territory spat—one of those ended up dead, too."

He held his silence a moment, then rolled out of bed. Too unsettled to pretend he wasn't, with the snow leopard so close to the surface—remembering that day, that fight.

Remembering that he'd gone looking for the man without much success—but that he hadn't looked all that hard. There hadn't been any blood on the ground, or the heavy scent of it in the air. At the time he'd chalked it up to the fact that he'd been pretty much on top of the attack when it happened—he'd stopped it short, and the man had quite wisely fled. There had been others approaching by then, their conversation rising uphill through the trees from a lower switchback—and Ian hadn't wanted to be found in the area.

But surely he hadn't left a man to die.

He paced over to his laptop, reached to flip it open… and didn't, resting his hand on the case instead. Realizing that his eyes weren't quite ready to focus, and not willing to let it show. "You're sure? The hiker died?"

She sat up and crossed her legs, as intent as he was. "That's what I heard." She watched him with a searching gaze. "I thought you'd know about it. You seemed so at home up there yesterday."

Left a man to die. Ian scrubbed his hands through his hair, the heels of his palms coming to rest over his eyes…pressing just a little too hard where the headache lurked. A dull throb of a thing, interlaced through his mind like a foggy lattice…making it hard to manage the duality of thinking he needed in this moment.

She wouldn't understand his upset. And he couldn't explain it. He needed to distance himself from the being he'd been on that mountain, feeling the surge of power in leaping muscle, the power behind flashing claws and the crunch of sharp teeth clamping down. He needed to be Ian Scott, think tank employee on retreat who simply enjoyed hiking in the high beauty of the Sangre de Cristo mountains.

Too late, of course. She asked, "Are you all right?" The question seemed to encompass all the things whirling around in his head, and seemed to do it with a perceptiveness he couldn't quite reconcile.

But then, he couldn't quite reconcile anything about this day—other than the time he'd spent with Ana.

"Headache," he told her, willing to let it take the blame for all. Rather than a glance at his watch, he checked out his window—easy enough to see the last rays of the sun creeping up the side of the mountain range. "I need to check on Fernie. On everyone." He scrounged for his jeans, foregoing the underwear… snagging a T-shirt from the back of the small desk chair. "You want anything? Ginger tea or aspirin? That's about all we have around here."

"Can I help?" She patted the bed in search of her underwear.

He found her bra on the floor and dropped it on the

bed on his way past. "Not that everyone won't be able to tell exactly what we've been up to—" Ian coughed, a meaningful sound.

"Right," she said. "They know anyway, don't they?"

"They don't care," he said. Sentinel culture was quite necessarily an earthy one, full of people who reveled in their senses and in their ability to enjoy one another. "They'll like you. Fernie already likes you."

"I like her, too," Ana said. "Let's see if she's feeling any better."

As it turned out, Fernie was—but she was taking a lesson from the ups and downs of the past day and keeping herself to quiet, restful activities in her tiny cottage. She'd advised the others to do the same, so Ian found them grateful for a snack but not yet ready to emerge.

"We should do the same," Ana said, returning to the kitchen with a tray now emptied of food. "And let's look at the trail map. I think a short hike in the fresh air might help us both, and there must be some trails that aren't anywhere near the spot where they found that man." She rustled in the food—pulling out a couple of croissants, slicing them for lunch meat and dabbing on some mayo. She plated them on the tray while Ian rummaged in the remedies cupboard to add a careful dollop of Ruger's herbal tonic to his tea mug. "Oh," she added, an odd reluctance in her voice. "My blazer. Fernie must have brought it inside."

He followed her gaze through the open archway of the kitchen to the coat rack inside the door, found the blazer hanging there. "I'll grab it if you're worried about losing track of it. I've got room in my closet."

"Yes," she said, tucking the sandwich makings away and appropriating the steaming tea for the tray before she picked it up to head for the back of the house. "Thanks. I guess that's best."

Her lack of enthusiasm seemed like another layer of something Ian should have been able to unravel on this day of amazing moments mixed with confusion. But he was starting to get used to the muddle, so he simply finished tidying the kitchen, flicked off the lights and detoured to grab up the light linen blazer, rearranging his grip to avoid the heavy little object in one pocket.

And then he went to be with Ana.

Chapter 6

Ana woke to a throbbing head and cool, rumpled sheets beside her.

No Ian. No sound of Ian. No sight of him. His clothes were gone; his phone sat on the dresser.

She sat, ran her hands through her hair, and very nearly flopped back down on to the pillow. Only the fact that it would jar her aching head and a glance at the bedside clock stopped her. *Past nine!*

There were aspirin on the little desk, beside the food tray. And a half-full glass of water. They beckoned her.

She slipped out of bed, realizing then that she wore one of Ian's colorful T-shirts and nothing else. Remembering that they'd returned to this room the evening before, eaten the light dinner and watched a sensationalist nature documentary that amused Ian more than not.

She'd been so aware of herself, cuddled beside him. As if every inch of skin knew of his presence and responded to it, her mouth pleasantly bruised from his kisses and every sensitive part of her body remembering his touch. She couldn't have been more comfortable beneath the weight of his arm, her head propped on his chest to catch the beat of his heart and the gentle rise and fall of his breath.

She hadn't been surprised when he'd flicked off the show and curled up around her, spooning snugly enough so she'd felt encompassed in a new way. *Safe* in a new way.

Able to sleep in perfect confidence.

So where was he now?

She squelched a little spear of hurt. Ian was a complicated man—a *busy* man. The surprise wasn't that he'd slipped out to do something around the retreat—it was that he'd spent so much time with her already.

Ana tossed back two aspirin and gulped down the rest of the water, ignoring the faint unease in her stomach. Her underwear was around here somewhere; she flipped the sheets over without finding it, then twitched them back into place, smoothing and folding the knitted spread at the base of the bed. Perhaps underneath...

Her ringtone gave a muted peal, buried somewhere and set to low. She glanced around the room and finally spotted her blazer, pushing it aside to find her purse beneath.

Of course it was Lerche. Her few friends didn't have this particular number. She accepted the call just in time.

"Can you talk?" he demanded without preamble. "If not, get somewhere that you can."

"I'm fine here," she said, but kept her voice to a murmur. Sentinels, she knew, had keener hearing than most. Than *all*.

"Report!" And then he didn't give her a chance. "What's happening with the second amulet? The first is giving us nothing but kitchen noises. The second is giving us little at all. If you've failed in planting them properly, you'll need to relocate—"

She took a bold chance, interrupting him. "It's in his private room," she said, looking at the blazer and failing to add that the spy amulet was completely muffled within her pocket, not to mention that it had only arrived here after their conversation—and lovemaking—had made way for the ridiculous documentary.

"Oh?" The single word sounded startled but also surprisingly pleased—given how little the location had yielded so far. And surprisingly neutral when he added, "I suppose you're still whoring yourself to him there."

She said, as steadily as she could, "I'm doing my best to fulfill the needs of this mission."

"And going above and beyond in ways I never imagined of you." His voice regained some of its cutting edge, but still held that hint of satisfaction.

"It would help if the posse kept its distance," she told him, dredging up the courage for it. If he took it as implied criticism of his management, he wouldn't forget it. "Ian isn't dulled by his time in his lab, whatever they think—he's got Sentinel instincts, and he trusts them. A lot more than he's going to trust me if this keeps up."

"It won't take much longer," Lerche said, cryptically enough. "You just play your role. And in the end, remember that you chose it."

He hung up on her, leaving her staring at the phone and trying to make sense of him—his moods, his implications, his underlying threat.

A gentle knock on the door startled her far out of proportion to the moment; she fumbled the phone and jammed it into her purse, although there wasn't a thing wrong with making a personal call. "Ian?" she asked, even as she realized he wouldn't knock on his own door.

"It's Fernie. I brought you some breakfast."

Ana looked down at herself, glancing around the room as if a robe might magically manifest itself, and finally snatching the light throw from the end of the bed to drape over her shoulders as she opened the door.

Fernie stood with a serving tray in hand, a smile in place. She wore a fresh housedress but hadn't put her hair up or applied any daily makeup; her face looked tired, but her eyes were bright enough. She let herself in, nudging the evening's tray aside to place the breakfast—bowls of homemade granola, fruit and two cups of steaming tea.

When she looked up, her smile faded. "Where's Ian?"

"I thought—" Ana stalled out on bafflement. "I thought he was out in the house. Helping."

"I haven't seen him," Fernie said, gathering up the used tray. "I didn't get up until nearly eight, myself." She shook her head at this. "We're a sorry excuse for a retreat right now, all of us!"

"Are you feeling better this morning?" Ana crossed her arms over the throw, letting it enfold her. If Ian wasn't in this house, she shouldn't be here, either. Just let the aspirin kick in…

Fernie shook her head. "Such a strange thing. I rest, I feel better, I get up to do some chores and feed some people and bam! I'm right back in bed. I'm beginning to think we picked up a mold with the summer rains." She gave Ana a sharp eye. "You don't look so good this morning, either, Ian's girl."

Ian's girl. Ana swallowed the guilt of the phone call.

"I don't feel so well. But that's not surprising. I've been with Ian on and off for days, and I've been here, too."

"You've been good for him," Fernie said, giving her a closer look—an unabashed one. Ana keenly felt the absence of her underwear. "I hope he's been good for you, too. I hope he's told you that no woman deserves whoever put those bruises on your face."

Ana gasped, realizing she'd been caught without makeup over the bruises, one hand clutching the knitted throw even more tightly and one flying to her jaw. It was much less sore today, and she'd hoped the bruises would be gone.

Fernie offered her a tight smile. "It's the reason they gave me this job," she said. "I meddle. Now have something to eat and get yourself dressed, and I'll see if I can't scare up Ian."

But Fernie couldn't scare up Ian—and a call to his phone revealed it to be on the desk beside his laptop. By the time Ana had shaken out her clothes and climbed back into her pants, appropriating another of Ian's T-shirts, Fernie was on her way back down the hall. Ana hesitated with the blazer in hand and then quickly flipped it out, doubled it and folded it tightly with the listening device in the center, tucking it against the wall behind the door.

She met Fernie at the door, tray in hand and headache somewhat ameliorated by the aspirin. Fernie didn't wait for her query. "This isn't like him," she said. "This isn't *anything* like him. Did something happen yesterday?"

Ana floundered, frowning and unable to think of a thing. "He's worried about you…he doesn't seem to feel as though he's done enough to help."

"Typical." Fernie frowned, giving Ana the most direct look. "This doesn't have anything to do with that phone call I overheard, does it? *Could* it?"

Ana froze, instantly trying to recall what she'd said—knowing it was certainly enough to indict her as far as Fernie was concerned, but reasonably certain she'd said nothing to reveal her Core affiliation. With utmost care, she said, "Not as far as I know."

Fernie said, "We'll talk about that later, then." She tipped her head at Ana, her expression somehow reminiscent of a satisfied mother bear. "Like I said, I meddle. But first, we need to find Ian."

"All right," Ana said faintly. "What can I do to help?"

Fernie didn't hesitate. "If this illness stays to pattern, we don't have much time before it's hard to be smart about this. I have some people to call. You check around the grounds—don't forget the fountain courtyard or the garden area outside the walls. And don't assume he'll be on his feet." Fernie shook her head, making a sound of disapproving dismay. "That boy is always putting his hands on things he shouldn't."

Amulets, Ana wanted to say—but didn't. She couldn't give that much of herself away, even if Fernie had already overheard her compromising words. "He has a keen curiosity," she agreed, and headed out of the room…but then couldn't stop herself. She turned, finding Fernie scowling around the room with a stern eye—one that stayed stern as it found Ana. "Why aren't you angry with me? Or showing me the door?"

Fernie snorted faintly. "That could come. But right now, whatever's going on, you're still Ian's girl and you've still been good for him. I'll let him make his own decisions."

Ana wanted to lift her chin, wanted to be proud and to be confident in herself and what she'd done. If the

Sentinels didn't want Core attention, they needed to practice self-control, and to quit taking advantage of their abilities at the expense of others.

Instead she could only stand in confusion, wondering at the sensations of acceptance even from this woman who so clearly knew Ana was more than she'd begun to say. Floundering in this nurturing atmosphere, where Ian had set aside his personal needs to take care of those beneath him in Sentinel hierarchy, and where Fernie's affection for her guests permeated this place like a physical embrace.

In the end Ana simply said, "Thank you," and went on, out into the yard to look for Ian.

At first Lerche had resented the number of silent amulets necessary to manage this endeavor—from the simplest tracking amulet used on Ana and on Scott's motorcycle to the complex layering in the amulets she had planted.

There'd been no choice—not with Ian Scott as their target. Intel on Southwest Brevis had identified the man as the only one capable of breaking the silence of those amulets, and he would most certainly detect anything not completely silenced, just as he'd detected the faint whisper from the feeble working used to discern whether Ana had triggered the second amulet.

But the expense was paying off. Even if Lerche hadn't gathered much information—the foolish woman had planted the first amulet in the retreat kitchen, of all places, and the second was full of so many muffled noises that it must have malfunctioned in that respect—Ian Scott was clearly sick. Clearly not thinking quite right any longer.

Not to have taken the motorcycle out into the mountains so early in the day, leaving Ana behind and leaving the Sentinel light-bloods worried and looking for him. Or so Budian reported, his phone pickup muffled with what must have been gloves. The man had moved in upon Scott's departure, confirming that the Sentinel had gone alone.

"Excellent work," he told Budian, thinking of Ian Scott—alone, sick and vulnerable. The one man who could bring them down—and the one man who could tell them how close he'd already come. "We'll take advantage of this opportunity. Find Scott on the trails and bring him to me."

Budian sounded cold—as well he might, after a stakeout in one of these stupidly cold desert mountain nights. "On the trails? He could be in his beast form."

Lerche dismissed the possibility with the ease of a man who wouldn't actually be on those trails. "Not with the amulet working on him to this extent. Ana said it was in his bedroom. Such concentrated exposure on a full field Sentinel will have resulted in profound effects by now."

"I'll send men to look for him," Budian said. "But it's a big mountain."

"Don't *look*," Lerche told him. *"Find."*

He cut Budian's response short with a swipe at his phone, and tossed the device onto his desk. Soon Ian Scott would be his—and then dead—and the only threat to the silent amulets would be eliminated.

It would be a good day.

Ana found no sign of Ian at the retreat, but the cool morning air refreshed her—clearing her thoughts, invigorating her body. The aspirin kicked in, and the granola sat well in her stomach.

She returned to the house to find that Fernie hadn't been as lucky. The older woman stood at the dining room table, a large map spread out before her and her own breakfast untouched to the side.

"Come out to the porch," Ana said. "It's a beautiful day, and you've been stuck inside since I met Ian."

Fernie regarded her for a moment, then nodded. "There's truth to that," she allowed, and gathered up the map. Ana picked up the cereal bowl and muffin, just in case, and brought it along.

Fernie sat in the porch chair with an undisguised weariness, opening the map on her lap. "Oh, Ian," she said, looking at it. "What are you up to?"

Ana set the bowl on a tiny round patio table, glancing at the map in belated recognition. "That's a trail map."

"Indeed it is." Fernie smoothed it. "Ian's not *here*, where he should be. And he's not himself—he's done well with this bug of ours, but you've seen it—when it hits him, it hits hard."

"It seems to," Ana agreed.

Fernie gave her the most perceptive of looks. "Ian is special, as you likely well know."

Ana gave her a surprised look, wondering if this was a direct allusion to Ian's field Sentinel nature. To his *other*. And if it was some sort of test to see how Ana reacted—if she *knew*.

The best she could do was not react at all. After a moment, Fernie said, "Things affect him differently—illnesses, medicines, even something as simple as caffeine. We can't assume he's thinking clearly right now. But when he's troubled…" She tapped the map. "This is where he goes."

Ana touched the map. "We were planning to hike today."

"Were you?" Fernie gave her a sharp look. "He was going to share this with you?"

"I didn't think of it like that," Ana admitted.

"You should have."

Fernie's short words sat on silence for a moment, and then Ana admitted, "I was worried, though, because of that mountain lion attack last week. The man who died." Worried because it reminded her that Ian had killed someone, she meant, even if Fernie didn't know it.

"What?" Fernie sat up straighter. Her eyes had brightened, and her expression looked livelier. "When? Where?"

Ana tapped the map. "Right here. Just over a week ago."

"No," Fernie said with some assertion. "I would have heard. Someone misspoke. Or they were telling tales."

"No, I—" Ana hesitated, her finger lingering on the map. The trail where she'd first seen Ian. The trail where she'd seen him *change*. It occurred to her that she'd never seen any news stories of the attack, no headlines in the paper.

Fernie saw her uncertainty. "Honey, when there's a lion attack around here, *everyone* knows. I don't know who told you that, but they were telling stories."

Ana couldn't quite fathom it. *Why* would Lerche tell her such a thing if it wasn't true? Why even bother, when it would have been so easy to double-check?

Except he'd known she wouldn't question him. That she'd believe him utterly, as she always had—and that in believing, she would not only be wary of Ian, she'd believe even more deeply in the task to which he'd set her.

What other lies has he told?

She pressed her fingers over her closed lids, searching for a way out of the confusion—in the end, she found nothing but the need to focus on Ian. *His safety.* "Okay," she said, releasing the rest of it for the moment. "Never mind that, then. What do we do about Ian?"

"I'm waiting for a call back from our company," Fernie said. "I want some help up here. It's one thing for us to get a passing virus, but this thing is holding on. And if Ian is reacting so strongly to it, it could mean there's something else going on." She didn't make any offer to explain her thinking. "Meanwhile, either he's gone out to clear his head and he'll be back, or he's too sick to get back and we should look for him."

"Me," Ana said. "*I* should look for him."

Fernie gave her a look. A reminder that she'd overheard too much of that last phone call from Lerche, even if there'd been nothing directly incriminating said. A reminder that Ana wasn't one of them, even if she wasn't truly supposed to know the significance of that fact.

Ana made a noise of frustration. "At least point out his favorite trails, if you know them—I can check the trailheads for his motorcycle. If we do need to go looking—or to send someone—then we'll know where to start."

Fernie took the deepest of breaths, glancing back into the house...quite visibly considering her options. At last, she nodded. "There's sense to that," she said, and shifted the map so Ana could see it more easily. "Here. Check this one. If he's not here, check the overlook parking—there are a handful of trailheads there, and some go directly to a wilderness area." Then she tapped the first spot, an assertive gesture. "But this is his favorite."

Of course it was. It was the trail where she'd first seen him. The one where her own people had first set him up for an encounter to reveal the depth of his true nature to her.

The one where he might or might not have killed an innocent man.

Ian wasn't sure how he'd made it to the trail. He had only an impression of those early morning hours—his vision bleary, his head a muddle, and his entire being driven by a singular need to find surcease in the wilds of the mountain.

Given that his lab wasn't available. Or the basement in the echoingly empty bachelor pad of his house, surrounded by earth and as deeply calm as his complicated world ever got. *His den.*

But here he'd found himself—not as the snow leopard, which surprised him. As plain old human, crouched by the side of the trail.

Only after he'd blinked a few times and oriented himself did he realize where he'd taken himself in that muddle. And only then did he realize he was growling softly in the back of his very human throat, a rolling commentary on his situation as a whole.

Now he still crouched here, not quite warm enough, accepting the fact that he wouldn't figure out his exact location until he found familiar features along the trail. For now he knew only that he faced west. And that he'd gone high.

Ian stood, hopping down to the trail—a single-footing thing that wound along the side of the slope, uphill on one side and downhill on the other. Little room for misstep there. He placed his feet carefully, drawing on his snow leopard—or trying to. That part of himself was obscured and hard to reach.

It was an unfamiliar feeling. The snow leopard was always there.

Always filling the heart of him.

But now his feet felt leaden...his senses dull. The part of him that seemed ever imminent—ready to burst right through his skin, full of energy and loud with life—

It simply wasn't.

The lack of it made him place his steps with extra care, as if they belonged to someone else. It made the world seem dull and distant around him, not quite as vibrant. As if he walked through it but not *in* it.

The moments passed, one step after the other, a painstaking effort to navigate a mountain he'd all but owned until this point. Until suddenly he stopped, a rebellion of sorts. He took a deep breath, then another a deeper breath and closed his eyes to inhale the pine-sharp air, the cool hints of juniper and the distinct scent of fall—oak leaves browning, the ground cover still faintly damp from the most recent of the area's brief but intense fall rains.

Inside, the snow leopard roused into clarity—irritable, demanding and tail twitching.

Ian released a gusting sigh, settling back into his skin. Not fully himself, but able to see it from where he was.

Just that quickly, he knew his exact location—which trail and which section of the trail. His favorite. And the very same trail on which he'd saved a man from a mountain lion, only to find him gone upon return.

The man had then supposedly been killed, although Ian had heard nothing of it—and no lion kill would go un-sensationalized by the local media. *Make sense of that, why don't you?*

Another fifteen minutes of walking brought him to

that very spot, as his mind grew increasingly clearer, and the hint of a bounce returned to his step. As if the very act of hiking in this place had pushed back the virus.

Or the *not*-virus.

For the illness gripping the retreat had *seemed* like a virus, but now—today, waking up in this place—Ian thought there was very little chance of it.

He'd seen Fernie recover and fade not in the natural wax and wane of such things, but just the same as he'd seen himself recover and fade.

Depending on where he was.

The first headache had faded after a few hours at Ana's. The next surge of malaise came the following morning after he'd cleaned up the retreat and taken trays to the others, and it had faded after he'd gone out to search the grounds—and faded even more thoroughly after an afternoon at the museum, leaving him alone until after he and Ana had quite thoroughly made love. After which it had descended again harder than ever—this time to include Ana.

In other words, as he spent time inside the retreat.

And there was Fernie, recovering inside her little casita and but fading each time she came out to tend the others—none of whom who seemed as affected as either he or Fernie, but who had more consistently sequestered themselves under the direction of Fernie and Ruger.

None of the others at the retreat were as strong-blooded as Ian, or as affected as he was when he did go down. For them, malaise. For Ian, blinding headaches, muffled thoughts and a delirious blackout that had brought him to this place, only to clear once he'd spent time here.

Not illness.

Amulet.

But if it was a silent one, he'd never find it—not by prowling the yard, and not by searching the house. And if it wasn't silent, he would have found it already. *Frigging silents.*

The only way to find the things was to solve the very riddle he'd been sent here to forget.

And he needed to do it without his lab—the place where he could isolate and deconstruct amulet elements.

Ian jammed his hands in his jacket pockets, searching…

Finding. The silent amulet he'd been carrying around. He crouched there, in the middle of the trail in the middle of the day, no one else within sight or earshot, and focused on the thing—for what must have been the millionth time—willing himself to be able to perceive it. Shifting up and down the long scale of energies he'd long ago learned to visualize and target, hunting any small sign of—

His head jerked up, eyes narrowed, nostrils flaring. *Core corruption.*

But not from the amulet in his hand. And not fresh. Not even particularly strong—just an afterthought of presence. The big cat in him flared whiskers, rising to interest—responding to a beckoning call he hadn't had a chance to notice the last time he'd been here, simply because he'd never gotten quite this far.

Not just a call, but a challenge.

He felt the solid undertone of a growl in his chest before he even realized his response to that call. *Territory. Invasion. Defend!*

With effort, he shook off the urge to take his *other*, to bound along this trail until he found an interloper—a leap and pounce and satisfying crush of jaw—

"Down, boy," he muttered at himself.

It was time for a different kind of hunt.

He rose to pace the trail, a slow and careful progress—hunting overturned ground matter, disturbed needles… exposed dirt.

Finding the solid trace of an amulet working. Following it. And then finding the small overlook, well-hidden, with the three equidistant gouges that could only be a tripod of some sort. There, he picked up a snagged section of someone's gillie suit. And, leaving that spot, he backtracked to the exact spot where he'd seen the mountain lion attack what had seemed to be a hapless hiker.

Had seemed to be.

Here, even though still muted by illness, his snow leopard bristled so strongly that Ian backed swiftly away.

It didn't matter. He didn't need to be on top of the site to see the lingering gouges in the earth.

And he didn't need to stick his AmTech nose in it to understand the setup. The lion had been a plant, lured here and excited into attack. And someone from the Core had watched—perhaps even filmed it, to judge by those tripod marks. Probably filmed his response to it.

If anyone had killed that man, it had been the Core.

What the hell?

What sense did this even make?

"None," he decided out loud. "Absolutely no sense at all."

Okay, Scott. Yours is not to wonder why. Yours is to figure out the whole damned silent amulet thing.

So he'd take this information back to brevis, fully aware that he'd never have found it at all if he hadn't been searching out Core energies—hunting any hint of the silent amulet right there in his hand. If he hadn't been so…

Receptive.

He stumbled over the thought.

Receptive.

Because a receiver was a passive thing. A thing that waited for energy to come to *it.*

His thoughts scattered, reminding him just how recently he'd not been particularly lucid at all. Warning him not to take any of it for granted. Unsettling him enough so he hunkered down beside the disturbed trail, getting closer to the earth…hunting balance. Finding it elusive—and finding himself, the man with the overactive mind and the endless energy, without the means to work through it.

Ana.

Ana had quieted his mind. Had calmed it, when he'd thought it might just hit terminal velocity. He closed his eyes, settling down to sit cross-legged on a carpet of pine needles and tiny broken branches and plant detritus. For that moment, he thought only of Ana and of the unexpected peace at her touch. He thought of her courage these past days, reaching out to him in spite of her obvious trepidation—and responding to him in a way that revealed her heart, her receptive and sensitive soul. From the way her breath hitched when she caught his eye to the unfettered nature of her cries in pleasure, the flush of her face as her body strained for and tumbled into completion.

The warmth of those thoughts suffused his body and settled his mind. For a moment he luxuriated in them, wrapping himself in them—along with the vague discomfort of rising desire that had nowhere to go. But the discomfort was of little consequence, coming as it did with the certain understanding that when he made it back to the city—when he found his balance—he and

Ana would have a discussion about exactly where following his feelings for her had led.

To more than just a carefree vacation fling.

When he opened his eyes he found the world clear around him. His thoughts, still hazy, no longer cascaded so quickly from one to another that he couldn't follow them at all. He picked his way through them to find the spot where he'd fallen into chaos.

The part where he'd for the first time characterized the entire Sentinel history of detecting Core amulets and workings. *Listening. Hunting.*

Active listening, to be sure, and listening by some incredibly skilled sensitives along the way. Always, in the past, a perfectly viable technique. Definitely the technique Ian had attempted to refine in his efforts.

But what if he'd been thinking like the wrong animal? Not a big cat listening for the rustle of prey or inhaling a drifting scent, but something equally elegant. *Dolphins and whales and sonar...*

Send energy out. *See if it comes back.*

And most importantly, see if it comes back *changed.*

He'd never done it. He'd never had to. He was snow leopard, stalking and bounding pounce. He was laboratory finesse and amulet study and deconstruction.

But he'd been in the field. He knew how to shield—and shielding was, in its modest way, a manipulation of energy.

Ian dug into his pocket for the test amulet, the one from which he'd never perceived any energetic signal at all. He tossed it aside—fifteen easy feet along into the ground cover.

Then he pushed through the hazy elements in his thinking and formed for himself a light shield—close to himself, good for protection against equally light workings. Nothing a light-blood or mundane human would notice at all.

But every field Sentinel knew how to protect others—how to push the shielding outward, even if only a little. He did that, enlarging his space…and then gave the concentrated shielding energies a quick, hard shove—expanding outward in all directions, and just about as much focused energy work as he had in him on this particular day.

And *then* he listened.

Then, the energy came back to him.

His heartbeat kicked up into overdrive. His hands, resting on his thighs, closed into fists—an alternative to releasing his burgeoning shout of triumph into the forest, where it would ring without understanding.

Ana.

Ana had done this. Ana and her calm, Ana and the distraction of her smile, Ana and the honesty of what she'd given him these past days.

For the silence was broken.

Chapter 7

Ian grabbed the silent amulet up from the dirt, jamming it into his pocket and hitting the trail at a jog. His mind already whirled off in a dozen different directions—wondering if, with experience and experiments, he'd be able to teach others to not only find the amulets, but identify their nature. He was eager to get back to the lab and try it—and eager to get back to the retreat and search it. Not to mention he wished he'd been smart enough to bring his damned phone when he'd wandered away from the retreat in the first place.

He'd have no reception up here. But down at the trail-head, maybe. Out on the road, definitely.

Beneath all that, he worried. He'd left Ana alone at the retreat; he'd left Fernie and the others sick.

And he had no idea how long he'd been gone.

He slowed to navigate a narrow section of rock-cobbled trail, then struck out again, a little faster this time. *Driven.* Running familiar ground now, and knowing when he could stretch his legs and when to gear down for rocks and single-foot sections. One mile... three... The trail finally widened as it looped back toward the trailhead, and he loosed a little more speed, freeing the power of the snow leopard that so often simply lurked beneath.

He rounded a final curve, breaking free of the trees to spot the trailhead lot—finding himself relieved that he'd actually parked the bike here instead of jamming it into some out-of-the-way niche during an insensible delirium.

It sat up close to the trailhead, but it wasn't the only vehicle in the tiny area in this early morning. At first he was simply relieved that he hadn't run into the SUV's driver out on the trail while he was so busy being Sentinel.

But then the occupants of the car disembarked, and a second car pulled in—a familiar-looking little city car.

Ana. He'd seen the car in her driveway, a little rental that she didn't seem to use much. Of course she'd come looking.

But as he approached, his pace steady, he realized that the men from the SUV weren't preparing to hike out on the trail.

They were waiting.

They were waiting for *him.*

He eased back, seeing Ana's reaction as she, too, exited her car, her initial wave faltering as she got a look at the men. His mind went back to a million miles an hour, wondering if these men had had anything to do with the bruises on Ana's jaw...or if they had anything to do with the sedan that had passed them two days earlier, the reek of a Core working trailing behind them.

He found himself running again as one of them snapped something to Ana. She stepped away, clearly fearful—but then stood up to them, a petite figure gesturing at them to leave, one hand clutching her blazer closed against a chill that looked as though it came from within.

The snow leopard surged at him, wanting to bound fully free—ready to leap between Ana and the men, and ready to take them down. *Ready—*

He didn't. He slowed, his breath coming hard now. His fatigue catching up with him. Realization catching up with him. For these men were Core if anyone was—the unofficial muscle uniform of a snug black T-shirt and black slacks beneath black jackets, dark hair pulled back into stubby clubbed ponytails, heavy silver glinting at ear and throat.

Threatening Ana.

Or were they? He hadn't felt any workings; he still didn't feel any workings. But he no longer took such things for granted. Clumsy as he was with the newfound amulet detection, he still pulled a shield into place... steadied it...*pushed* it at them.

And staggered to a stop when a silent amulet pinged back.

Not from the two men.

Not from their car.

From Ana.

Ana held herself as still as she could, caught between two worlds.

What has Lerche done?

She couldn't warn Ian without giving herself away—not to Ian, and not to the two giants who stood in her way.

Ian hadn't hesitated. He moved with the grace of a wild thing and the power of a predator, his strides full of purpose and intent. Even a week ago on this very mountain, the snow leopard hadn't ridden him so clearly, painted him as *other* so distinctly. It wouldn't take knowing his nature to see it—to make way for him on this trail and to yield to the temptation of simply standing openmouthed to watch him move.

Ana felt the tug of that temptation, the lure of knowing she saw the extraordinary—and the realization that she'd not only been with that man, but that he'd chosen to be with her.

That until she'd felt his embrace, she'd never known what it felt to be safe. To be revered. To be *respected.*

And here she was, standing beside his enemy. *Being* his enemy.

"Stay out of the way," one of the posse goons growled at her. She didn't know him—didn't know the other one. They were enforcers, far too noticeable to manage everyday surveillance and public chores. They were muscle and force and proud of it, and she had no idea what they were doing here.

"Leave him alone," she told them, knowing it pointless. "This is my operation!"

The biggest of them glanced at her. Bigger than Ian, who, for all his power, packed leaner muscle on a more graceful frame. "Things change," he said, and she would have bet anything that he had no idea of her role in the situation and no concern about it one way or the other. He paid her no more attention.

That, she could understand. Because Ian had pulled up only fifty feet from them, standing loose and ready, his breath coming fast. And his expression…

Ana wanted to cry—and discovered that she was, tears dampening her cheeks.

He'd recognized the goons as Core, no doubt about that. But his initially cautious expression turned startled as his gaze jerked to Ana. He took a step—as if he might come to her, torn between a demand for explanation and the need to gather her up in his arms.

He knows.

Not just guessing, not just hoping it wasn't so. Somehow, he *knew*.

Because of who and what he was, and how strongly it shone from him now. Oh, he definitely knew.

She lifted a hand in supplication; he shook his head ever so slightly, taking a step back again—the recognition of her betrayal coloring his eyes, painting his face with shadow.

"No," she said—not loudly, but knowing he'd hear. "It's not like that."

"Shut up," the biggest goon said, stepping out in front of her. "And stay out of the way."

But Ian was already poised for flight, glancing at the distance to the motorcycle.

Too far. She knew it, he knew it…and the goons knew it. And still…

"Run!" she cried at him. "Ian, *run*!"

Ian broke for the motorcycle, an astonishing sprint of speed. Ana ripped her blazer off as both goons leaped to follow, their movement slow and clumsy, compared to Ian's, but far more inexorable. She threw herself at the smaller one from behind, wrapping her blazer around his head and yanking the sleeves tight, falling away almost in time to miss the sharp backhand blow of response.

She tumbled away from the impact, losing her bearings for that instant. When she oriented again, her shoulder throbbing, Ian had flung himself on the bike, jamming the keys in for a quick start and barely settling in the saddle as the bike came alive beneath him, spitting dirt and gravel and finally grabbing traction. It leaped away—not over the barely paved lot, but cross-country over cactus and scrub.

One goon threw himself into a hopeless effort to take Ian off the side of the bike, missing to land in scrub. The other pulled himself up short—and Ana pushed herself away from the ground, daring to come up where she could see the heavy bike wallow and spurt across the ground, cutting across to the curving drive where he could gun it and *run*—

But he didn't. She didn't believe it at first, scrambling to her feet as he targeted not freedom, but the lot just behind her car—letting the bike slew to a stop while he beckoned to her.

He'd come back for her.

He'd known of her betrayal, and he'd come back for her.

Why?

She stared at him, stupified. Because he'd seen the goon hit her? Because he wanted to question her? Because he…

Cared?

Cared *enough*?

"Ana!" he shouted, glancing over his shoulder because *yes, they were coming.* She broke her stasis and ran for him. Not swift, not powerful, but small and determined, her hands clenched into fists and with not the faintest idea how she could ever make her actions right with either Ian or the Core.

"Ana!" But this time his shout was a warning, as

he came off the bike saddle in alarm. She barely had a glimpse of motion from the side, shooting out from behind her little rental and then slamming into her with smashing force—hurling her into Ian, who twisted aside to free himself from the bike and still went down beneath her.

But not for long, because he'd quite clearly had enough of playing fair. Preternatural light flared around him as goon hands grabbed at Ana, lifting her…tossing her *through* the sudden play of light and energy and into the thorny scrub.

By the time she landed, a snow leopard crouched by her side—so close that the pale splendor of its pelt brushed against her, its long tail slapping against her leg—altogether not quite as big as she'd expected, but every bit as magnificent. Only for an instant before it leaped, broad paws spread wide and claws unsheathed, a wild snarl of warning in the air.

The first goon went down before him, and went down screaming—legs flailing, fists beating against the big cat's head and deterring him not at all. A whiskered muzzle closed around the man's thick neck, flesh giving way with a grisly crunch—

The second goon had grabbed a tire iron on his way, and he came in swinging. Metal thumped against feline ribs, and the cat—*Ian*—tumbled away, his teeth tearing free. He landed in a crouch beside Ana, already prepared for another leap.

But the goon had also brought out a gun. And he yanked Ana to her feet and jammed the muzzle of it to her temple, grinding metal into tender flesh. He snapped, "Your choice!" and gave Ana a little shake as if that would make his point more clear.

Ana gasped, knowing all too clearly that Ian understood her betrayal. She was the enemy; the Sentinels gave no quarter to the Core. He'd come for her on the bike, but he'd surely never intended to give himself up for her.

The goon wrenched her arm, jamming the gun against Ana hard enough to torque her head aside. She cried out, twisting in that grip—feeling small and insignificant and helpless and yet unable to ask Ian to do this thing.

And yet Ian did it.

With a final snarl, he disappeared into that blinding fog of energy and light, and when it cleared he still crouched there—blood smeared on his face, one arm clamping protectively against his ribs...bright blue eyes locked to Ana's.

"Ian," she whispered. "Ian, no..."

The goon shoved her aside and slapped the gun across Ian's face, and it turned out that was enough to take even a Sentinel down.

The stench of Core workings permeated Ian's head, throbbing along in time with the pain of his cheek and brow. His side radiated with stabbing pain against a lumpy excuse of a mattress. He absorbed the faint surprise of finding himself alone and unbound, and pondered opening his eyes.

And remembered, then, exactly how he'd gotten here.

Trusting Ana.

Trusting her right up until the moment he'd found her carrying the silent amulet—and even then, he hadn't been able to leave her to the fate her Core compatriots would have dealt her.

Or *might* have dealt her. Hard to know for sure. She might well have orchestrated the whole standoff. The

Core was rarely kind or respectful to its women, and those who made it out of low-level support roles tended to be both the best of them and the worst of them.

Either way, she'd played him like a pro.

Thanks to his delirious midnight departure from the retreat, the Sentinels had no idea where he'd gone—and no idea that he'd been taken. Worst of all, he had no way of telling them what he'd learned. That finally—*finally*—he had a way to detect the silent amulets. One that with refinement, might even allow the Sentinels to identify the amulets as they detected them. Right now the technique was nothing but a clumsy thing, baby steps that could at least alert them…

If they knew.

They needed to know.

He'd bet anything that his illness, Fernie's illness… *everyone's* illness there at the retreat—had come from one of those silent amulets. Although Ana had seemed to feel the faint effects of that illness, as well…

Nothing that couldn't be easily faked.

He took a steadying breath, full of a new pain he hadn't expected—a hard twist in his chest, radiating up the back of his throat to mingle with the effects of the blow he'd taken.

Probably broken.

The thought made him snort in faint laughter, figuring *broken* in more ways than one, and in turn the faint laughter sent bright shards of pain lancing along his ribs, wringing a gasp from him.

The tire iron. Right.

Eventually he opened his eyes, expecting a cell or some crude containment, and blinked at the sight of a textured paint ceiling. A careful turn of his aching head revealed similar walls done up in a classic Southwestern taupe, and a small window with tasteful decorative bars. A closet door, an opening at the corner he was fairly certain led to a tiny bathroom, and a bedside table and chair completed the furnishings. The table held a glass of water and what looked like two aspirin.

All the comforts of home.

With much care and several false starts, he eased off the bed. Healing swiftly wasn't the same as healing instantly, no doubt about it. A quick tour of the bare space revealed a small desk and nail holes in the wall where someone had been smart enough to take down the pictures. If it had occurred to them to rip up the comfortable carpet underfoot, they could have removed the tacking strips, too. As it was, he kept them in mind.

The bathroom was indeed tiny, tile floor and a corner shower, plus a securely locked second door to another room. The mirror was just big enough to give him a glimpse of his face—blood streaked and swollen over the angle of his cheek, a split over his brow—and, when he pulled up his shirt, his ribs. Just about what he expected there—bruises blooming purple unto black, the worst of them gone white in the center.

Dammit.

He availed himself of the facilities and went back to the bed. Whatever this particular Core mastermind had planned for him, Ian would meet it as well-rested—and recovered—as he could. Napping in relative comfort seemed like a fine idea when his painful ribs meant he wasn't going anywhere anyway.

Except that his fingers twitched against the covers, drumming to a silent song. There was no nap waiting here, only the tangle of his thoughts.

His mind whirled with *Ana*. His heart whirled with *Ana*. His body ached with mingled hurt and remembered touch, and his mind's eye gave him Ana laughing and Ana uncertain, and Ana's face lighting up in response to him.

He had no idea how to reconcile what he knew of her. What he felt of her. What she'd done to him.

In the end, with the most ultimate irony, the memory of the peace she'd given him allowed him to fall back into a meditative quiet. Relative rest, his body burning with the attempt to heal.

By the time quiet footsteps sounded outside his door, he'd had time to settle into himself. To resist taking the form of the snow leopard, no matter how close to the surface it lurked. The leopard was a hunter—it knew how to wait. How to persist.

So did Ian.

And Ian wanted answers.

But he hadn't expected Ana.

To judge by her uncertainty as she slipped through the door—as it locked behind her—she hadn't quite expected to be here, either.

She pressed her back to the door and regarded him, biting her lip. Definitely uncertain.

Or pretending to be.

He didn't rise to greet her. She'd changed to slacks that fit her petite, rounded form perfectly, and a stretchy shirt that molded to her slender body. Her face held a new bruise—from the morning's struggle or something fresher, he couldn't tell.

He tried to tell himself he didn't care, but that was a lie.

"Ian…" she said, and stalled out.

"Ana," he said, much more flatly. A lie of disinterest, as his heart rate kicked into gear and his fingers gave him away, twitching against the plain green bed blanket.

Her eyes flicked to the corner of the room and he saw what he'd missed before—the tiny dark spot of a camera lens. Well, that only made sense. Of course they'd keep an eye on him.

"They must think they can get in here pretty fast," Ian said, making his voice hard. "Or else they don't care what I do to you."

She flinched. "This wasn't supposed to happen."

"No? What in particular? The part where I end up with broken bones? The part where you make wild passionate love with me? Or just the part where your cover gets blown?"

"We both had secrets," she said, but her voice held a note of desperation.

Ian shook his head. "My secrets were my own. Yours were there to hurt me."

"No!" She moved forward from the door, just a step, her entire body tensed, her fists clenching—and then releasing in defeat as she retreated, turning away. Her voice came strained. "I guess maybe that's turned out to be true. But not like *this*." She looked up, but he didn't think the glare was meant for him. "*This* wasn't part of the plan. Not that I knew."

"So no broken bones, no incredible intimacy and no ever knowing who you really are." He gave no quarter. "What *were* you supposed to do?"

Her mouth twisted in some emotion he couldn't quite read. "Get inside your retreat. Plant a listening device. Spend time with you—get a sense of you. Fill out our dossier on you. And I thought… I *hoped*—I could start some sort of dialogue between your people and mine."

Ian couldn't help but bark a laugh, one that ended in a grunt of pain. He stiffened against the lash of his damaged ribs. "Is that what they call it where you come from? *Dialogue?*"

She glared at him. "These bruises?" She pointed at her jaw, where she'd either done a better job than usual of covering them or they'd faded faster than he'd expected—maybe they'd never been that bad after all. "I got these because I was only ever supposed to *talk* to you. I wasn't supposed to get—" she swallowed hard, looking away "—close to you."

"You *weren't*," Ian said, hard words to match the hard sensation in his chest. "You have no idea what *close* even means. Nice try, though. You had me fooled."

"That's not fair!" She rose to that, pushing away from the door and this time holding her ground. "I had nothing to do with this! You *saw*—" She stopped herself, visibly gathering up her thoughts and something of her emotions. "You saw what happened at that trail. I had no idea they'd be there. I came looking for *you*. I was worried. Your friends were worried."

"Awesome," Ian said. "I guess they'll be even more worried now."

She held her silence for a long moment. "There's not going to be any talking to you, is there?"

Ian felt the finality of that to his bones. "Not for a while."

Not for a long while.

Defeat enervated Ana, leaving her with nothing else to say.

But then, she'd known this wouldn't be something she could fix. She'd known it from the moment Ian recognized her as Core.

That the muscle goons had threatened her along the way made no difference—it hadn't surprised Ana, and it likely hadn't surprised Ian. The men who worked enforcement for the Core were trained to accomplish their task regardless, and Ana would have been a fair enough trade for Ian.

She stepped away from the door to look up at the camera. It was enough. She heard movement from the other side—a long, curving hallway that ran along the wing of this luxurious house, only ever meant to be a Santa Fe mansion and now altered by interior locks and latches and camera feeds so it could serve as Hollender Lerche's little posse hideaway—and Ana's home—since their flight from Tucson after *Core D'oíche*.

After only a few moments of silence—she couldn't bring herself to look at Ian, as aware as she was of his painfully uneven breathing. She'd barely been able to look at his face in the first place—the ugly puff of his cheekbone, the angry split at the edge of his brow. She certainly hadn't been able to ask how he felt beneath it all—if he still carried the headache and illness that had driven him away from the house to start all this.

She rubbed the side of her head, perfectly well aware of the lingering headache and trying not to think too much of it. She carried her own bruises, both physical and emotional; she'd been just as ambushed as Ian on that trail, if in a totally different way.

The room locks disengaged; the knob turned. Ana moved away from the door, tucking herself into the corner beneath the camera—barely making way for Lerche and the remaining posse goon.

Ian didn't move as they entered—not really. But something about him changed, his gaze going from Ana to Lerche, his eyes narrowing to shadow the bright blue. Lerche might not see the anger there—he was far too busy gloating over the coup of capturing Ian—but Ana did.

Anger for her. In spite of what she'd done. For she knew, seeing that expression, that Ian had instantly identified Lerche as the man who'd dealt her those earlier bruises.

It left her naked. Vulnerable and revealed and naked.

She swiped desperately at welling tears, swallowing against the barely controllable sob in her throat and perversely glad for the blur that kept her from seeing that look on Ian's face.

But humbled, too.

By Ian.

By a man who cared more for what had been done to her than for his own grudges and hurts.

"I want to thank you," Lerche said to Ian, characteristically unaware of the subtle byplay. "For you to have stumbled out of your safe little retreat and onto the mountain while we happened to be paying such close attention to you…for you to have done so while so clearly out of your head…it was a tremendous opportunity. I know you'll forgive me for taking advantage of it."

So many things Ian could have said in response. He was brilliant; he was never without words and never without dark humor and never without attitude. But as Ana regained control over her emotions, she found him silent, regarding Lerche with such a simmering anger that she couldn't imagine how he restrained himself at all.

"Well, perhaps not," Lerche acknowledged. "But I'm sure you'll see that I couldn't waste the chance." He shot one cuff, adjusting it with a twitch. "In any event, here we are. Do I need to mention that the more cooperative you are, the easier these days will be?"

"How about if I'm not cooperative at all, and you cut to the chase and kill me so you can see how I tick inside?"

Ana startled at Ian's words. Lerche didn't. He assumed a thoughtful expression. "But that would deprive you of the chance to pretend to cooperate while you look for ways to escape."

Ian barely lifted one shoulder. "True."

Lerche waited a moment for Ian to say more, and made a brief disappointed moue when Ian did nothing but watch him. "Well, then. Let me make your circumstances clear. Not only does no one know you're here, once your motorcycle is discovered, they'll think that you met your demise on the mountain. No one will look beyond that convenient little parking lot. I own you, Mr. Scott."

"You've captured me." Ian didn't look captured, sitting against the headboard with an aplomb Ana couldn't begin to muster. "It's not the same thing."

Lerche tipped his head, a casual *point-to-you* gesture. "Not yet." He left the obvious promise implicit. "You'll have a day to recover from your illness—I'm afraid I need you thinking straight for my purposes, at least to start with. By then your broken ribs should be tolerable, from what I understand of your healing proclivities. Future persuasion will be more exacting." He smiled unpleasantly. "You do intend to need persuasion, don't you?"

"Probably," Ian said.

"Excellent. You expand my opportunities by the moment."

Ana couldn't stop herself. "Ian—" *Don't play with him,* she wanted to say. *Don't doubt him.*

Lerche offered up a cruel laugh. "Ana, dear, he knows

what he's up against. That's more than I could ever say for you." He gestured to the walking wall of a posse bodyguard.

The man reached for the doorknob, opening it just enough to indicate he'd done the job and then waiting for further sign from Lerche—one eye very much on Ian. "As you can imagine, at that point I'll be asking you a certain number of questions, as well as using the opportunity to test some of our new workings on you. Nothing mortal, of course—that would be wasteful. But I wouldn't look forward to it if I were you."

At his nod, the bodyguard pulled the door open and stepped back so Lerche could precede him. Ana held her breath on a sigh of relief, prepared to make her own escape.

From what she'd done. And from what she was no doubt about to do.

She should have known better. *Lerche.*

He gestured at her. "Since it causes you such discomfort to be here, Ana, I'm happy to strengthen you with a new assignment—you will be the liaison for our prisoner. You'll see to his every need, and keep a log of his meals and other requests. You'll report to me on the schedule I provide. Of course, someone will make sure your records correlate with the camera footage."

Humiliation washed across her face, heating it. She couldn't help but glance at Ian—preparing herself for his annoyance, and for the rejection she expected to see there.

But the anger was directed at Lerche, not at her. When he did meet her gaze, she found an expression she couldn't quite fathom—something with compassion behind it.

For the merest instant, she didn't feel quite so alone.

And then his expression shuttered and he looked away, his eyes gone cold and his body quiet, and she tumbled back into the realm of the utterly bereft.

Chapter 8

Lerche left the Sentinel alone for the rest of the day—not so much as a mercy, but to provide him with time to think about his situation. To let his resentment toward Ana build, and his worry about his little friends at the retreat.

Not to mention the reality of his capture at Lerche's hands—the inevitable unpleasantries and ultimate death.

And, yes, the man needed time to heal. Not that much time, being what he was, but Lerche wanted to start with someone who was robust enough to take the process. He hadn't wanted the Sentinel damaged at all, but he supposed it had been inevitable—he'd had too much recovery time away from the retreat amulet to be taken easily.

Those at the retreat continued to sicken in a satisfying manner. No doubt they had help coming—perhaps even as soon as today, to judge by what the spy working had relayed—but Lerche expected it to be deliciously too late. Even if the healer guessed there was a working in play, he'd never find it in time.

In another several days the amulet would slowly disintegrate, destroying all evidence it had ever existed. That, too, was a skill that the Sentinels had not yet discovered.

Lerche smiled to himself, heading toward the small amulet workshop housed in what had, most incongruously, been a baby's nursery. Now the bright windows illuminated specialized sorting cabinets and wooden work tables alongside the man who called this place his domain. Budian waited for him here as well, no longer taking pains to hide himself from Ana.

Lerche gave them no preamble. "Which amulets have you chosen?"

The specialist, a man named Peter, glanced up from his work and gestured to a wooden tray of samples, each labeled with a neat, hand-printed card. "Experimental inducers," he said without ever turning away from the notes he was making. "Having primary feedback on the efficacy of these would be most helpful."

Lerche looked them over, only skimming the identifying cards. The amulets themselves were a variety of shapes, each with its own meaning, and each was also incised with precise, delicate glyphs—an ancient language known only to the specialists. That the glyphs were formed with such precision told Lerche all he needed to know—only complex, upper level amulets received such exacting attention.

Peter pushed two amulets across the table with one finger each and withdrew to his notes again, a disrespect that inspired Budian to look at him askance but which Lerche had learned to accept as part of the man's brilliance.

In truth, at this level of craft, the only specialists left were the brilliant ones. The others didn't survive.

Peter said, "Get this one into his room today. It should lower his resistance. He'll detect it, of course, but I assume you can overcome that."

"It won't be a problem."

Peter grunted as if he'd expected it to be just so. "The second of these will tell you whether his shields are still up. Don't waste any of these amulets until you've broken through."

"No," Lerche said, amused at Budian's stiffening posture. "I have no intention of wasting this opportunity."

Peter nodded to himself, as if checking that point off a list. "I've arranged the amulets in order. The first ones will be quite subtle in effect, and I'd appreciate careful monitoring—pulse, respiration and a camera on his face. Once you reach the red dot amulets, the effects should be perfectly clear—but of course you'll continue with the notes."

"Ana will," Lerche said, and smiled when Peter glanced at him. "As I've said, this is an opportunity not to be missed."

Peter only shook his head slightly and went back to work. Lerche chose to interpret the gesture as admiration, and left Peter to his work. It was time, he thought, to put Ana through her paces...and to remind her of her place.

Breakfast was good, and Ian ate it without reservation. If Hollender Lerche wanted to drug him or poison him, he'd do it either way—he'd already planted amulets to keep him isolated from other Sentinels, to chip away at his shields. Meanwhile Ian was healing—healing fast, in those dark restful hours of the night, and in need of fuel to keep doing it.

When lunch came, he asked for seconds.

Ana brought them, duly noting the fact in on her clipboard page for the day—along with the readings from the glorified fitness band he now wore around his wrist. She'd readily shown him the notes—had even taken his suggestion in a spot or two.

But now, as she brought the second tray, she also sat in the room's single chair for the first time, tucking it back in the corner under the camera. "I think he'll be in to talk to you soon," she said, her hands folded on the clipboard in a way that might have seemed casual if it hadn't been for the whitened knuckles. "I don't know what'll happen then."

"He'll torture me somehow," Ian said, so casually, dipping a forkful of grilled steak into barbecue sauce. "And he'll probably ask me a lot of questions while he's at it. Because, as we know, your Hollender Lerche isn't one to let opportunity pass by."

"He's not *my*—" But Ana stopped herself, openly gripping the clipboard now.

Ian shot her a look, not inclined to be charitable. "Ana, I get it. However you got tangled with this guy, he's got power over you. Easy for me to say you should have walked away before things came to this. So, yeah, I get it. It's complicated."

She gave him a wary look. "I *got tangled* with him by being born," she said. "And because I believe in what I do."

Born Core, just as he had been born Sentinel. No telling what she thought she knew of Sentinels. "Right," he said. "You believe what you did was justified, then?"

Her mouth flattened. "I believe what I *thought* I was doing was justified. That I'd be helping the Core to learn more about you. And after I met you—after I *knew* you—I believed that I could bring a new perspective to the Core's understanding of Sentinels. I thought…if the Sentinels are like you, at least some of them, then why can't the Core and the Sentinels come to some sort of understanding?"

He laughed shortly, pressing his hand against ribs still stiff and sore if not nearly as bad as the day before. "Did you think you could undo a couple thousand years of trouble with one short assignment?"

She flushed. "I thought I could try!"

"Yeah? How's that working out for you?"

She looked away, her expression troubled. "It's confusing," she said, taking his sarcasm and turning it into truth. "How things are for me in the Core…it's never been easy. My family isn't favored, and it's only right that I should have to prove myself more than others—"

Ian snorted, reaching for the glass of milk beside his plate. "Bullshit."

She blinked. "But—"

"Bullshit," he said again, and drained half the glass with a few big swallows before setting it aside. "That's just another way they control you. Keeps you useful. Keeps you from asking too many questions."

"What are you talking about? I *want* to be useful. I want to be—" She stopped, took a hard breath and struggled to control her voice. "Accepted."

"Only because they've made so damned sure that you aren't," Ian told her. He tossed his napkin on the tray, his appetite gone. "*I* accepted you, Ana. Remember that."

She blinked again, this time rapidly, with the glisten of tears on her lashes. "That's not fair."

"It's true." Ian would have scrubbed a hand over his face, had it not been still bruised and aching.

She sat a little straighter. "Your people have taken advantage of your abilities from the start!" But she couldn't hold her gaze on his; she looked down at the clipboard. "Mine have simply made sure you don't get out of hand. It's a thankless task, and it takes hard choices."

Ian sucked in a breath to snap back at her—and then let it ease away, making room for the ache that filled his soul as much as his body. She'd been conditioned since childhood, no doubt about that. Accepting the way her own people treated her and yet condemning him. His heart pounded—a peculiar thing, not racing with effort, but each beat deep and strong, as if these seconds mattered so much more than any others.

After a moment during which she kept her gaze fixed to the clipboard, he finally said, "Okay, you believe that. Nothing I can do about it, right? But I should warn you—I won't be answering their questions. And it's not going to be pretty." She jerked her gaze up, her eyes widening at his meaning, and he gave her no quarter. Not with his eyes, as hard as they ever got. Or his voice, dark with warning. "So be prepared, Ana."

"Ian...*no.* They'll break you!"

No kidding. If Lerche was right, then his choices were between a slow and lingering death or a quick and merciful one.

But if someone at brevis thought to send a skilled tracker up here, they'd know. And they'd come looking.

So he'd bide his time as best he could.

And meanwhile he regarded Ana with something akin to pity. "Listen to yourself. Are those the words of a woman who believes in how her people are acting?"

"Hard choices," she whispered. "Sacrifices..."

"Right. They've sacrificed you from the start, bullying you into compliance." He wanted to get out of the bed and take her into his arms and hold her until she understood just how badly the Core had done by her. Instead he only glanced up at the camera, knowing it a lost cause and knowing the price, at the moment, to be too high. "Ana, the big difference between your people and mine isn't what we can do. It's how we do it."

She made a stricken sound—part denial, part distress. And then, at the sound of a faint digital alarm, she pulled herself together and lifted her phone, checking the fitness band app and dutifully noting the readings in her neat, tiny print—no doubt understanding, as Ian did, that if Lerche wanted those readings he need only check the download himself. Forcing Ana to chart them was just another way to exert control over her.

Ian picked up his fork again, resolute.

The hardest choices for both of them still lay ahead.

Darkness fell before Lerche returned. Another meal gone by, another several visits for Ana—during which Ian held his silence and Ana tried and failed to hold her detached demeanor, the tip of her nose gone red with emotion.

Now she trailed behind Lerche, who had brought an assistant—a man he introduced as David Budian, which Ana took to mean he'd be here as often as not. Budian wasn't one of the bodyguards, which spoke of Lerche's confidence, but was a smaller man whose features looked faintly familiar and not terribly reflective of the Core.

As Ana's hadn't been. Too delicate of nature, her skin

tones not quite as deep, her hair not quite as dark, her eyes too close to a honey glow.

Budian placed a soft-sided briefcase on the small desk and unzipped it, flipping it open to reveal neat rows of secured amulets and closed partitions. Then he wrestled a restraint chair into the small room, leaving little remaining space and relegating Ana back into the corner beneath the camera.

"First things, first," Lerche said. "As much as I'd love to goad you into changing into your beast form so you can discover we've made it impossible, I have more important things to deal with and don't want to risk damaging you in a way that would delay us."

Ian hadn't intended to respond to Lerche at all, but hadn't counted on that little revelation. *Not possible?* He reached within himself, brushing against the leopard… looking to rouse it just enough to reassure himself, and only then realizing that he hadn't felt the leopard stir since he'd woken here.

It must have shown. Lerche smiled. "You feel it, don't you? Excellent. We can move forward with efficiency. Because, as you've surely guessed, our Ana did more than plant a simple spy amulet in your pathetic little retreat. She also planted a working we've been developing—a clever idea, if I say so myself."

You might as well. No one else will.

"It interferes with the manifestation of the Sentinel *other*, among other things," Lerche said. "It made you all quite satisfactorily ill."

Ian stiffened, his gaze shooting to Ana. She gasped, clamping her mouth closed too late.

"Yes, dearest," Lerche told her, his smile far too close to a smirk. "You made that household sick. If you weren't so reliably problematic with such details, you would have been informed ahead of time. As it is, you performed admirably. The kitchen was too noisy to yield much in the way of information, but the location worked nicely for our other purposes."

Ana.

Ana had planted a spy amulet.

She'd planted the very thing that had made them all ill—from Fernie to the kid who'd barely manifested his full potential.

Ian understood it all in one dizzying swoop of horror. The pattern of his illness, and Fernie's. The way he'd been so badly affected—but recovered so quickly, only to falter again.

The strength of his *other* dictated both his weakness and his strength.

Ana had done this. Ian speared another look her way, hot and furious—only to see how pale she'd turned. How clearly she'd believed the amulet to be of no harm. *To understand you all better*, she'd said of her role.

Just as manipulated as he'd been, in her way. And yet—

Ana had done this. To him. To his people.

And he'd never seen it coming. She'd been the perfect operative—nothing of the Core about her appearance, her presentation, her actions…

Or the way she'd touched him.

But Lerche wasn't done making the moment about Lerche. "Eventually we believe it will kill a field Sentinel such as yourself, but for the moment…the related amulet currently residing in this room is of a more refined nature, if just as effective. So if you were counting on being able to shield yourself from the consequences of declining to participate in our conversations…well, I'm assured that isn't possible, either."

Blah-blah-blah. Ian got it. The evil overlord, strutting his stuff.

And he got the underlying message well enough.

They'd rendered him defenseless against their tricks. No resistance, no delays.

If his people were going to find him, they'd have to do it quickly.

Ana sank into the chair in the corner, too stunned to do anything else.

This was her fault. All of it.

Not *fault.*

Accomplishment.

That's what Lerche would say. What any of her early teachers and remedial tutors would say. What any of her low-level coworkers would have said. *This is your break. Don't blow it.*

But inside, it wasn't what she felt. Instead she felt a flush of shame, a cold, heavy guilt...a sickness in her stomach. She hadn't ever wanted to do things *to* others. She'd only wanted to further the Core cause of controlling the Sentinels.

Controlling the Sentinels...

Just as she'd been controlled.

What she'd done suddenly didn't seem at all the same as understanding the enemy, or finding ways to communicate with them, to allow them to understand how dangerous their ways were. How potentially disastrous.

Understanding was what she thought she'd had with Ian, during those moments she'd allowed herself to forget why she was there with him in the first place. Understanding and respect and a response that she couldn't even quantify at all. The one that had kept her at his side, yearning for more of his touch, for yet one more dry snap of humor, for the glimpse of vulnerable truth in his eyes when he moved beneath her.

In his bedroom.

Where she'd taken her blazer. Muffled the amulet, thinking to secure privacy…and never knowing that she poisoned him all the more.

No wonder he'd stumbled away in the middle of the night, out of his head.

She'd sent him out into the mountain, creating the circumstances under which Lerche couldn't help but come after him. She'd made it possible for Lerche's men to accost him…to capture him.

Not the same as *understanding him better* at all.

So much for her lofty goals of creating better communication between the Core and the Sentinels. Could she have been any more naive?

She spared Lerche a quick, blurry-eyed glare. *I trusted you.* She'd known herself to be bullied and controlled, and she'd known it to be because she hadn't yet proved herself.

Now she wondered who she was trying to prove herself *to.*

And if Lerche had lied to her about all these things, then what else?

Ian sat against the headboard, his expression unreadable behind the healing bruises—or nearly so. Ana saw the understanding in his eyes, and the mixture of resignation and determination.

He knew what was coming. He'd known from the moment he'd seen the posse musclemen in the parking lot.

She thought that, just maybe, he'd understood better than she had all along.

Lerche gestured at the restraint chair. "If you would be so kind."

"Yeahhh," Ian said, drawing it out. "I don't think so."

"I'd prefer not to damage you."

"Much as I hate to inconvenience you..." Ian let it trail off into a shrug. The corner of his mouth crooked into something wry. "The way I figure, the sooner I get this over with, the better."

Ana didn't follow his meaning, but Lerche understood well enough—and was displeased by it, his mouth thinning in a way that Ana had learned to dread. He rapped lightly on the door without turning away from Ian, stepping aside to admit two of the posse—the big man from the parking lot and another who could be his twin, both of them wearing full posse getup of black slacks and polo shirts and heavy silver and arrogance. Not men that Ana knew—except she knew their nature.

Ian, she thought, suppressing a shudder. *Don't do this. He's not bluffing.*

But she saw the gleam in Ian's eye as Budian withdrew into the bathroom with the chair, getting himself out of the way with no apparent need to prove himself equal to this task. The men approached one on either side of the bed and Ana knew with a certain horror that this was what Ian had wanted. What he'd intended. He understood Lerche's nature and had used it, even as Lerche had thought to use him.

You can't possibly be healed enough...

They were bigger than he was, and they were professional. And Ian sat quietly on a sickbed—

Except then he didn't.

He rolled off and came up from beneath the man on the left, driving a fist into his groin and rolling aside, sweeping a leg alongside to bring the man down in that small space, awkward and clutching himself. Ian rolled up not to his feet but in a crouch, barely a hesitation. He launched, briefly airborne, adding momentum to the knee that jammed down on the side of the man's neck.

Ana gasped—to see again Ian's speed, his precision—the sharp strength behind his movement. To know she saw the leopard within him, the very thing that made him such a danger.

This man had touched her. Had loved her. Had brought her more pleasure than any man before him, and never once made her fear for pain.

Bone cracked, and still Ian brought the rest of his motion into play, slamming the edge of his hand along the man's throat.

The man's partner gave an inarticulate cry of rage, but he was hampered by size and the bed between them, and he launched himself over it far too late to do the first man any good. Ian met him on his way, jamming the heel of his hand upward, stiff-armed and precise and into the man's face. Another crack of bone and blood spurted, and Ian drove farther upward, driving his forehead into the nose he'd just broken.

The man went limp, stunned past the scream that had bubbled on his lips. Ian ducked aside but went down under that limp bulk anyway, his grunt of pain barely audible.

Silence.

And then Ian crawled out from beneath the vanquished guards and straightened to face Lerche—or nearly straightened, bent over his damaged side, his arm clamped tight to it. "Sorry," he said, and the calmness of his voice belied the look in his eye—dark and wild and barely controlled. "I hope you brought more."

Lerche's mouth had thinned to near invisibility; his

sharp rap on the door brought the pounding feet of reinforcements. "I had hoped you'd be sensible about this."

"Hollender," Ana whispered, using that first name exactly for the sharp glance it got her. "Please. Stop this."

Leave him alone, she meant. And *let him go. Just let him go.*

Lerche held up a hand to forestall the two men who reached the door. They stopped short, looming beyond it. "Perhaps you're right, my dear. Clearly I failed to strike the balance between keeping him whole and keeping him controlled. An expensive learning experience." But he left the door open, and Ana knew it for the taunt it was.

"Yeahhh," Ian said, drawing it out as he had before. He stood apart from the two men on the floor behind him—standing still and protecting his side, and yet his whole being filled with a sense of imminent action. The fallen men filled the space between the bed and the wall, and only one of them moved, groaning over the ruin of his face. "But I've got my own plans."

It's not going to be pretty, he'd said. Ana had thought he'd meant what would be done to him. Now she knew he'd also meant what she'd see him do in return.

Lerche saw it, as well. This was no rebellion—this was Ian, taking his fate into his own hands. Escaping, either way. Lerche's hand darted into his jacket, and Ian snarled a laugh and *moved*—moved so fast Ana hardly saw his intent.

But Budian did. The restraint chair shot out from the bathroom and into Ian's path, bringing the chair down and Ian with it—but only for the instant it took before he sprang up again.

By then Lerche had drawn his streamlined weapon,

jamming it into Ian as they collided with a force that drove Lerche back into his men.

Ana flinched in anticipation of gunshot and instead heard the arc of electricity. Ian stiffened with an involuntary shout, and Lerche, full of disdain, shoved him away. Ian fell, a clumsy caricature of his normal movement in collapse.

"No," Ana said, barely out loud. *No, don't do this. Don't hurt him. Don't break what he is.*

Lerche straightened, distancing himself from the supporting hands of his men and brushing a hand down the front of his suit. He tossed the Taser to Budian with a jerk of his chin, and Budian bent to apply another shock. Ian's eyes rolled up; his grunt was purely involuntary, all the air pressed from his lungs with the force of his reaction.

"No," Ana whispered again, tears spilling over once more—more tears in this past day than she'd allowed herself for years. *Don't break what he is. Can't you see the wonder of it?*

Lerche stepped aside so his men could finally enter. With cold indifference, they hauled Ian into the heavy-duty chair and strapped him down, and then helped—and carried—the fallen men away. Within moments, Ian was right where Lerche had wanted him all along, already stirring—blinking, jerking his head to shake off the effects of the stun, his hands in an involuntary tremble that quickly faded.

"Recovering already," Lerche said. "That *is* interesting. I see I'm going to learn a lot from you, my friend."

My friend. Just as he'd always called Ana by various pet names. Never meaning it…meaning only the opposite.

But as Ian came back to true awareness, jerking

against the restraints with an instant of obvious panic—*the leopard, a wild thing, caught and bound*—Lerche reached over to the soft-sided briefcase and withdrew several amulets, sorting through the knotted lanyards with swift efficiency and making a sound of satisfaction as he found the one he wanted. He briefly closed his hand around it, his face blanking with an instant of concentration.

The unpleasant taste of an invoked working flooded Ana's palate, making her blink and swallow hard. Ian made a sound she'd never heard before, an involuntary gasp filled with pain—she found him rigid, his fists clenched and every inch of his body straining against his bonds, as if some invisible force flooded him with nothing but pain.

"No," she said again, a little more loudly this time. "Hollender, you've won. You've got him. But he can't tell you anything like this!"

Lerche laughed. "My dear," he said. "I'm not doing this to get information. That will come. I'm doing this because I *can*. And because I want to." He spared her a meaningful glance, and she saw he was more affected than he'd let on by his close call, his face flushed and his expression not nearly as controlled as he probably thought. "And, Ana, dear—I very much hope you're making notes."

Ana swallowed a sound of despair, her hands clenched around the clipboard as her pen and smartphone tumbled to the floor. As she bent to retrieve them, Ian moved his head just enough to catch her eye. His struggle to draw breath was a palpable thing.

She understood that glance perfectly—the pain of it, the meaning of it and the intent still lurking behind it.

It's not going to be pretty.

Chapter 9

Ana hadn't done him any favors.

If she hadn't interfered, Ian would be that much closer to useless as far as Lerche was concerned. That much closer to one escape or the other. Or that much closer to the point where Lerche would have to leave him to heal. *Buying time.*

Sitting in this chair, bound at ankle and wrist and across his chest, Ian knew where things would lead now. He was helpless—damaged just as much as Lerche wanted and no more—as Lerche had so amply demonstrated by leaving him here to recover.

No matter Ian's intention, there would come a point where he would betray his people simply because he no longer had the control over his mind to prevent it. He would become weakened and befuddled and confused, and he'd mutter something important without even knowing it.

He had to put an end to this before things reached that point, one way or the other. That meant pushing Lerche harder and faster…making him go too far.

So Ana hadn't done him any favors at all. But Ana still didn't understand—not the way Ian had understood all too well from the moment he'd opened his eyes in this room.

"Ian," she whispered—not that there was anyone here to listen, or that he cared if they heard anything he might say to her.

She might still think they had secrets, though. Or that they *could* have them.

Her clothes rustled; the clipboard made a subtle sound as she set it on the small wooden desk. "I think you're awake."

More than awake. Awake and still throbbing with pain, a gripping lattice of pressure around his bones and trickling along nerves. A low-impact working as far as the Core was concerned—one chosen purely to punish him and restore Lerche's authority.

He reached for his leopard with caution, found…

Nothing.

Frigging effective, that particular working.

But it hadn't stopped the healing. Slowed it, he thought. But not stopped it.

"Ian, I'm sorry." She reached him, soothing his nose with her scent and a tentative brush of her fingers in his hair. "I'm in so far over my head right now… I don't know how to help."

"That's a start," he said tightly without opening his eyes. "Knowing this is complete fuckery."

She drew in a breath, holding it only an instant before acceding, releasing it with a sad sound. "It shouldn't be like this."

He couldn't restrain a snort, much as it pained him in all ways. "Babe," he said, "It's *always* like this."

She continued as if he hadn't spoken, determination in her voice. Determination to be heard, if nothing else. "Maybe I can't undo it, but I need you to know that I *want* to. If I could only turn this into what I thought I was doing—what I *wanted* to be doing…"

"You never had that power." He had no energy for anything other than blunt truth—barely that, as another shudder of the fading amulet effect gripped him tightly, scraping along rebroken ribs and forcing a desperate gust of air from his lungs.

"I'm sorry," she said again, and this time she rested the back of her hand just beneath his jaw, the touch of a lover.

The rush of quiet took him by surprise—his mind calming, the churning excess making way for peace. It hastened the retreat of the lingering pain, such a sudden surcease that he choked on it, struggling for composure.

She seemed to understand. She gave him the time he needed. And when he finally opened his eyes, she gave him an uncertain smile. "Better?"

He shook his head, not only unable to respond, but simply unable to fathom. The understanding of what they'd been together, what they somehow still *were*…

Heartbreak.

She seemed lost in her own thoughts. "I'm grateful that you aren't…taking this out on me. I wouldn't blame you."

"Hey," he said, making no attempt to soften his harsh voice. "Don't get me any kind of wrong. I'm mad as hell, and what you've done…" He shook his head. *Carefully.* "But I'm more than just *Sentinel*. I'm a whole person.

With layers. I'm as complicated as anyone. So don't go making assumptions about what I'm going to feel."

She bit her lip, blanching tender skin. "I really thought I was doing the right thing. A good thing."

It wasn't a conversation he could have right now and stay sane. *Ana, his lover, versus Ana, Atrum Core pawn.* He forced himself to more practical matters. "It doesn't make any difference. As soon as Lerche thinks I'm ready, he'll be back for more. And I'm going to give it to him."

She sat on the side of the bed in this tight space, still able to let her hand linger—this time on his thigh. The long muscles tensed involuntarily under her touch, but then relaxed into the bliss of it. She said, "I don't understand. Or I hope I don't."

He forced himself to relax his grip on the chair arms, flexing his fingers. "I mean that I'm not going to be a very good guest."

She gave the chair a meaningful look; he shrugged in response. Tied, he was. Utterly helpless, he wasn't.

She must have decided to let it go. "I'm to feed you," she said. "And to stay here with you—*observing*—although I'm allowed to return to my own room to freshen up after you've eaten. Are you up to that now?"

He was nowhere near *up to it.* But the better he ate, the stronger he was...and now, more than ever, he had to stay physically strong. So he said, "Go for it."

She fussed with the monitor on his wrist, straightening it. "When I get back, I can feed you." She glanced up at him with some uncertainty. "Or I can release one hand so you can do it yourself. But—"

Right. He'd just pledged to be a bad guest. And even if she'd always obviously known, deep down, the precarious nature of her position with the Core, now she was in the process of recognizing it out loud. "Ana," he said, "I won't ever do anything to make your situation worse." But in all honesty, he had to amend those words. "Not directly."

She gave him a faint smile, the tension around her mouth relaxing. "Okay, then," she said. "Let me go get a tray. And, Ian…" She faltered, glancing up at the camera as if reminding herself how closely they were watched. "If I find a way to help…"

His words came out harder than he meant them to. "You want to help? Fine. Then promise me this—whatever happens here, once this is over, you break from these people. You don't belong here, and you know it. *They* know it. Just get out of here and into the rest of the world where you can live your life the way it should be lived."

It startled her. She opened her mouth for a protest, and he shook his head sharply. *"Promise."*

She glanced at the camera again, doubt and fear evident. Of course she wouldn't believe that she *could*; she'd been conditioned against it. Whether she believed that she *should* was something Ian couldn't glean. She lowered her voice to near silence when she said, "I'll think about it."

He hadn't expected that much. It was a start. And convincing her of it might, in the end, be the only thing he had left to accomplish.

Ana made it back to her room with the neutral expression she'd learned to cultivate from childhood—never disapproving of anything she'd seen and never showing weakness.

But once she closed the door, leaning against it as if that would ensure privacy, she tipped her head back and allowed the emotion to release—her mouth trembling, her face quivering out of control, and again, those tears. Silent tears, but tears nonetheless.

For herself. For Ian. For what could have been, and for what she'd always thought had been.

Because she wasn't what she thought she was. The Core wasn't what she'd thought it to be. The Sentinels…

She had no idea.

After a long moment and a gulping breath, she decided against trying to sort those things out. There was too much, and she had too little information to go on. She began to think she'd always had too little information to go on.

But she'd been lucky earlier, when Lerche had been too busy to take true notice of her pleas to stop hurting Ian. She'd never seen him taken off guard so thoroughly—his authority challenged, his dignity lost. He wouldn't like it when he had the time to realize her quiet witness from the corner.

But that, too, she would face at another time.

For the now, she simply had to get through the moments. She rubbed a circle on her temple, massaging the dull ache there, and pushed away from the door—headed for the shower with her mind's eye full of the past hour.

Never mind that Ian was Sentinel. She'd believed his promise not to give her trouble in a way she never would have believed one of Lerche's posse members. She'd released one arm from the restraints and positioned the tray on his lap, eating her own meal beside him while lending him a hand as necessary—but allowing him to feed himself.

The small things, she knew, made a difference. A grasp at the illusion of control.

And now, with the weak shower sluicing water down her sides, she let her hands linger on her body—not pleasuring herself, but recalling the sensation of Ian's touch, and how it had felt so natural. How she had felt so safe.

Once out of the shower, the contrast struck her hard.

She wasn't truly safe in Lerche's posse. She'd never been. Not since she'd arrived here in adolescence. Not truly before then, in the hands of tutors and a communal Core household where she somehow quite naturally ended up as the one to blame for whatever happened while her father took no strong stand for her and her mother remained absent.

It was something she'd grown used to, until she'd felt Ian's touch.

She blotted her wet hair with a towel, rubbing her temple again. The ache had grown. In fact, when she took the time to think about it, it had never quite left.

It made her think of Fernie with that weary look in her eyes, and of the others at the retreat, hiding in their rooms without ever realizing they truly had something to hide from. That the amulet Ana had planted was making them ill when they spent time in the kitchen.

She faltered, looking around her room—a space no larger than Ian's prison but more comfortably appointed, if with little in the way of personal touches. Her eyes fell on the closet door, and she tossed the damp towel onto the bed and crossed the room to open it.

Because, of course, her blazer hung here—along with the clothes someone had already recovered from the vacation rental home. She slipped her hand into its pocket without removing it from the hanger, her fingers closing on the small button of cool metal she'd never bothered to remove.

She pulled it out, turning it over in her fingers. The

sleek, barely marked object had once struck her as elegant in design, unfettered by any lanyard with its braided or knotted cord. Easy to invoke and endowed with the ability to cling if pressed against a surface at the moment it was activated.

But it was poison. It had poisoned Fernie, and it had made Ian deathly ill. And that, she knew now, had been the point. To kill Ian. His capture here had been a change of plan, a moment when Lerche had seized opportunity. If Ana had a headache now, it was only just—even if this amulet couldn't possibly be affecting her.

The polished brass button evoked sudden revulsion in her—the impulse to fling it across the room and as far from her as possible. Instead she closed her hand around it and before she could think twice, strode back into the bathroom and dropped the thing into the toilet, flushing not once but twice.

Sudden trepidation trembled through her as the empty toilet stared back at her. There were always consequences for such small rebellions and misbehaviors. One day soon, Lerche would ask about the location of the amulet, and she'd have to say she lost it.

She made herself breathe slowly, lifting her shoulders back to completely fill her lungs. Then she snagged her robe from the door and slipped into it, wrapping it snugly to ward off the sudden chill chasing goose bumps along her arms.

Footsteps outside the room door gave warning—a man's footsteps, the tread slowing at the last moment. She pushed the uncombed hair from her face and made it to the bathroom doorway before Lerche entered.

He never knocked.

At some point during the afternoon, he'd taken a minor blow to the side of his mouth—as likely from his collision with his bodyguards as anything else. Ana found the sight of that insignificant abrasion gave her some small, mean satisfaction. It was enough to provide her the strength to stand here before Lerche in a short, light robe that offered not nearly as much coverage as she'd felt when she'd slipped it on.

He said, "Tomorrow you'll return to the Sentinel retreat and retrieve the amulet you planted."

It was the last thing she expected. The last thing she *wanted.*

She wanted to be here with Ian—if not able to stop what was happening to him, at least *knowing*. At least *here*, so if opportunity arose…

She'd learned to think like Lerche in that, at least.

But she knew better than to challenge him, so she did what she so often did, and offered confusion. "I don't understand. I thought it served a purpose there."

He scowled at her, his eyes raking over the vulnerability of her exposed neck, the easy handhold of her tangled hair. "Ana, I begin to despair that you will ever understand." He didn't sound despairing. He sounded disgusted.

He sounded as if he believed her and as if he'd always believed her—never understanding just how much she'd always managed him.

Maybe that, too, would be opportunity.

But now he only looked at her with his patronizing, disapproving mien. "On the whole, it isn't necessary that you do understand. You will simply carry out my orders. But in this case, it happens that I'm removing evidence. It wouldn't serve me for you to be caught, so be forewarned—Sentinel reinforcements have arrived at the retreat. Field Sentinels in truth, unlike the laboratory squint you were able to fool. Do not play with them."

"No," she said, fervently enough to convince anyone. "I would never."

"They're looking for our guest, of course—they won't find him, although they've already found his motorcycle. We spread obfuscation workings all over that trailhead, and we're fully surrounded by them here."

She nodded, struggling with the understanding that he'd been ready for this—this completely forbidden direct move against the Sentinels.

Because the Core, as a matter of course, didn't take action against the Sentinels. Not directly. They worked only to prevent their egregious use of the Sentinel power that no one else had.

So she'd been taught.

Lerche evinced no sign of noticing the whirl of her thoughts. "Get in on the pretext of looking for Ian—tell them you, too, have been ill."

"Misdirection," she said. "So they won't think it's a working aimed at them." As well as explaining her absence after she and Ian had connected so strongly, so quickly.

He gave her a sharp look. "Exactly so." His gaze scraped her up and down. "In truth, you aren't quite looking yourself."

She stopped herself from narrowing her eyes at him. He wasn't one to notice the subtleties of her disposition unless it suited him somehow. "I have a headache," she said, and didn't miss the satisfaction in his eyes. "I'm sure I'm just unused to the intensity of this day."

"No doubt." He dismissed her well-being with a flick of his hand—and then closed the distance between them with swift purpose, grabbing her jaw as he so often did, pushing her up against the bathroom door frame. "I am not pleased with your interference at the trailhead," he said, grinding the back of her head into wood. "You would have no doubt of this if it wasn't necessary to leave you unmarked for tomorrow."

Ana gasped at the brute ugliness of his grip, and the escalation of his threat. Never had he handled her so much before, so cruelly—so frequently. Bruises on her arms, yes; the red welt of a slap on her cheek, the hot, puffy feel of an inside lip bruised against teeth. Rarely something she found so hard to cover. His hold muffled her words, but she managed them anyway. "I understand."

No excuses. No explanations. No crying out that he'd lied to her and taken her by surprise, and how could he expect her to be a team player that way?

No spitting back the words of accusation that on this day he'd been everything he'd ever accused the Sentinels of being. Or everything she'd learned from childhood that the Sentinels were.

While Ian had never been any of it.

"Good," he said, and thrust her away from him, leaving her to grasp at the gaping edges of her robe, her mind spinning. "I might have left a mark at that. No matter. You've always healed so conveniently fast."

He spun on his heel and left before she could ask what he'd meant by that, not bothering to close the door and thus leaving her exposed to the sneering curiosity of the posse member who passed by.

No matter. She pushed the door closed without haste, too stunned by events for her thoughts to do more than hover and clash.

After a lifetime of wanting to be part of something—to do *more*, to be involved in *more*, it seemed that now she very much was. Just not nearly in the way she'd imagined it.

And now she had to decide what to do about it.

* * *

The Sentinels' compound was the last place Ana wanted to be. And the last people she wanted to be with.

But morning found her here anyway, searching—and failing to find—the confidence to approach Ian's friends. Knowing she'd been the cause of their illness and that even now she remained complicit in his captivity.

Uncertainty left her just down the block from the retreat where the odious David Budian had dropped her off, and where he would pick her up again at her call.

"Don't dawdle," he'd told her, his voice bored and bossy as she disembarked from the nondescript sedan he'd chosen.

"I'll take as long as I take," she'd told him, no longer finding herself so automatically respectful of those in Lerche's chosen posse—even if she'd once aspired to join it.

Budian had merely grunted and waited for her to close the door before he pulled away from the dirt and gravel lane.

Leaving Ana to gather herself and move forward.

Each time she steeled herself to walk confidently to the door and innocuously inquire after Ian, she also thought of Ian himself—restless in the chair restraints, his body stiffening in leftover waves of pain while Ana pretended to sleep in the bed beside him.

She'd wanted to kneel beside that chair and unbuckle every single restraint, kissing away the marks of them. She'd wanted to brush his hair from his eyes and take away his pain.

Instead she'd done what she could, slipping a hand from beneath her light blanket and letting it rest on his wrist through the night. Giving him the peace he craved, and seeing the visible signs of how much more easily he rested.

Come dawn she'd fed him and managed his needs, knowing he wouldn't betray her even though she'd betrayed him, and knowing her presence here was Lerche's way of reestablishing his control over her. She would pay for giving herself to Ian; she would pay trying to protect him.

And Ian would pay, too. Lerche had never wanted her as a woman, and he'd never bothered to notice her brief, obligatory encounters with the Core members who'd shown any interest. But her intimacy with Ian had triggered something in the man.

It was the first weakness she'd seen in him.

The thought startled her. It meant that in her own way, she'd had control over Lerche—that his reaction made her important in a way she'd never understood.

She didn't truly understand it yet. But she'd use it, if she could. If only to bolster her confidence.

She drew the deepest of breaths, shook her hands out and moved out down the lane with a confident stride. Armed with purpose and carrying only the one small protective amulet she'd slipped out of the amulet room.

Ian's motorcycle sat not in the barely visible driveway, but off to the side—out of the way of the two cream-colored SUVs in the driveway and the several economy cars behind them.

The Sentinels were here, all right.

One man sat on the porch, brown hair and bright eyes and jeans beneath a pale plaid button-up shirt. Not a large man, but a lanky one who lounged with what Ana considered remarkably alert insouciance. He lifted his chin in greeting as she hesitated, as if quite certain she meant to come into the yard.

She did.

"Mornin'," he said. His eyes were brown and she thought they might just see right through her. "Ana."

She raised a brow at him in question.

"We've been hoping you'd stop by. Fernie'll be out in a moment." He seemed to reconsider this. "Probably Lyn and Jet, too. Maybe Ruger."

Sentinels all, no doubt. But unless they'd already figured out who she was—*what* she was—why come out at all?

"We've been worried about you," he said—and she had the sense that he didn't read her mind, no matter what horror stories she'd heard, but that he'd simply read her face, seen her confusion. Those eyes were too alert to miss much.

Like Ian's.

They were *all* that way, she discovered, as two women pushed their way out of the house, followed by Fernie at a more sedate pace and by a looming form that remained just inside.

"Fernie!" Ana said, relief spilling out. "You look better!"

Fernie nodded back at the house, her gaze on Ana openly assessing. "Ruger has his ways. We worried about you, Ana. We're worried about Ian, too. What can you tell us?"

Ana looked at the other two women—one no larger than she was, graceful and petite and tidy, and the other a tall, lithe form with a dancer's movement and wild whiskey eyes, her dark hair cropped short and mussed, her body clad in leather from snug black pants to a black vest and her bare arms strong with muscle.

The shorter woman eyed her without any friendliness. "Where is Ian?"

Ana's heart kicked up a notch. She had no chance of fooling these people—field Sentinels, all of them. If they couldn't read her mind, they'd read her body. And they obviously weren't taking anything for granted.

"She is already frightened," the dark-haired woman observed. "You just made it worse."

"Stop it," Fernie told them. "This woman is important to Ian. She's our guest." She came down the porch steps to take Ana's hand and give it a comforting pat. Today she wore her hair in a bun again, and her square features looked more relaxed. "Are you well, Ana? And yes, we need to know—have you seen Ian?"

Ana was supposed to say *I've been ill. I left early yesterday to look for him and had to go home to bed. Haven't you found him yet?* She was supposed to make her way into the kitchen—not so hard to ask for a glass of water in this climate—and quietly reacquire the amulet.

But when her mouth opened, the words wouldn't come out.

And the words that wanted to come out would probably get her killed. By these people, or—

She thought suddenly of the man on the trail—the one who'd been bait for the amulet-enraged mountain lion, and for Ian. The one who'd died without garnering any attention from local authorities.

Because the lion hadn't killed him and Ian hadn't killed him. But Lerche's posse…

They could have done it. They no doubt *had*. Because, no doubt, it had served Lerche to convince Ana of Ian's perfidy.

That man had been assigned his role as a consequence of his failure in the field. If Lerche had discarded him for failure, what would Lerche do to Ana if she…

Betrayed him?

Even if he had betrayed her first. In so many ways. Controlling her, lying to her, *shaping* her…

She couldn't think. She took a step back. Another. Her hand fell from Fernie's, and only then did she realize how long the Sentinels had watched her—silent, waiting.

"You see," the leather-clad woman said, her whiskey eyes wise and wild. "She is prey."

"Jet!" the other woman said, and the man on the porch smothered a laugh. "That's not appropriate. And she's more than prey. She's…" The woman trailed off, taking a step forward—which Ana mirrored by taking a step back. The woman wrinkled her nose, held up a finger…and sneezed.

From the giant shadow behind the screen door, a voice rumbled. "She's Core."

Ana froze. Jet's whiskey eyes narrowed. Fernie made a sound of dismay. But the woman only looked thoughtful. "She's certainly been exposed to their workings," she said. "But there's nothing active here."

Ana's knees went to water. She stiffened them, bracing herself—readying herself. She would never outrun them, but surely it was better than not even trying—

But she didn't run. And no one pounced on her.

They didn't have to. They could afford to bide their time when she had no chance of escape in the first place.

But the smaller woman circled to the side, frowning—and then quite surprisingly closed her eyes, while the others just as surprisingly—and obviously—waited on her.

Finally the screen door opened, and the man who stepped through was every bit as big as his shadow had suggested. Tall and rugged and full of shoulders and a hint of pure brawn. "Lyn?"

The smaller woman shook her head, opening her eyes. "Don't ask me to explain it. There's Sentinel blood here."

No. No there wasn't.

The woman Lyn gave Ana what seemed to be a sympathetic look. "Not much," she said, glancing back to her friends. "But it's there."

Ana took yet another step back. She couldn't think. She couldn't begin to understand, and yet so many things suddenly made sense. The outcast nature of her parents; the way she'd been taken from them just a little bit early—and the way no one had ever expected her to amount to much anyway. The way Lerche treated her.

The way Ian had responded to her.

Lerche had known.

She touched trembling fingers to the side of her head, where the ache still lingered. *The amulets.* The ones that were only supposed to be spy amulets, and yet were so much more.

He'd known they'd sicken her. Maybe he'd even looked forward to it—taking the *opportunity* to assess how strongly her Sentinel blood ran.

"Ana," Fernie said, reaching out to her with a look that warned Lyn back. "Let us help."

"No!" Ana said, not rejecting Fernie so much as the entire situation, the overwhelming waves of understanding—her life rewritten in whole. She took a step back, and another. "Stay away from me! All of you!"

Chapter 10

Ian sat silent before the camera, waiting with the patience of the big cat.

Even aching and battered from the inside out, he heard things they probably hadn't meant him to hear, drew conclusions they likely hadn't meant him to draw.

They were packing up. Preparing to withdraw and relocate.

It meant that brevis was coming. Was maybe even here.

It meant Lerche wouldn't have as much time as he probably wanted—and the man would cut his losses rather than risk moving Ian.

But not until he'd wrung as much as he possibly could from the situation.

In the midst of the bumping and thumping of the packing, Ian easily heard when Lerche approached—knew there were three of them altogether and that Ana wasn't with them.

She'd been gone for hours.

The door opened to reveal Lerche and his soft-sided amulet case. He put it aside on the creaky little desk and faced Ian with some satisfaction. "It's time for a little blunt conversation."

"I hadn't noticed any particular niceties so far." Ian flexed his wrists against the restraints, finding them as snug as ever. He didn't waste energy on shields. His had never been profound, and Lerche had already demonstrated he could dispense with them at will.

"Nonetheless," Lerche said, "Ana has a propensity to interrupt, as you've seen."

Ian looked not at Lerche but at the two walking walls he'd brought for backup. Not a bad thing, perhaps, to have the man so wary of him that he brought muscle even under these circumstances. "What is it about her, Lerche? Why keep her so close, when you don't think much of her at all?"

"I see she did this particular job well, if nothing else." Lerche smiled in a way that made Ian want to hit him. Hard. Nothing of the leopard behind it, and everything of the man. "She betrayed you in the worst possible way—she continues to betray you—and still you care. One of your Sentinel weaknesses."

"I consider it a strength." Ian spoke as evenly as he could. He didn't defend Ana. No matter how impossible her situation, or his belief that she'd been misled and used…

Her choices had been hard, but she'd still had choices. She was still responsible for them. And the ones she'd made still hurt like hell.

"As you will." Lerche unzipped the case, flipping it open. Amulets gleamed more brightly than the limited window light should have allowed; a sickening ochre taste oozing out into the room. "Although the truth about Ana might amuse you."

Ian doubted it. He flexed his fingers, his ankles… tensing and relaxing the long muscles of his legs as he'd done all morning. Tied he might be; willing to let himself stiffen, he wasn't.

"Once upon a generation or two ago," Lerche said, running his fingers over the amulets with appreciation, "one of our *drozhars* met one of your Sentinel bitches and found he had a point to make. The incident resulted in a child. Naturally, he couldn't allow such a child to remain in Sentinel hands, so he took it, and kept its mother on hand until the child was raised far enough along to be interesting." He glanced at Ian. "If you had a chance to check, you'd find your records back this up."

"If," Ian said. Not believing, not disbelieving. Just filing away the words for another time. Trying to keep the impact of them from rousing emotion. *Anger. Desperation.*

"As happens from time to time, we found it convenient to have Sentinel blood for experimentation," Lerche said. "We allowed the child to breed, in a limited fashion—and we kept the bloodline ignorant of its heritage."

"To control the experiment," Ian said, finding in Lerche's satisfaction a convincing truth. One that churned inside his chest as he understood, all over again, how deeply and perversely the Core had continued to work against them. Generations earlier, the Sentinels had thought the detente successful and had focused on protecting their world from the burgeoning environmental costs of industrialization.

"Ana is the end of that line," Lerche said. "The blood has become too thin to remain interesting, while still thick enough to render her deeply flawed for our purposes." His face flickered with annoyance. "I had hoped the spy amulet would deal with her, but her blood is apparently too thin for that. A shame she hesitated on triggering the second working."

"Bummer for you," Ian said, trying to still the clamor of his pounding heart.

"Still, it gives me the chance to play with her a while longer." Lerche seemed genuinely cheered by the thought. "Make no mistake, Ian Scott. You might have temporarily had her body, but she remains mine."

"Can't argue with that." And he couldn't. Not when Ana had been the one to snug his restraints back to the tightest setting. Whatever the pain on her face as she'd done it, her regret didn't begin to echo what that decision had done to *him*. "As long as we're gloating, you want to tell me where we're going with this? Because my people are coming, and I'm guessing you won't leave me behind as a welcome gift."

Lerche made a noise that Ian couldn't quite read. Derisive, perhaps. Amused, maybe. "As you wish." He patted the soft briefcase as if it were a pet. "Fabron Gausto once thought he could create a working that would eliminate your various bestial advantages."

"Right. As I recall, he simply turned himself into a monster. And then he died."

Lerche made a dismissive gesture. "He wasn't looking at the situation from the correct perspective. Why change us, if we can change *you*?"

Of course. All of the recent amulet developments had focused on destroying the Sentinel *other*, from the bullets that had poisoned Kai Faulkes over the summer to the very working that now held Ian's leopard at bay.

He hadn't meant to clench his fists against the restraints, but of course Lerche noticed it. "You," he said, lifting a shoulder that in no way offset his smug expression, "were an opportunity I couldn't pass up. I had hoped to wrest more information from you—you're really quite the prize—but..." Lerche shrugged. "As it is, I'll simply focus on permanently peeling you away from the beast you call your *other*. Being the first to accomplish that will be equally as rewarding."

Ian fought for composure through throbbing head and aching ribs and fury. "I don't suppose it's occurred to you that after those interlopers crashed our party outside Ruidoso this summer, we'd be better off working together? Because they're after us both, and I can tell you right now we don't know crap about whoever was behind that."

"I'm sure we have people working that situation," Lerche said. He nudged the amulet case into the exact center of the desk. "In any event, Ana will be back soon. I care little whether you tell her any of this. Her fate is sealed regardless."

"I'm not sure why you even bothered to tell *me*."

Lerche smiled. "You're smarter than that, Ian. Obviously, I knew it would distress you."

Ian grit his jaw on the snarl rising to break free, the tension of it aching down his spine.

Lerche only laughed. "I have things to do," he said. "When Ana returns, I'll be back to play." He gestured at the open case, laughed again, and swept out the door with an exit worthy of an evil overlord. Ian glared after his back, then glared at the muscle who had never deigned to notice him in the first place—and then found himself glaring at the closed door.

Alone. And waiting. And, just as Lerche had intended, anticipating. Not only his own fate, but Ana's—

spread out there before him in the open case and its sickly gleam of metal.

Spread right out before him.

None of these amulets were silent; there was no need for it.

Lerche, perhaps, didn't understand the intuitive nature of Ian's work with amulets. Didn't understand that his strength, the thing he did better than any other, was combining that intuition with the logical process of deconstructing the things in the same layered, rote fashion of their construction.

Didn't understand, perhaps, that while even a Core expert required the cords, knots and braids to identify an amulet at a glance, Ian found them convenient but needed none of it—not so long as he'd encountered the basic elements of any given amulet in the past.

Ian rolled his shoulders within the confines of the chair, and began to explore the amulets.

The big man facing Ana from the porch made a harrumphing sound. "If we want you," he said, quite matter-of-factly, "you're ours. You must know that."

She glanced from one to the other of them, utterly unable to think. The lanky man on the porch bench gave her a modest little shrug, confirming the big man's words. Jet waited in readiness and Lyn stood back slightly as if leaving it to the others, now that her job was done.

Fernie said, "Don't you dare push her. We just turned her whole life inside out...and I don't think she ever meant to hurt anyone in the first place."

The lanky man snorted. "If you say so, Fernie. That's your thing, isn't it?"

"Yes, Shea," Fernie snapped at him, "it is. So have

some respect. And remember that Ian—" She didn't finish that sentence, glancing at Ana as she started another instead. "Remember that Ian thinks much of her. He's no fool, our Ian."

But he'd been a fool to trust Ana, no matter that she hadn't meant for any of this to happen.

Fernie reached out to her again, palm up and fingers gently beckoning. "Ana. Let us help. We can keep you safe here—and you can help *us* help Ian. I know that's what you want."

True enough. But a single clear line of thought broke through her confusion, and she grasped at it. She couldn't stay here. Lerche would know something had gone wrong. He might well shut down the house, cut his losses and relocate.

He wouldn't leave Ian alive.

"Start over," Lyn said, very practically. "I'm Lyn Maines. I take the ocelot, and I'm a tracker."

"*The* tracker, you mean," the lanky man said. "You don't want to be a Sentinel on the run if Lyn is on your track."

Ana looked more closely at him, then, floundering in her assumption that Lyn tracked not those from the Atrum Core, but Sentinels.

Lyn caught her expression well enough. "We do police our own," she said drily. "As well as get them out of trouble."

The lanky man made a noise that Ana couldn't quite interpret and said, "I'm Shea. I take the coyote and handle shielding." Ana glanced around them somewhat warily, and Shea nodded. "Right. This whole place is shielded now. Including you."

"Jet," said the wildest of them. "I am wolf." She frowned, glancing at Fernie.

"Yes, that's a good way to say it," Fernie agreed. To Ana, she said, "Jet was born wolf. One of yours got hold of her."

"Gausto." Ana winced. She'd heard things—the Southwest *drozhar* gone rogue. And she knew how quickly Lerche had dissociated himself from the Southwest *drozhar* when things went bad—but also that he secretly admired the man. She'd never known details.

"I'm Ruger," said the big guy on the porch. "I'm the reason Fernie is up and walking around when she shouldn't be."

"The healer," Fernie interposed, more drily than was her wont. "And a very bossy one, too. Not in the best of moods, with Mariska newly brooding back home."

"Bear," Ana guessed, looking at him—though she hadn't quite meant to say it out loud.

Ruger showed his teeth in a laugh. "Kodiak."

Ana said with some hesitation, "My name is Ana Dikau. I'm not anyone important to the Core. I guess… now I know why."

"You're important to *us*," Lyn said. "You can help us with this illness. Maybe help us find Ian."

The illness. The amulet. She glanced at Ruger.

"It's all I can do to stay ahead of it," he said. "We're all feeling it. It's silent, isn't it? And you know where it is."

She took a breath. A deep one, not caring how visibly it revealed her nerves and her lack of inborn courage. "I do," she said. "I'll get it. But not until everyone comes away from the porch."

Of all of them, Jet seemed to understand most readily. She moved off the porch and over toward the driveway, and seemed surprised when no one else did. "Come," she said. "She is prey. She will not go past us to enter.

And she will not enter if she thinks we'll be waiting outside the door for her to come out."

Prey. Exactly so, in far too many ways and for far too many years. Ana crossed her arms and looked at those who hadn't yet moved. Ruger made a sound deep in his chest, and she thought it might have been amusement. He followed Jet, and Lyn and Shea moved more reluctantly but still ended up beside the cars.

Fernie held out her hand to Ana—most assertively this time, nodding at it. "We're vulnerable, too," she said. "We go together, you and me." When Ana hesitated, she said, "Ana, I take no other shape. My blood probably isn't all that much thicker than yours. At some point, we must trust."

"Follow the feeling," Ana murmured. Ian, she trusted. Fernie had less reason to trust her than Ana had to return it, making her continued understanding a gift.

She took Fernie's hand.

But when they entered the house and reached the kitchen together, Ana pulled away. "You should stay away, now."

"My kitchen," Fernie said in dismay. "Of course, the kitchen. This is where you were, that first day."

"I didn't know," Ana said, unexpected bite in those words. "Not *any* of what I thought I did." *I didn't know the amulet would hurt anyone, I didn't know I would find good people here, I didn't know I would follow one of them right into love.*

Fernie said nothing, her mouth flattened, the strong morning light and her recent illness making her face severe.

Ana knew the feeling of being unforgiven. A familiar thing, now that she knew she could pin it on the way Lerche had never forgiven her murky heritage.

Somehow, that feeling mattered more with Fernie. It mattered deeply with Ian.

Maybe because this time, she deserved it. She hadn't known what she was doing…but she'd done it. She'd deceived them all, and she'd deceived Ian, and she'd hurt them.

And Ian was captive. *Captive.* In what world did that even make sense?

"It's a lot to take in," Fernie said—and if she was upset, she was still understanding. At Ana's sharp look, she said, "Oh, yes. That's what I do. Empathy of a sort. Who else would manage a retreat for overworked, damaged and recovering Sentinels?"

Ana hesitated beside the counter, suddenly panicked all over again. "If you could read my mind, you'd have known about this from the start."

Fernie laughed. "No, *hija*. I've known you to be troubled, and I've certainly known you were mistreated. But I have only the sense of your reactions. And Ian's. Or did you think my defense of you was simply blind faith?"

"I didn't have much time to think about it at all," Ana told her, and ran her hand along the underside of the counter overhang until she found the smooth button of the amulet. A simple twist of thought released the working that held it there, and it dropped into her hand. She held it out to Fernie. "I'm supposed to return with this, but I can cover that if you need it."

Fernie wrinkled her nose in distaste. "Leave it there. Shea brought one of Ian's warded isolation cases."

Ana gladly dropped it to the counter, wiping her hand along the side of her jeans. Jeans and minimalist crosstrainers and a waffle-weave shirt that would allow her to move.

She'd come ready to run. Now she said, "Please. Make sure they're still back from the door."

Fernie gave her a look that might have been pity. "Child, if they want you, they'll take you."

She knew. But she held Fernie's dark gaze anyway, and Fernie shook her head and went to clear the way. Once Ana left the house—cautiously, finding them all still clustered by their vehicles—she kept right on walking until she'd made most of the distance to the lane.

"Wait," Lyn said—a little closer than Ana wanted now, but not threatening. "Don't go. We can protect you. We can *help*."

"A whole lot more now that we won't be fighting that amulet," Shea said, tipping his head at her—eyes narrowed, as if trying to figure her out. "And we need your help to find Ian. We know that matters to you."

"I've stayed too long," she said. It was truth. "And I'm already returning without the amulet. Lerche will suspect something, if he doesn't already. He's had someone watching this place all along."

Shea coughed into his hand and nodded at Jet.

Jet said, "The wolf likes to run in the greenway. It was a good chase."

Ana's eyes widened. "You didn't—"

Ruger interrupted her with a snort. "He's downstairs, nice and tidy. And you should stay. Help us find Ian. We know him best from his lab and his work. You know him best *here*. Now. With what the illness has done to him."

She found it hard to breathe, facing reality all over again. "I can't," she said, struggling to say the words. "Lerche… Lerche has Ian." The pronouncement brought the Sentinels to a tightly strung alert, and Ana shrank away. "If I don't return, he'll shut down the house. He'll hurt Ian—he'll *kill* him, if he can't control him."

"He can't begin to control a field Sentinel," Ruger said tightly. "Not Ian."

"Where is he?" Lyn moved closer—too close. She might be no bigger than Ana, but she was Sentinel, faster and stronger and dangerous. "Where's the base?"

"It's got to be a big house," Shea said. "They always are."

Ana shook her head, a quick and nervous gesture. "No," she said. "You don't *know him*. You don't know what he'll do. I don't think *I* knew what he was capable of until these past few days."

"We know he's cruel," Lyn said, and tipped her chin at Ana.

Ana clapped a hand over bruises old and new. *You've always healed fast*, Lerche had said. Now she knew why, and how he had taken advantage of it. "Yes. He's cruel. He's been cruel to Ian. And I think he had a man killed just to convince me that Ian was as awful as I was supposed to think he was. That you *all* are. You have to believe me—if you push him, he won't hesitate to make Ian pay."

"Ana," Ruger said, and that deep voice of his, that size of his, that unassuming lurking *strength* of his as he, too, moved closer—

It was too much. Too big, too close, too *Sentinel*.

Ana fled. She wasn't as strong as they were or as fast, but she was fit and ready to run, ready to take the chance she could reach the end of the lane and witnesses before they caught her.

Lyn's sharp command followed her out. "Let her go! I can follow her anywhere, now that I have her—"

No, Ana thought, sprinting hard—driven by the need to return to Ian, no matter how little control she had over Lerche. She made it to the corner, turned sharply north to cross the bridge over the greenway canal and plunged abruptly into the pedestrian population of Santa Fe. *No, you won't.*

She found the silent shielding amulet in her pocket and gave the necessary twist of will to invoke it.

I'm sorry, but you won't.

Because if Lerche saw them coming, Ian would be dead.

Chapter 11

Lerche ignored the bustle of packing to focus on the security camera feeds on display in the mansion's dining room. Half a dozen views showed on the large-screen monitor, but only one was enlarged. *Ian Scott.*

The man seemed to doze, impressing Lerche in spite of himself. Conserving energy was indeed the smart thing to do, but Lerche hadn't thought the man had it in himself to tame his own restlessness.

It wouldn't do to give the Sentinel too much recovery time. Especially since Lerche had decided to use another, possibly more effective weapon against the Sentinel's silence.

Ana.

Lerche couldn't countenance the loyalty Ian Scott had shown to the woman. She'd thoroughly betrayed the Sentinels, and quite specifically betrayed Ian Scott himself. And Lerche had no sense that Scott had taken that betrayal lightly.

But he knew, without qualm, that Scott would be more affected by threats to Ana than he would to the ones aimed at his own person.

Stupid Sentinels. They could never, ever be trusted to use their powers properly. Far too emotional, all of them.

Activity at the house entrance caught his eye, and he discovered Ana on approach—not with Budian, who had escorted her to the retreat, but emerging from a taxi, after which she hurried up the long ornamental walk to the house. As she grew closer, her harried expression and disheveled state became evident. She stopped at the door and attempted to finger-comb her tousled hair back into place, straightening her colorful tank top. One of his favorites, the way it exposed the delicate sweep of her collarbones and the graceful rise of her neck.

She had always been a pretty little thing. Too bad she couldn't have been more useful in other ways.

An interior camera caught her slipping through the entryway, avoiding several of his posse on the way—shrinking away from them, as she well might. They thought no more of her now than they ever had.

He assumed she'd look for him—coming to report. It took him a moment longer than it should have to comprehend that she was heading toward the opposite wing of the house.

Ian Scott.

He watched with rising anger as she entered Scott's comfortable little jail, her back to the camera, her expression hidden from Lerche. She glanced over her shoulder, a moment of trepidation that told Lerche she knew someone watched, and then knelt beside the restraint chair, her hands folding over one of Scott's.

It took the Sentinel a moment to rouse. She reached

up to stroke the side of his face, a visage no longer satisfactorily covered with bruises, once-deep cuts healing. Scott's eyes fluttered open—Lerche was pleased to see that groggy response, at least.

She spoke urgently to Scott, as aware of his state as Lerche was, and sent another, more urgent, glance back at the camera.

She had, somehow, surmised that she and Scott had little time left. She had, somehow, actually learned something on her little mission to retrieve the amulet.

That she rushed to Ian Scott's side to give him this news first only sealed her fate.

Righteous anger suffused Lerche's body, stiffening his back and bringing warmth to his face. Lerche pushed the chair back from the security desk, full of intention to show her just how gravely she'd erred—and then stopped himself.

He was not, after all, a man to pass up opportunity.

These moments she spent with Ian Scott would be a bittersweet final reminder of what she'd come to mean to the Sentinel, no matter how she'd betrayed him in the end.

And *then* Lerche would interrupt them. He'd learn what Ana had discovered, and more.

After which they could die together.

Lerche stood, straightened his suit and strode toward his office with great purpose. Budian was still out in the field, and Lerche hadn't sent him unprepared. Now that Ana had removed the evidence of his illicit Core strike, Lerche could buy that time.

Not with the subtle amulets that Ana had used, but with those that Budian had been planting along the retreat perimeter.

Silent, strong and just waiting to be triggered.

* * *

Ian sank deeply into meditation—giving his body a chance to heal itself, such as it could. Preventing the endless and exhausting spin of his mind.

Hunkering down to wait.

He was slow to come back to the surface, floundering off balance as the effort of maintaining his quiet gave way to an effortless silence of internal clamor.

"Ian." Ana's voice came in a whisper. "Wake up. We need to talk—quickly, before Lerche sends someone to join us."

"I'm awake," he said, making it so and opening his eyes to her concern, to her brows drawn, her lip caught between her teeth. "I'm good and awake. Means I remember very well what's happened between us." *Love and betrayal. Loss.*

"I know." Her features took on an intensity of determination he hadn't seen before. "I get it—you can't truly trust me. But you know what else I know? I've been a pawn all along the way. Around here, truth seems to be a moving target. So I figure I'll forgive myself if I miss it now and then."

She had his attention. Not so much her words, but her manner. Anxious, yes. Definitely aware of the precarious nature of her words here deep in Lerche's private little lair. But no longer a woman waiting to see what might happen.

Just maybe a woman who was about to *make* things happen.

He worked his jaw a little, getting moisture to his mouth. "What's going on?"

"Lerche sent me to retrieve the amulet I planted at the retreat. I ran into your friends."

"Who?" he said, shifting in the chair as if he could

sit more upright—but he was too restrained to do any such thing.

"Ruger. Shea. Lyn. Jet. And Fernie and the others are doing well." She saw his intensity and shook her head. "I got away from them, Ian. They're not coming after us. *You.*"

They let you go. If they hadn't, she wouldn't be here. And they were looking. With Lyn on the track, they'd find him.

She shook her head again. "Believe me, Ian. They're not coming. I know Lyn thought she could follow me, but I used a working to cover my tracks."

The reality of it hit harder than he'd expected. He struggled to breathe past the hard, cold disappointment. *"Why?"*

She scowled. "Why do you *think*? Lerche is already preparing to run. If he sees them coming, he'll cut his losses—he'll kill you outright and be gone."

He tried to absorb her words and ended up absorbing only the sincerity of them—the realization that the courage he saw in her face, the determination, had come from her need to protect him.

Or to try.

"You could have stayed." He couldn't help the bemused tone in his voice. "You would have been free."

"Ian Scott." She said it firmly, her hands closing around his wrists and holding tight. With meaning. Her face uplifted to reveal the honey depths of her brown eyes, and he saw the truth there, absorbing the impact of it. "You're here because of me. Because of the way I feel about you. What makes you think I could have walked away, and ever truly been free again?"

Ian Scott, rendered speechless.

She was the enemy. She had betrayed him. But she

had always been sincere. She had given him everything of herself that she'd been able to give—and now she'd gone beyond. Now both of them were captive.

He opened his hand, turning it over, and she slipped her own into its grasp. Ignoring, for the moment, the cameras. "Ian, I—" But she stopped on a gasp when he tightened his hand around hers, a grip too firm.

"Not here, Ana." He hadn't meant for his voice to have so much grit. "Not under Lerche's terms."

Even if it meant saying those words never.

She didn't respond immediately—and then her hand gave his the faintest squeeze in return. She sat back on her heels, her demeanor nothing but practical. "Then let me see what I can do for you before he gets here." This time she did glance at the camera, if only with a flick of her eyes. "I'm sure he's on his way."

She poured him a glass of water, unstrapped one hand so he could drink, and sat on the side of the bed while he downed it in a series of deep gulps. Then she exchanged the glass for the container he could use from the chair and turned her back to stand between him and the camera, giving him what privacy she could.

Not that Ian cared. If Lerche wanted to watch him pee into a bottle, that was his problem.

The necessities finished, Ana fetched a damped washcloth from the bathroom and allowed Ian to wash his face around the healing areas, even to wipe down his arms and chest.

The big cat in him appreciated it.

But in the end she returned his wrist to the restraints. "I have to," she said, though she didn't tighten the strap nearly as snug as before—and she took a quick moment to loosen the other one, very nearly loose enough for his hand to simply slip free. "For the same reason I always have. If he sees you unrestrained—"

"I get it," he told her. Their interactions had become remarkably tacit, a quiet teamwork in an untenable situation. "He'll come down all over both of us. It takes things out of our hands."

Not that things were very much in their hands to start with, especially not with distant footsteps on approach, perfectly clear to Sentinel ears. Ian let a piece of his attention slide away, returning to the amulets that had been left to intimidate him. Feeling their various natures, the sick taste of them on the back of his tongue and the slick feel of them beneath the touch of his mind. Amulets of pain and persuasion. Amulets of sickness and power. And a number of amulets that served no purpose in this context—a noisemaker, a spy-eye, even an amulet of pleasure.

She lifted her head as she finally recognized the approaching footfalls as headed for this room. Her calm deserted her in a blurt of words. "Try to hold on," she said. "You know your people are looking—and I think they'll find us. This place stinks of Core. I just needed some time to be ready for them. And to let you know, so together…somehow…we can try to last that long."

That's the plan. But it didn't mean he didn't have a backup. Because Lerche had his friends surrounded by silent amulets, and Ian was the only one who knew how to find them.

"Ana, listen." Ian pulled on reserves to bring the room into sharp clarity, his thoughts with them. "Listen," he said again, enough urgency to it that he pulled her attention from Lerche's approach. "Lyn had every reason to believe she would be able to follow you. If there's Sentinel energy out there, she can find it—along with almost anything Core. *Sentinel* energy, Ana."

"Oh," she said, and flushed, her hand over her mouth. "I can't believe I forgot…so much to say—"

He understood in an instant. "They told you."

Her eyes shone in a way he hadn't expected. "It explains everything," she said. "It explains my *life*."

"Then you know she can find you. You just have to hang in there."

"She should be able to find *you*, too," Ana said, a certain stubborn note coming into her voice.

"Yeah, yeah. Here's the thing." Ian didn't hesitate. He should have told her this first thing, before the personal stuff, before the wash up. But he'd been groggy and hurting, and, without those very personal moments, he simply hadn't been willing to trust. *And now Lerche was at the door.* "My team needs to know I can locate the silent amulets."

Ana gave him a startled look, freezing as the doorknob turned. "That's not possible."

"There's a reason Lerche was so happy to get his hands on me. I've been working on this for over a year—and I got the last piece while I was out on that mountain." Ian lowered his voice, drawing her in closer even as Lerche entered the room, his musclemen behind him. Noisy and self-assured. *"Tell them to use sonar."*

But he saw from her expression that she absorbed only the implication that Ian wouldn't be able to tell them himself. "Ian, no—"

He clamped his hand around her wrist. "Tell them to quit listening and—"

Ana cried out as a huge hand landed on her shoulder, another on her arm—tearing her away from Ian and sending her sprawling into the corner to collide with the chair. A growl burst from Ian's chest; he jerked against the restraints, leather scraping skin, freedom only an inch away—

But already the posse muscleman returned, his hands clamping down over Ian's wrists, his weight grinding bone against the thin padding of the chair arm. The second man entered to tighten the straps hard—looking back at Lerche for approval.

"Not so tight that his hands fall off," Lerche said. "I need him able to answer questions."

Together the men loosened the straps by a single notch, retreating to stand outside the door of the small room and relieving it of their bulk.

Ana pulled herself upright, steadying herself with the chair and pinning Lerche with the wariest of looks, sparing only a glance of apology to Ian. Apology and a quick scowl of demand. *Survive, Ian Scott.*

Well, that was the plan.

It just wasn't a very *good* plan.

"I expect you to pay attention when I enter a room, Ana dear." Lerche's mild tone belied the look on his face. "Sit, please. I'm quite sure you'll want to take notes for this."

Slowly, Ana sat, bending to pick up the clipboard and its disarrayed papers but never taking her eyes off Lerche.

"Ian Scott," Lerche said, playing to his tiny audience. "Southwest Brevis AmTech." And then smiled, as if just thinking of the words that followed. "And former snow leopard."

Ian let the leopard show, lifting a lip to expose the canine tooth that wasn't quite human.

"Excellent," Lerche said. "Bravado. Let's see how far it gets you."

* * *

Lerche had changed.

Or maybe he'd just revealed himself.

Ana stared at him from the chair, shocked by the rough handling—her arm stinging from impact, a myriad of small pains pricking at her mind. Pains she would normally have tended, but which suddenly seemed insignificant.

For Lerche had lost his classically condescending mien and now displayed a harder expression. A meaner one.

He wasn't holding back any longer. He was looking *forward.*

They'd run out of time.

Ana cast a frantic look at Ian, and found that he already knew.

Lerche ran a caressing hand over the amulets, plucking one up along the way. "You're familiar with this class of amulet, I'm sure." He let it dangle from one outstretched hand, spinning quietly at the end of its cord.

Ian gave it a glance. "Targeted," he said. "Point and shoot, so to speak. And if I'm not wrong, it's a series working. Turn it on, turn it off, rinse, lather, repeat." He shrugged, but Ana saw a faint tension on his face and knew there was more to it than just that.

Whatever this amulet did, it would be ugly.

"Excellent," Lerche said. "Then you see this coming."

Cloying bitterness from the invoked working flooded the back of Ana's tongue, pushing a sound of dismay from her throat. Ian's eyes widened ever so slightly—and then his body stiffened and his head jerked back. His features contorted, a grim, involuntary sound harsh in his throat.

"Stop it!" Ana screamed at Lerche. "He can't tell you anything like this!"

Lerche dropped the amulet into his waiting hand, closing fingers around it with satisfaction. Ian slumped forward, sucking in air. And Ana scrambled not only to make sense of it all, but to understand where it was going next.

She flinched when Lerche reached into his suit coat pocket, and then again when he extended an object in her direction—only to wilt in relief when she recognized his fancy phone. "You don't seem to have yours active," he told her, a patently gentle tone that felt more like a lash. "Use the app to monitor him, please."

Gingerly, she took the phone, fumbling it—risking a glance at Ian, who lifted a face wet with involuntary tears and drew the deepest of breaths.

Preparing himself.

"Excellent," Lerche said once more. "Please keep notes, Ana."

Ana dutifully scribbled a line of unintelligible nonsense—knowing she had to pull herself together or she'd be of no use to either of them.

She'd known Lerche to be cruel. She hadn't known him to be a monster.

A monster nurtured by the organization in which she'd been so eager to excel.

Lerche dangled the amulet again, letting the cord slip through his fingers with appreciation. "Ian Scott," he said, clearly relishing the moment—his glance at Ana told her as much. "Would you care to share your progress regarding detection of the silent amulets? And while we're at it, who else has been working that project with you?"

Ian showed his teeth, as clear a threat as Ana had ever seen.

"You see, my dear," Lerche said. "He has no intention of answering questions. Not yet." He smiled, raising the amulet in an entirely unnecessary fashion. Ian's head snapped back, his hands splayed and body jerking within the restraints.

Ana knew better than to cry out this time. She pressed her mouth closed and breathed through her nose in careful, even rhythm, refusing to acknowledge the hot and steady tears that ran down her face and dripped from her chin.

And she made herself watch. Because this was *her* fault. *Her* responsibility. She'd drawn Ian in, and she'd never seen this coming. Seeing his agony was her penance. Watching him slump in the restraints as Lerche released the amulet—seeing that this time his eyes fluttered open to a dazed expression, and blood trickled from a bitten lip, and from his nose.

At that she couldn't help but whisper, "What are you *doing* to him?"

Lerche affected a modest expression. "Hurting him, mostly. But yes, there will be cumulative damage. To the small vessels…and then to the large. It's always a question of which will go first—the heart or the brain. Won't it be a shame to see your brilliant friend turn into a vegetable?"

Ian's gaze sharpened with obvious effort, even as Ana drew a sharp breath—understanding better than she would have, days earlier, the depth of that threat.

"I'd wanted to experiment with the new workings, of course," Lerche said. "To see how carefully I could peel the layers of his Sentinel *other* away." He glanced at her. "It's a shame *you* couldn't serve me in that capacity, Ana dear. Once again, a failure."

Ana stiffened at this blatant reference to the Sentinel blood he'd not mentioned to her directly. Her mouth felt clumsy in response. "I don't understand—"

"Of course you do." Lerche shot her a look of false patience. "They told you, didn't they? They're like that, and since they're looking for your friend here, they surely sent someone who could easily sniff out your insipid nature." He smiled. "I'm honestly surprised you returned to me, Ana."

"You shouldn't be." She snapped the words at him, the fervency not coming at her bidding, but simply welling up from inside. "I've always been loyal, Lerche. And now I have reason to be. It's just not to *you* any longer."

Ian managed to shake his head. Barely. His voice came ragged. "Ana, no. Don't."

Lerche laughed right out loud, short but delighted. "Excellent," he said. "You're still with us. The truth is, I don't want your mind destroyed before I have the chance to sift through it—and although we're dealing with your Sentinel friends at the retreat, I'm sure more will be along quite promptly. So I have very little time." He set the amulet aside, quickly plucking out another—a smaller thing, with less complicated knotting and rough, scribed surface. He sent Ian a meaningful glance. "I've warmed you up nicely. Now let's see how you feel about watching Ana suffer."

Ana sprang to her feet. The clipboard fell from clumsy fingers; the chair toppled backward. Protest sprang to her tongue and she swallowed it—terrified, knowing herself not strong, not brave and nowhere near as well-trained as Ian.

But she would not give Lerche her terror.

At least, not yet.

"Don't do this," Ian said, and his voice was gravel. Not desperate...not pleading. *Warning.*

Lerche's expression shifted to the one that frightened Ana the most—his response to defiance. The one that meant he would reassert control. Swiftly. Decisively.

The one that had always left marks on Ana.

He lifted the amulet, the subconscious little *tell* of his triggering effort. Ana drew breath, bracing herself—knowing she was defenseless even as her senses flooded with the ugly stench of the amulet invoked.

One of the men behind Lerche made a startling sound of surprise, lifting to his toes as though by some invisible force as he staggered backward and bent over himself. In the stunned silence that followed, he straightened with extreme effort—his deep olive skin tones gone pale, his expression still stunned.

Lerche scowled, pinning Ana with a scowl—focusing on her with deliberate effort and lifting the amulet—

The second bodyguard jerked, his arms flailing as he fell back from a faintly audible pop of impact, as though the very air before him had exploded in directed force.

The amulet steamed, used up and darkening into tarnish. Lerche eyed it with an expression Ana might have called baffled if she'd seen it in him often enough to be sure. She sought Ian, looking for answers, but he met her gaze only briefly before resting his head against the high chair back.

Lerche dropped the amulet onto the table as his men recovered themselves, looking both sheepish and still a little startled. "Not a great loss," he said, but frowned nonetheless.

Ana could well understand their confusion. Directing an amulet to a specific target took practice and a certain focus, but someone like Lerche took the ability for granted.

With less ceremony than before, Lerche selected another amulet from the case. "I do hope you're not awash in relief, Ana dear. I still want my answers."

He displayed the amulet to Ian, smiling as Ian's jaw tightened. Ana wasn't close enough to see the details of the thick metal disk, only that it was more complex than the last. Lerche said, "Nerve pain can be a terrible thing."

"I know what the amulet does," Ian said, his voice still stuck in that gravel register, his throat working.

Lerche tipped his head at Ana. "She didn't. And now she can anticipate. Are you ready, Ana? Or perhaps your *friend* would like to discuss his progress on the silents, or share the name of the colleague most likely to pick up on that work."

Ian rolled his eyes at that prospect, and Ana wanted to cry *no*! Because here came that look on Lerche's face, fury lighting his eyes into something not quite sane. Ana found herself backed up hard into the corner, bracing herself.

But it was Ian the working struck, stiffening his body, forcing a choked cry of what sounded so very much like *laughter* that Ana stopped breathing for an instant, too torn by threat and fear and horror to take in the moment.

Lerche clutched the amulet hard, his fury at the misfire giving way to satisfaction as Ian made another sound, a more primal thing of unendurable pain, and Ana covered her face with her hands, dropping to a crouch and rocking slightly in the awfulness of it all—as if she could simply wish it all away.

"Stop it!" she cried. She lost her balance, dropping to one knee. Something hard ground into her kneecap, a trivial pain. "What kind of man *are* you? Just *stop it*! He's not going to tell you anything, and the Sentinels will surely be here any moment—just pack up your things and *go*!"

Ian fell free of the working, his gasping groan holding that same edge of dark laughter. "Ohhh, yeah," he said. "*That* hurt."

"What kind of man am I?" Lerche said, and his voice held a cruel edge that seemed all too sharp to Ana after years of pretending it wasn't that bad, or that she deserved it when it was. He laughed just as darkly as Ian had. "Of all people, you should know that." He took two swift steps in the small room and crouched before her, taking her jaw in that cruel grip over bruises still tender to the bone.

"Leave her," Ian said, words that scraped in his throat. "Leave her *alone*!"

Lerche paid him no mind, giving Ana's face a little shake. "And you *would* know, if you weren't so unrelentingly dense about the bold tactics needed to manage these beasts. Your mother was allowed to have you for far too long, little Ana. She damaged your thinking beyond what I could repair."

"Lerche," Ian said, his voice louder. "I am about *done* with you—"

The bodyguards shared a laugh over that one. Lerche smiled, fingers grinding into Ana's jaw. Her knee slipped over the object beneath it and she suddenly knew—*the pen.* She felt herself break from terror to anger to *I. Have. Had.* Enough!

She groped for the pen, found it, fisted it and jammed it into Lerche's thigh, years of defiance crammed into a single instant and driving the sleek metal deep.

Lerche roared with surprise and fell back from her,

the pen embedded halfway up the barrel. He scrabbled at it as the bodyguards swooped in, snatching Ana up one on each arm and yanking Ana to her feet. Ian made an inarticulate sound of frustration, jerking within his restraints, and Lerche scraped his fingers across the floor to sweep up the amulet, glaring at Ana with an intent so clear he might as well have spoken it.

"—Goddam sonnuva *bitch*—" Ian snarled, fighting with an animal intent, and she wanted to cry out *no, don't wear yourself down* but there was Lerche, thrusting the amulet right into her face while she lifted herself up in the grip of the bodyguards, kicking out at him—

Only delaying the inevitable, the first electric slice of pain down her arms, down her legs and scattering into branches of lightning through her limbs. And the last thing she saw before her vision flashed into white and red and stark bright bursts of light was the satisfaction on Lerche's contorted face, and the last thing she heard was Ian's rising shout of demand, his chair crashing over—

And the screams in her own throat.

Chapter 12

Ian's shouts rang impotent to his own ears, eclipsed by the sight of Ana strung between the two bodyguards—her body taut, her screams strangling in her throat.

As if Lerche hadn't done enough to her already.

The restraint chair lay on its side, trapping him just as thoroughly. He'd missed his chance to divert the amulet from Ana—he'd underestimated Lerche's cruelty, had been too stunned at Ana's explosion of defiance.

The lower restraint shifted against the floor, grabbing his attention. The stiff buckle jabbed against the carpet, pushing back at the buckle tongue. He grabbed the hint of room it gave him, twisting his wrist and jamming the thing down again—doing it again and again, gaining space until a final twist and his wrist slipped free, his fingers stiff and clumsy.

A quick glance showed him no one had noticed—showed him, too, that Ana no longer strained against the working but dangled limply. And still Lerche plied the amulet, the bitter, broken taste of it a thick corruption of the very air around them.

Dammit. He plucked at the stout leather around his other wrist, stiff fingers slipping and making no headway. *Dammit it to—*

His gaze fell on the amulet case. The amulets he'd so carefully explored the evening before, learning of the tools Lerche would ply against them.

Do it. Take them.

Lerche hadn't expected that Ian could redirect the amulets; he hadn't yet figured it the cause of those failures.

Or realized that Ian could trigger them, as well.

Do it.

But triggering them from a distance wasn't easy—even Lerche needed them up close and personal. And triggering them from a distance and then directing them with any precision…

Do it.

If he didn't do it right, he'd kill them all. He'd send every bit of power raging through his body and through Ana's, including the workings that would shred his very nature.

But what a grand bright beacon it would create for Lyn, for any Sentinel within the region. What an unmistakable warning, and a neon-bright cry for help.

And if he didn't do it, Ana would die. If she wasn't already—

Lerche stepped into her, taking her jaw in that favorite grip of his, shaking himself out of his own satisfied reverie to check in with Ian—to revel, too, in that.

"Yeah?" Ian said, his upper lip stiff with dried blood and his body tensed with the understanding of what he was about to do and what it was about to do *to* him. "You think that's impressive? Suck on *this*, why don't you?"

He couldn't shield; Lerche had seen to that. Hell, he could barely think. He just *knew*. And he followed the moment to the only conclusion left, wrapping the amulet case in his awareness, touching each and every one of those cold metal disks, the buttons, the miniature tablets…

Twisting.

The room flooded with the thick taste of ichor. Lerche flung him a look of astonishment—an utter awareness of what Ian had done, his expression giving away his instant understanding of Ian's earlier interference. "You *imbecile*—!"

Ian lifted a lip in what was left of his snarl—and braced himself.

The bodyguard farthest from Ian cried out, his face twisting horribly and his skin sagging, squirming as if a colony of bees swarmed beneath it. He threw himself away from Ana to writhe on the carpet, his flailing legs tangling with Lerche's so the amulet went flying and Lerche staggered away, hands slapping at his body one moment, then twisting terribly, unnaturally, in the next. The crack of bone came at the same time the second bodyguard cried out, and someone else in the house shouted in surprise and then screamed in agony, and the wall across from the open door split from top to bottom while dust sifted down from the joints and seams above them and—

And Ian saw nothing more, because not all the workings took direction. Some of them simply sought targets.

Sentinels.

The leopard twisted within him, robbing him of sight and sound and pouring chaos into his mind. Dark agony ripped along his limbs, filling his ears with an insensate yowl. He felt claws ripping through carpet and tail lashing, teeth bared and whiskers bristling.

Screaming filled what was left of his mind and he had no idea from whose throat it came. He lost track of the world and of himself in it. Just a swirl of motion, sensations sweeping over him, most of them scraping through with jagged edges and stinging hints of insanity.

A blink of reality swam before him—*Ana at his side, tugging on his hand, urging him into blinding sunlight, the mansion creaking into a new tilt behind them.* Gone, and he stumbled, but at least felt himself do it before he fell away into bright darkness again. Another blink and *he slammed up against a tree, the rough bark a familiar comfort and the scent of pine strong in his nose. The ground rose steeply before him, unmarked by any trail. Fingers closed around his arm and he jerked himself to freedom, turning on the perpetrator with a snarl. Striking out and hearing a woman's cry and then falling away...*

His mind tumbled. It grasped at the clarity and brilliance he once knew to be his, seeing just enough of it to know it had been there but now was not. Reality turned *shivering in darkness, still moving, still climbing. The night should be awash with the scent and color of moonlight, a Sentinel's unique vision of the world after sunset—*

But it wasn't, and it continued to tug and roil and snap at him until it used him up. Until he heard nothing but a steady groaning that came with each exhalation, and each inhalation sounded like a forced thing, a thing to be endured instead of a thing that came as naturally as life. Endless running, endless movement, endless pain and confusion.

Endless...

A twig snapped, echoing unnaturally in his mind. A hand touched his shoulder, and he felt it to the bone. A whisper of comfort scraped against his ears. The air felt stifling against his face, scented heavily with sap and musty old needles.

This is real.

The groans were his. The whispers were hers. The night belonged to the mountain, cold and crisp and alive around them.

"Ian?" she said as if she somehow knew he'd emerged.

"For now," he managed, and fell asleep.

Ana jerked awake with the dawn—not that she'd ever truly slept.

She barely remembered escaping that horrible house she'd once called home. She'd come to her senses to find the bodyguards dead and Lerche moaning into the carpet, and her own body barely responsive to her demands.

She'd thought Ian dead at first, too. He'd sagged limp in the chair, on his side—one hand free and still clenched around the restraint for the other, his wrists and ankles chafed into ragged, bloody abrasions and blood at his mouth and fresh from his nose.

My God, Ian, what did you do?

She had no idea. Her senses rang, her body echoed with pain and trembled with weakness. She'd not given any thought to her actions—she'd only done them. She'd pulled herself over the strangely squishy body of one of the men beside her, reaching Ian to tug and scrabble at the remaining restraints—freeing him and rousing him and tugging on him until they made their way out of the house, quite instinctively heading for high, wild ground.

Their progress had been more of a mutual tumble than flight. Ian had struck out at her without warning, connecting more than once. He'd snarled at nothingness, and he'd fallen into trees. There'd been no sanity in his eyes. No sign that he'd seen Ana, no sign that he knew her. And still they ran, because she'd rather be with Ian in this state than anywhere near the organization to which she'd once been so loyal.

To which she'd subsumed herself and for which she'd doubted her sense of right and wrong, allowing others to devalue her for simply being who she was and burying the small, still lessons of her early years.

At least now she knew where those values came from. And why.

Ana shivered in the brisk fall air. She'd had the sense to snatch a blanket from the bed, wrapping it around her shoulders. Still, a blanket was no match for high country fall, and even the warmth pouring off Ian—an unnatural warmth, as though his body fevered itself with healing—had been unable to hold the cold at bay.

She had no idea where they were, only that this mountain was plenty big enough to get lost in. The sun gilded the slope across from them, painting the thick forest a glimmering tint of gold over green, the shadows still deep. She and Ian had tumbled beneath an overhang; a giant tree had lost its grip on the earth to slant above and beside them.

For the moment, Ian slept on. His silvered hair stuck out in disarray. Dried blood smeared across his face and down his chin, and she remembered what Lerche had said about the first working—the one that weakened all the small vessels and thinned the blood.

Please, not his mind. Not the brilliance and compassion and essential *Ian.*

Or maybe he'd just run headlong into a tree during their flight. He'd certainly had the opportunity.

Ana shivered again, tucking herself back in beside Ian. When he woke, when they could move, they would find some sunshine and let it blaze against them.

But they also needed water. Dehydration came quickly on a desert mountain no matter the green around them, and free-flowing water was a scarcity. She and Ian needed such things as civilization could offer—and Ana had no idea which direction would lead them home.

Or if they were safe to go.

Lerche had not been dead, after all. Hurt, most certainly—but still alive enough to cry out threats as she'd fled.

Another shiver, one that rattled her bones. She ached right down to the heart of herself, and couldn't tell what of that discomfort came from her treatment at Lerche's hands and what simply came of being so cold.

Ian moved not at all. He breathed lightly but not quite steadily, with an occasional exhalation that verged on a groan.

"I'm sorry," she whispered to him with nothing to offer but her presence and a ragged blanket. She wrapped herself around him, soaking up his unnatural heat and letting herself fall into memory. In memory he'd lost his breath in pleasure, not pain, and the lines of his body had been hers to explore. Muscle layered tightly over ribs, all long lines and grace and that sense that he could, at any moment, put his body exactly where he meant it to be. Precision and brilliance wrapped in power and masculine beauty.

He had been the one to grin at her, as irreverent as a man could be, and talk about following the attraction between them—faster and further than she'd ever expected. He'd been the one to treat her so tenderly, so respectfully, that she'd let herself go, taking chances with her heart and with her fate.

If I could do it over again...

Who was she even fooling? She'd do it just the same. She didn't have the courage to give up the things he'd offered her—the look in his eye as he made himself vulnerable to her touch. The hint of surprise at her effect on him, and the deep gasps of his response. And there, too—the way his expression grew just a little bit fierce when he offered the same back to her, drinking her cries with a greed she found as arousing as his touch.

Ian.

She pulled the blanket more tightly around them both, resting her head on his shoulder while his body heat radiated into the chilled lump of her torso, warming her from the outside while memories warmed her from the inside.

But they couldn't stay this way forever. If he didn't wake soon, she'd have to find some way to mark this spot—and then she'd have to find her way out of these mountains, with no idea what awaited her once she did.

Or she would die here, and Ian would die here, and the Sentinels at the retreat would die under renewed attack, never knowing Ian's secret to finding the silent amulets.

And Lerche would have just what he'd wanted all along.

One broken arm. One dislocated shoulder. Three badly wrenched fingers, and one badly bruised kidney.

Those things had come from the mass release of the amulets—but his ferocious headache came from the intrusion into his space. From the loss of so many of his posse, and the rebuilding to come.

But opportunity remained. In the wake of his report—the "unwarranted attack by Ian Scott gone rogue"—there were Core reinforcements on the way. An investigation of the Sentinels to come. And plenty of work to do so they all got the story straight.

Ana, a low-level support admin, had a chance meeting with Ian Scott, and none of the wiles to recognize how he used her. He wooed her. He conquered her. He discerned the location of Lerche's safe house, and somewhere along the way his mind snapped—he was, after all, in the area for enforced R & R due to the strain he'd been under.

No one had realized how far gone he was, however, and it allowed him to launch an attack the likes of which no one had realized was possible—triggering amulets in bulk from afar. Ana had then tried to stop him the only way she knew how, by seeding amulets at the retreat.

Such a shame the rest of the Sentinels would die before anyone realized what she'd done. Or that Ian had given way to his beast, taking Ana deep into the mountains to kill her.

With the few men he had left—with the final card he'd already put into play—Lerche would make certain of that. And if his story had some weak spots, there would be no one around to naysay it.

He'd already ascertained that the retreat amulets—one at each corner of the property—had done their work well. The Sentinels at the retreat had quickly fallen ill. The tracker, Lyn Maines, had finally given up on locating Ana and returned to the unnatural silence of the house—wary, he'd been told, but not wary enough to save herself.

No doubt there were reinforcements on the way—this time, in likelihood, a team that would make no bones about its presence. There would be no *playing nice* from the Sentinels at this point.

But they'd have no means to contradict his story.

Because they'd be too late.

Ian burned.

He burned hot and then he burned cold, and the jumbled sensations of his escape and his journey to this rough shelter had faded into a dully overwhelming throb of pain that silenced all else.

"Ian." That was Ana's whisper in his ear.

Come to think of it, that was her body pressed up against his, soft where it should be soft, yielding where it should yield—but nonetheless shivering with the cold.

It was a cold that hadn't penetrated further than Ian's fingertips, held at bay by the burning.

"Ian," she whispered again, this time her hand closing over his shoulder. Agonizing spikes of fire spread from that touch. He didn't mean to groan, or to curse, but he apparently wasn't in control of such things just yet.

"I'm sorry!" But she still whispered. "I won't do that again. But, Ian, you have to wake. They've come for us."

"Killed the bastards," he muttered.

She released what might have been a sob of relief, touching her forehead to his back. "Not all of them," she said. "Not Lerche, I don't think. And there were others—men who weren't in the house when you did… whatever you did."

She wouldn't know, of course. She'd been insensible when he'd triggered all those amulets.

Pretty much like Ian was right now.

"They might not find us here—but they shouldn't have found us at all. How could they track us so quickly?" She released a breath he felt along the back of his neck. "I only saw them because I had to, you know, find a bush. They're down in the gully between these two rises."

The words should have made sense; they didn't. They floated away along with his grasp on the immediate situation, leaving him only the understanding that he was missing something. It eluded him no matter how he swam though his thoughts, grasping at threads of reality.

A firm but careful hand turned his head. Cool lips found his, molding to his mouth and moving in a gentle rhythm that grabbed every bit of his attention. Her teeth nibbled; her tongue teased him, a touch and then gone.

Complete and utter clarity folded around him, cutting through inner chaos to present him only with Ana. Ana's scent, Ana's mouth, Ana's hands on his shoulders and slipping into his shirt.

Ana's cold, cold hands.

Ian gasped something between a laugh and a protest, grabbing those hands and enfolding them in his, chafing them slightly. She shivered and he went one better, pulling her to curl up in his lap and wrapping his arms and the blanket around them.

There they sat, with the morning settling in and the sky brightening ever so subtly as the sun's angle changed, starting to fill in the gaps and shadows of the folded mountainside. A faint mutter of male voices reached Ian's ears, rising from below as sound was wont to do in the mountains. He caught no words but heard a tone of frustration.

They were looking, she'd said. And Ian would guess they had good reason to expect their fugitives to be here—or they wouldn't have arrived so promptly in the first place.

The woman in his arms held the answer to that. She held any number of answers.

Ian could fill in some of the empty spots on his own. His memory held pieces of crystalline detail—moments of agony, the awareness of his body bruising inside and out. The look on Ana's face when the two bodyguards took hold of her. Deep fear as he'd reached for not one amulet but all of them, doing that which might save them or might kill them. Trying to direct them away, still knowing that the ones meant specifically for Sentinels would find him.

After that…

They'd gotten out, he knew that much. Must have been Ana's doing. And they'd run—farther and faster than he would have countenanced under the circumstances.

Ana's doing.

"You betrayed me," he said, and heard the surprise in his own low voice. Not that he hadn't known it before… just realizing it all over again. Especially in the wake of the world's sweetest kiss, his salvation through inner chaos.

It hadn't fixed the internal bruising or the lingering ache in his face, or the angry burn of his body healing just as fast as it could. Sentinel advantage, not without its costs. If he didn't get food soon, the whole process would collapse on itself. If he didn't get water, it would be a moot point.

Ana lifted her head from his chest, drawing back enough so she could meet his eyes. Cold air drifted between them, wringing another shiver from her. She didn't seem to notice. "Yes," she said, murmuring the words to keep them here inside this scant shelter of theirs. Her restraint somehow only leant them more meaning. "I did betray you. And then I betrayed my own people *for* you. And then they betrayed me. It's a horrible, confusing mess, and right now all I know is no matter how crazy it is, I love you and I think you know it."

He had no response for her, no matter how it felt to hear the words in the moment. Couldn't turn his feelings for her off; couldn't turn his trust for her back on. Not just like that.

She dove into his silence, still barely audible in her intensity. "Let's just get through the mess, Ian. Just feel what you feel right now and so will I, and let's get out of this and we'll see how we feel *then*."

He let the words sink in. *Feel what you feel right now.* "Yes," he told her, seeing relief in the faint sheen of the tears she blinked away. "Let's do that."

"Good," she said, nonsensical words with a tremble that told him she wasn't nearly as certain of herself as she'd seemed. She breathed deeply. "Yes. Okay."

He took a breath, scrubbing his hand over his aching face. They needed food and water, and to get off this mountain past Lerche's men…two of whom had tracked them with unlikely certainty. "Okay," he echoed her. "First things, first. How are you?"

She hesitated to answer, lifting her head to listen to the movement of the two men still significantly below them. "Cold," she murmured. "But that's probably obvious. Thirsty. And I'm afraid I pretty much used myself up last night. You?"

He tucked the blanket around her shoulders and answered only with another question. "And from the working Lerche used on you?"

"Ah," she said. "*That.* If there are aftereffects, I can't feel them." Her low voice took on a bitter note. "I think it was all about the pain."

In that bitter note, he heard all kinds of self-recrimination. "Ana, look at me." When her startled gaze met his in the shadows of the slanting tree trunk, the surrounding scrub oak and jut of rock, he shook his head. "Be grateful you didn't truly understand the man before now. That you couldn't says more about you than it does about him."

"Naive?" she suggested. "Malleable? Downright stu—"

He growled, finding himself suddenly closer to the big cat than he'd thought he was, the human veneer scraped away by the events of the past days. She startled into silence, a flicker of fear on her face—but it quickly passed, replaced by a wondering openness as he found the words to say, "Don't talk about yourself like that. It's no shame to have a fundamentally good nature. Or to be taken in by a man like Lerche when he's had so much control over you for so long. But *now*—" he tightened his hold on the blanket "—*now* you know better. Now you move forward, as you said. Now *we* move forward."

She blinked. "Okay," she said, and her whisper this time came from emotion and not from their precarious situation. She swallowed quite visibly, took a deep breath and said, "Well, that's it. Nothing from the amulet. I'm hungry and tired and cold, and I don't feel as if I can be of much help when it comes to these men, but I'll try."

Relief swept through him. Maybe she'd been affected by his mass amulet release, maybe not. But not so much that it dogged her.

"*We'll* try," he said, and followed sudden impulse—

kissing her forehead, her cheeks and then lingering a moment on her mouth. But not long, because they didn't have long.

The men had started to quarter the slope beneath them, no longer traveling up the easy gully bottom.

Ana's cold hand closed around his arm, above the deep abrasions left by the restraint. Under other circumstances, that wound and the others like it would have been well on the way to healing by now. But too much other damage had been done, and they were far from life threatening, and his overwhelmed body hadn't even tried. Ana said, "But you, Ian? What *happened*?"

Of course she had no idea. She'd been unconscious. And even if not, she'd have had a difficult time deciphering the abrupt chaos he'd unleashed. The targeted workings had no doubt been drawn directly to Ian himself. Not just Sentinel, but full field Sentinel.

Juicy target, at that.

"Lerche underestimated a few things," he said. "You. Me. And how familiar a Sentinel AmTech could be with all his precious amulets."

She just looked at him, a frown starting at her brow.

"I triggered all his toys," Ian said. "Aimed what I could at them and deflected what I could from us."

The frown turned to horror. "And absorbed the rest? *Ian!*" That last came in a furious whisper that threatened to break free of their little respite.

Ian shrugged, not a little abashed. "Hey," he said. "I knew what was in that case before I did it."

For a moment, it appeased her. And then the frown returned. "So you could have done that at any time?"

A random spike of pain shot through Ian's head; he winced, and wished their hunters would hurry it up. He needed the element of surprise that leaping from this hidey-hole would produce, and he needed it to happen before this spate of functionality faded.

For he had the distinct feeling it would fade. *Was fading.*

"Lerche didn't leave the amulet case in the room until that morning," he said, briefly splitting his attention—making a tentative foray outward with his inner awareness—brushing against the men below. Brushing against the amulets they so foolishly carried. "It was supposed to intimidate me or something. I doubt he realized I could identify them *or* trigger them from that chair."

"But after that," she said, persisting, "you could have done it?"

Suddenly he understood. "Ana," he said. "I am so sorry Lerche hurt you. I'm damned sorry he hurt *me*. But triggering those amulets…it was a last stand kind of thing. It could have gone wrong in so many ways." He hesitated. "Do you remember the first time he tried to aim the amulet at you? The way it went wrong?"

She worried her lip, her gaze gone inward. "Vaguely. Yes. It hit his men. And then it hit…" She looked at him, startled. "You. It hit *you*."

"Just stalling for time," he said, drawing breath at another stab of pain, closing his eyes against it. "Took him a while to catch on. I don't think even then that he had any notion I could trigger them all. He might not have figured it out yet."

She stroked cold fingers across his brow and down the side of the cheek that hadn't been broken. Soothing. "So you waited…"

He tipped his head into her touch. "For all sorts of reasons. But mostly… I didn't know what it would do to you. Or to me." He opened his eyes to pin her with that gaze. "If not for you, Ana, I would have died in that room."

"If not for me," she said bitterly, "you wouldn't have been in that room in the first place." But she quickly shook her head. "No, I'm not going there. We have other things to do."

As became ever more obvious, with the men quartering upward, the tension in their voices making it clear they knew they were closing in.

Ana dropped her voice so the words barely had sound at all. "What can I do?"

Ian swept another feathery touch over the men—men who would be invisible to that touch had they been without amulets. But they weren't, and they were closer than he'd thought. Close enough to recognize the tracker they carried, and close enough to find the far-from-silent offensive amulets—pure energy of the sort that would release with concussive violence. He smiled darkly, only to be struck with another shaft of sharp pain, a thing that shot from one temple down the side of his face and radiated out along the nerves of his arms, spreading to encompass damaged ribs. He couldn't help his grunt of response, the snarl against his awareness of the blanketing fog that closed in on his mind in the wake of it.

"Ian," she said, desperation giving her murmur a new intensity. "Please, tell me how to help!"

"Come here," he managed to tell her, although there was hardly any distance between them to start with. "Hold me, and put yourself back in your mind to how you felt when you kissed me. When you *woke* me."

He was asking the impossible, and he knew it. *Trust me enough to make yourself just that vulnerable while death creeps ever closer.*

But she didn't argue. She didn't ask how that could

possibly help, wasting what little time they had. She twined a leg over his, slipping her hand beneath his shirt to avoid his ribs and hold him low over his belly. Her head tucked into the hollow of his shoulder and neck, her breath the only warm thing about her.

Except for the warmth that came from within, seeping into him like a balm. Clearing him. Giving him the focus to reach out one more time, keeping the sense of those approaching amulets until they came within the range he could manage without risking misdirection.

One final effort, reaching out to embrace the acrid sense of the repulsive things, twisting them awake as the taste of them washed across his senses, making Ana flinch—

The sound of the workings rang across the mountainside like twin gunshots, echoing away into silence.

Ian shuddered in the wake of them and let the fog wash him away.

Chapter 13

Somehow the lingering sensation of the amulet working felt even uglier this time. Ana swallowed hard against a dry throat and managed a raspy whisper. "Are we safe?"

She couldn't quite bring herself to ask the real question. *Are they dead?*

By way of response, the tension drained from Ian's body; he sagged against her, his head lolling down to rest against hers.

"Ian!" She ducked out from beneath him, and then knew it for a mistake as he continued to fall and she struggled to control his descent. In the end all she could do was cradle his face from the impact. For all his lean grace, he was heavy with muscle—she didn't imagine she could do much to move him.

Though she was almost certain that if she put herself in the calm, open state of mind that seemed to most affect him, she could bring him around. She just didn't know if she *should*. His cheek still burned against her hand; his breath stuttered against pain. She had no way to know how much damage had been done—by Lerche, or by the explosion of workings Ian had triggered himself.

Best let him sleep. And heal.

Besides, there wasn't anything to be done here that she couldn't do herself. Not if the men were disabled.

If they weren't, then she was in over her head to start with.

Ana pulled the ragged blanket more tightly around her shoulders with one hand and lifted the drag of it with the other, stepping out from their scant shelter to scan the hillside below—a view of tree trunks and scattered underbrush, everything scrubby and stunted and dry. Only as she shivered in renewing panic did she finally locate the three men—a little cluster of lumpy forms that slowly resolved into awkward bodies in awkward poses, each equipped in camouflage outfits and equipment packs and what looked from here to be holstered pistols.

To her shame, her first thoughts were utterly selfish. Instead of regretting their deaths—for they surely looked to be dead—she found herself relieved. Not just because they so likely carried the supplies that she and Ian so badly needed, but because Lerche had sent three of them.

With those three now down and so many others affected by Ian's amulet explosion, Lerche would have fewer yet to send after them again. Hard to imagine herself so callous.

Then again, hard to imagine herself taking up against the Core.

It doesn't mean they're wrong. It doesn't mean the

Sentinels aren't out of control. It just means that Lerche is an awful human being.

After all, he'd been in control of her life since those preteen days when she'd arrived, grieving and confused. He'd kept her so isolated that she had no idea how other major Core posses functioned.

Take your own advice, Ana Dikau. Now was not the time to worry about such things. It was much better to scurry on down the hill, grasping at tree trunks for support and losing the blanket along the way as it snagged in a prickly scrub oak.

Didn't matter. The men had coats.

She reached the three of them and looked back up the hill, only then realizing how close she and Ian had come to disaster. From here, the fallen tree that canted over their tiny hollow of a shelter was clearly visible. From here, since she knew what to look for, she could see glimpses of Ian's shirt.

They'd been close enough to unleash these workings, if they'd but known it. But she put that, too, aside, and went to each man in turn, ascertaining that they were, in fact, dead—or close enough to it that she couldn't tell the difference, cold fingers against the cooling skin of their necks.

It came as a relief, in the end. It meant she could rob them without compunction. And she did.

Each man had water—bottles at their waists, water bladders and tubing in their packs. She snagged a bottle that was almost empty and forced herself to a single swallow, then put it aside to wrestle away the man's pack, and then, with more difficulty, his coat.

Not so easy to handle the dead weight of a large man, after all.

The coat swallowed her, instantly trapping warmth.

It was activewear, thinly insulated and full of zippers, toggles and pockets, but it made all the difference in the world. She luxuriated in it for a long moment, and then jostled herself into motion—adjusting it at the waist and tightening it in all places so she could continue her plundering.

By the time she was done, she'd emptied the water bottle and gathered two more, along with three packs, two more jackets and a vest—not to mention the gloves and hats. It took two trips to get everything up the hill, after which she no longer felt cold at all.

She sat beside Ian to riffle the packs, finding a gold mine of energy bars, a trail map marked with the men's progress and several precious heatable MRE packets. She tore into one right away, heating the stroganoff bag and dipping the spoon inside to hold near Ian's nose.

His face twitched; she ate that portion before it cooled and then presented another. As the third spoon approached, he opened his eyes. "What?" he said, and sounded annoyed while he was at it. "Seriously?"

Ana grinned, as out of place as it seemed. "I know, right? Not quite manna from heaven, but…pull yourself together, Ian. Eat up. We've got decisions to make." She reclaimed the spoon to swallow its contents and kept it in her mouth as she helped him straighten up, settling one of the jackets across his shoulders. He still frowned, expression bleary, but she decided first things, first and thrust the food at him, relinquishing the utensil. "Eat that," she reiterated, and unwrapped an energy bar, breaking it in half. "And then eat this."

He gave her a halfhearted disgruntlement of a growl, and she waved him off. "Whatever. I'm warm, I've got food and water, and I've got a *map*. You just go ahead and growl, see if I care."

"That was supposed to be impressive," he said, digging into the bag of food.

"And I'm sure it was." She tore a bite from the energy bar and wrestled with its cold chewiness, bending over the open map. "Remind me to make some sort of suitable reaction later. Right now I want to find us the fastest way out of here."

The spoon hesitated on the way to his mouth. "It's not that easy." He cleared the rest of the ragged feeling from his throat and took that bite, swallowing—eating faster now. "They found us, Ana. They *followed* us."

Her tenuous cheer evaporated. "I don't see how."

"The same way they always do. One of us is marked somehow." He offered her the food, and she shook her head—knowing well enough that the accelerated healing took a toll on him. It was Core Education 101.

He tipped the rest of the stroganoff into his mouth for a high-calorie chew-and-swallow and set the bag aside, pushing the jacket off his shoulders to check his pockets and coming up with nothing but lint.

Ana quickly did the same, going so far as to check the rolled cuffs of her pants. "Nothing," she told him—and then muffled a startled cry when he reached for her, patting her down as thoroughly as anyone could, hands impersonal as they traced the seams of everything from her shirt and pants down to her bra. Her face flared with a new and unwelcome warmth. "I suppose I deserved that."

He cast her a startled glance. "*Deserve* has nothing to do with it. Right now I think it's safe to say that I know more about how the Core works its enemies than you do."

"Enemies," she said, musing on it with a prick of

hurt. She'd never done anything but try to be what they wanted…without losing herself in the process.

"Don't get tangled in it," he said. "Isn't that what we decided?" He rubbed his temple with a weary gesture.

On impulse, she reached for his hand. They sat together for a long moment of silence during which she was ridiculously aware of the way his fingers overlapped hers, the faintly rough nature of his palm and warmth of it. His fingers twitched slightly, and she found a wince at the corner of his eye and reached to soothe it.

Gratifying that he closed his eyes to rest briefly against her touch. Once he straightened, he said, "They tracked us somehow. We need to know how."

"Can't we just make a run for it?" Ana asked, thinking herself sensible. "Surely once we return to the retreat—"

"Don't count on my people for help," Ian said, more sharply than she expected. "Not if Lerche told the truth about seeding that place with silents—and triggering them."

"I thought…if your brevis is already on alert…won't they send more help?"

"On wings," Ian said. "If they're not here already. But they'll be in crisis mode. And who knows if they'll be able to shield from the damned silents, no matter how careful they are. Although if they can get Maks on the scene with his uber-shields…" He trailed off, stopping himself. "Never mind. The point is that they're vulnerable. There's no way I'm leading the Core straight back at them."

"Then you should rest." The contents of one backpack sat on the ground before her, and Ana spread them out with one hand. A change of socks, a compass, a first aid kit, energy bars—and most importantly, in the middle of it all, a thick stack of chemical warmers, bundled together with a rubber band. "We've got what we need for now, if we're careful."

His grim smile disabused her of that notion. He said, "We bought some space, but not much. Lerche absolutely can't afford for me to live—once he doesn't hear from those men, he'll act quickly. He has too much understanding of what I can do, even if he has no idea I solved the silent amulet."

Ana reclaimed her hand, threading her fingers into her hair, head bent to look at the ground before her—the scattering of supplies from the pack, the coat that overlapped her crossed knees and then some. The evidence that they'd killed and fled and killed again. "I just can't even believe this," she said. "In what world does *any* of this make sense?"

"No particular world," Ian admitted, and recaptured her hand. "Look, Ana. You had the right of it. We can't stop to make things make sense. We just have to trust. And to follow."

"Follow you, you mean," she said bitterly. "Just like I followed Lerche for so long."

He sat silent for a long moment. Far *too* long. When she dared to glance at him, she found the weariness she expected, and the strain on his face. But she also found a less expected grief.

He gave her hand one last squeeze and released it. "Not if you don't want to." He rubbed a hand over the back of his neck, rotating his shoulders within the drape of the jacket. "But give me a chance to work out this tracking thing before you make up your mind."

Ana froze on understanding. He didn't intend to *make* her do anything. He didn't even intend to insist.

He was hurt and tired and doing his best, and yet he was willing to let her walk away.

She didn't know whether the realization pierced her heart, or freed it.

Ian wouldn't force her. Not after what she'd been through, and especially not because of what she believed him—the Sentinel—to be.

In the end, he didn't even know if he'd be willing to let her go her own way. But if he couldn't stop her, then he'd damned well make sure she wasn't carrying a tracker. Sure, he could have done with a little more time. He didn't have it. So be it.

He'd tasted the posse concussion amulets in spite of his illness and injury—he'd been able to perceive them from afar and been able to trigger them. So he trusted that he'd have similarly felt any tracker planted on Ana.

Not that they hadn't searched her—and him—thoroughly enough.

It meant that if they were being tracked by amulet, it was a silent one. Silent and so well hidden that there was no point in continuing a physical search.

He was about to put his new system to the test.

Not ready.

Not physically, when he still burned from the inside out, his thoughts slippery and his bones sore. Not skillwise, either. No finesse, no established parameters—only a blind fling of energy. "Just give me a moment," he told her as grimly as before. Not that she'd leaped to her feet. She was, he thought, still processing the fact that her choices from here were entirely her own.

Not a situation in which she had practice.

Besides, he still held her hand. In fact, he drew strength from it—knowing, if not understanding, why it made all the difference in the world. Enough so he was able to close his eyes and find one small, quiet, still place inside himself. From that he drew the purest note of energy he could find—a fine-tuned thing of highest clarity.

He sent it out in a single smooth pulse.

Chaos instantly pushed in on him, and he held it off—listening from that same quiet place, the only place from which he had the faintest chance of hearing—

That.

The response bounced back at him so quickly he almost missed it—and then again, three quick pings tumbling over one another at not quite the same strength.

He lost hold on the quiet, shuddering faintly as the chaos slammed in around him again.

"Ian," she said, bending close to him, the scent of her hair a soothing spice and her breath warm against his neck.

He opened his eyes to find her there. That close, with the daylight reflecting into the deeper honey glow of her eyes and the faint freckles completely revealed, concern written all over her face.

She had no idea.

And they didn't have time to soften the news.

"It's you," he said. "And them, for what it matters. But mostly it's you."

She understood immediately.

Almost.

Her hands flew to her blouse, leaving him to fight the impinging chaos alone. "I'll change," she said, glancing down the hill where three men lay still clothed. "If we can't find the thing, I'll just leave it all behind."

He put his hands over hers, stilling them—getting a frown of response. Cold still blushed her cheeks and nose, but behind it her complexion had pinked up to a healthier warmth. No point in getting her cold all over again. Especially not when he was pretty sure it wouldn't do any good.

"I mean," he said, "it's *you*."

She looked at him with a distinct horror. "What do you mean, it's *me*?"

"*In* you," he said. "I'd bet on it. Just as Fabron Gausto did to Jet."

"I don't—" Her confusion said it all. Ian knew more about the activities of the deceased regional *drozhar* than she did. Knew more about the Core altogether—if not about how those such as Ana lived within it. Or about how the Core managed them.

Although he was getting a pretty damned good idea.

"Ian," she said, pulling her hands away and tucking herself inside the absurdly oversize jacket. "My very own people are using me—they're trying to *kill* me. And now my very best ally, my *lover*, is the enemy I've always known couldn't be trusted at all." She worked herself up to a glare. "I've had *enough*. So you just come right out and *tell me what you're talking about*."

He blinked at her. Felt amusement welling up and didn't try to hide it. "When you put it that way, babe, it does seem only fair." He rotated his shoulders again, taking the stretch through to his torso—testing his ribs. Wincing at the scrape of pain but nonetheless lifting his arm to brace against the tree trunk. Testing himself. Limbering himself.

Because now it was about to get ugly in a way he hadn't anticipated.

And she was waiting.

"Short version," he said. "From scratch. Gausto was developing a working to force a shapeshift on non-

Sentinels. He wasn't getting anywhere, so he worked it from the other direction—forcing the change on animal subjects."

Unexpected understanding crossed her face, a startled distaste. "Jet," she said. "The woman I met yesterday."

"She's here?" Ian felt a surge of hope. "Excellent. Lerche's workings aren't likely to affect her the way they'll affect the others."

Ana took that in with a nod, but not without vexation. "What's that got do with me?"

Ian released a gust of impatience. "God, my head is a mess. The point is that once he had Jet, he used her—but she was and is a wild thing. So he found a way to keep track of her that she couldn't thwart. He implanted an amulet." The amulet had been a multitasker, full of less benign workings, but Ian left that part alone.

Ana froze, looking down at herself with renewed horror. "*In* me," she said, suddenly understanding. "Oh, my God, he can track us just because I exist!"

"Unless," Ian said gently, "we can do something about it."

"I don't—*how*—" But she froze, understanding. "Take it out. You want to take it out. You want to *cut me open and*—"

She jumped to her feet, clumsy in the cold and the jacket, and Ian made no move to stop her. He could hardly blame her. Even if he wasn't Sentinel, even if she wasn't wrestling with her whole world flipped inside out. She turned her back on him and took the three stumbling steps to the edge of their little scoop of shelter, and he didn't try to stop that, either.

He said, "I'll be back in a few moments."

She made a muffled sound he didn't even try to interpret as he stood and slipped his arms into the jacket sleeves—slowly, carefully, unwinding muscles stiff from the night and protesting all the abuse they'd taken along the way.

He was just as glad Ruger wasn't here to tell him what he'd done to himself with that explosive release of amulets. Or to tell him what he was doing to himself by interfering with his body's attempt to heal.

He ducked out beneath the massive tree trunk and made his way downhill to where the two posse members lay—sans their jackets, their bodies already taking on that peculiar stillness of death. The concussive amulets, released from such close proximity, had left them splayed as if trying to escape themselves, resulting in an instant rigor that must have resisted the removal of their jackets and now made searching them even more of a challenge.

But before he searched, he circled them—alert for the stench of amulets that might have gone untriggered when he'd targeted the concussive workings. Perceiving nothing, he steeled himself, slipping around the edges of the necessary focus to ping them for silent amulets.

Come on. *Get it together!*

But he didn't and couldn't. Not until he extended his awareness back up the hill to where he'd meant to leave Ana her privacy—not intruding so much as reminding himself of the peace she'd always given him. From that first moment in the retreat yard, in the kitchen… even in those moments when she'd been planting that first lethal amulet.

She was right. There'd be no untangling this mess between them. There'd only be allowing what they felt and seeing where it took them.

Where it took him now was into the quiet zone. A

brief respite, and just enough to ping for silents, sending that faint pulse out and away.

From the men, he got three faint, damaged pulses.

And from Ana, he received the same quiet response he'd felt before.

Just frigging awesome.

Ian made short work of his remaining tasks—searching and finding the men's more conventional weapons. Two handguns, about which he knew little other than the fact they were semiautomatics. A Leatherman multitool and two combat knives of modest length. Their phones, which might come in handy if he and Ana ever found a signal.

He stuffed the bounty into the various pockets of his newly acquired jacket and let his mind drift as he circled a little farther out, found a moment of privacy behind a cluster of little junipers, and slowly made his way back up to Ana.

She greeted him with eyes reddened but dry, delicate features pinched with both the cold and resolution. "Okay. Then how do we find it?"

"The amulet?" He barely waited for her nod. "We can try to triangulate. Don't know if I'm up for that, honestly. It's a kind of fine work I've had no practice in, and my ability to concentrate at that level is fractured at best." He gave her what felt like a lame grin and no doubt was. "On the other hand, even with healing workings, it should have left a mark. We can just look. Starting with here." He touched her neck, slid his hand down beneath the jacket to stop at the grace of toned muscle where her neck met her shoulder. "This is where they put Jet's."

Her eyes widened; her hand raised to cover his.

"There's a spot there…" she said. "It always itches. Since right before we came here…"

"Don't tell me. Right about then you had some sort of twenty-four hour bug."

She gave him a skeptical look. "You couldn't know that."

Ian laughed without humor. "I know how the Core works, babe. I know they made you sick so you wouldn't notice the clues that they'd done this thing. Probably just a day or so, but pretty miserably so."

"I had an awful headache—it lasted two days." She closed her eyes, struggling with the reality of it. "I'm not prone to them. I should have—"

"No." He said it with such vehemence that it shocked her into looking at him—unguarded, eyes wide. "You can't blame yourself. They were very careful to make sure you never had reason to suspect what they could and would do to control you." He stepped closer. "What they were doing *all along*. Don't ever forget that, Ana."

She held his gaze for a long moment, then sighed. *Acceptance.* "Fine," she said. "So now…?"

Ian couldn't help his grim look. "Now," he told her, "we get it out."

Easier said than done…but done as quickly as Ian possibly could.

He raided their acquired first aid kit, not surprised to find disposable scalpel and hemostats. And with Ana's jacket and blouse open and pulled aside far enough to expose her bra strap and the swell of her breast, he found the faintest hint of a scar. The stroke and prod of his fingers located the tiny lump of an implanted amulet.

She drew back in alarm when he produced one of the combat knives, but settled back even before he reassured her, curling her fingers into the exposed roots at the base of their shelter.

"Silly," he told her with much affection, and bounced the knife pommel against the old scar fast enough to set up a vibration and long enough so she frowned at him again.

"What—?"

"Now," he told her, and made the quickest of incisions, feeling the faint bite of metal against the blade and swapping the scalpel for the hemostats. Ana squeaked with surprise and jerked, biting her lip hard, and by then Ian had the thing.

He swabbed her shoulder and made swift work of the butterfly bandages, placing a gel skin bandage over that and leaving Ana with a stunned expression on a pale face.

"You're done?" She ran her fingers over the thin and flexible covering.

"Aim to please," Ian told her. "It might need stitches when we get past all this, but no big deal."

"I'm not even sure I felt that." She laughed, if not quite convincingly. "You and your bouncing knife."

He held the nubbin of an amulet up for her inspection, and then flicked it down the hill toward the dead men. "Just in case they have any trouble finding their own."

"Goodbye, Lerche." Ana's words should have held finality, but Ian heard a sadness there, too.

Not that he could blame her. Goodbye to a way of life, to a way of thinking. To a big part of what she'd always been and always believed.

He tucked away the first aid kit and the trash he'd generated, grabbing the meal wrappers while he was at it—leaving Ana to her silence while he distributed the contents of the third pack between the first two, and then helped her to her feet and adjusted the pack to fit—as best it could, sized as it was for the man who had worn it.

Ana glanced down the hill. "We just leave them?"

He understood her reluctance. "We do. Someone from the Core will track them down. They had their own trackers—damaged with concussion release, but yours is there, too." For above all, the Core knew better than to leave the evidence of its behavior lying around for the mundane world to stumble over. "They would have found us, too, if we hadn't made it."

She tucked newly gloved hands around the pack straps. "I know. It's just…none of this seems right. I just can't help but wonder if this isn't so much about the Core as it is about Lerche, and if I head on in…report what's happened…"

Something in Ian hardened. "Lerche," he said, jamming an arm through his own pack strap. "Eduard Forrakes. Fabron Gausto. And all the men who ever thought it was okay to belittle you and demean you and keep you so beaten down. Who think it's just fine to hurt Sentinels whenever it suits them. What happened here isn't about any single person, Ana, and it's not even about you or me. It's about a culture that sees bullying and *taking* as their right."

Ana sent him a strange look. "Funny," she said. "That's what Lerche would say about you."

Ian settled the pack into place. "Then you've got some decisions to make, don't you?"

"I don't—"

"Stay," he said, "and your Core will find you. Probably not Lerche's people by then. Or go on your own way, and find the Core. Or come with me. I'm heading to the Sentinels, and I'll take down as many posse members as necessary to get there."

"That's hard," she said, the faintest tremble at her mouth—and anger lighting her eyes. "That's damned hard."

He knew she wasn't talking about the choice. She was talking about *him*. And he couldn't disagree. "I want you with me, Ana. But I'll do what needs doing, and I'm not going to debate it at every turn. So, by God—" he shook his head, the words stuck in his throat for that instant "—I hope you'll come with me. Just be sure you know the choice you're making. And that you can live with it, one way or the other."

"No," she said, and her voice wasn't strong—nor that steady. "I won't let you define my terms. I can come with you now...and walk away later."

He reminded himself of how she'd grown up. Of what she'd been told. Of what she'd been plunged into the middle of. He reminded himself that he would probably never know how much strength it had taken her to say those words.

"Yeah," he agreed, and didn't do what he wanted so badly to do—snatch her off her feet like some caveman, keeping her safe. Keeping her *his*. Knowing that if he strong-armed her, he'd simply lose her altogether. "You can. But not without consequences, if you're wrong about the Core. And, just so you know, probably not without ripping my beastie little heart into some ugly pieces. But it's up to you."

With that, he struck off—his thoughts already whirling off into chaos with the distance he'd just put between them, and his body one large smoldering bruise except for the parts that simply hurt worse—his side, his face.

And, yeah, his heart. Even though it should have known better all along.

Chapter 14

They hiked with unerring purpose, making Ana glad she'd worn her minimalist cross-trainers the day before but also sorry she hadn't put on hiking boots. Ian led them from sun to shadow and back again, cresting unexpected slopes and curving around sharp points. Always one foot slightly lower than the other on slanting ground, her feet straining to find purchase among the accumulated bedding of needles and snagging in the sly tangle of underbrush.

She drank when Ian suggested; she ate the energy bar he dug out of the pack. She unzipped her jacket to let the cool air circulate beneath, finding herself plenty warm even without the rising temperatures of the day and the direct beat of the sun. Her feet turned leaden early, and she learned to place them with even more care. When she asked if they'd make it out before nightfall, he'd said only, "Maybe."

She didn't press. She heard the strain in his voice.

She knew what it had taken from him to walk away from their discussion, leaving her the space she needed—she knew how he cared. How deeply. Because she knew, now, how passionate he was about his people. What they did. What they'd suffered at Core hands.

No matter why the Core had done what they'd done. They'd caused suffering. That, Ana knew.

Because he was right. She'd experienced it all along, in her own way, even before Lerche had turned a torturous amulet on her. Or sent three men to kill them. Or before she'd known he'd hidden a tracker in her body.

She shifted the pack straps away from the tiny wound Ian had dealt her to free her of that tracker. Even in hurting her, he'd touched her with more care than she'd experienced since she'd been torn from her home.

Ian made a sound she hadn't expected, stumbling—righting himself against a tree and striking out again. Another dozen steps and he tripped again, this time landing heavily on his hands and one knee. He didn't bounce back up.

"Ian?" She ran a few hasty steps to reach him, and then wasn't quite sure what to do when she got there. She couldn't fix this any more than she could undo the moment she'd planted that amulet in the retreat kitchen.

"Awesome," he muttered, sitting back on his heel and dusting his hands off. "Big bad Sentinel."

"You're pushing too hard," she said as if she had the right to tell him of his own needs.

Ian glanced up at the sky; without thinking, she followed his gaze.

The sun was well on its way back down toward sunset, low enough to shine in her eyes if she'd been looking up instead of at her feet.

She'd had no idea they'd lost so much time tucked away in their little shelter. She'd been judging by the warmth of the day, unable to factor in the chilling effect of the altitude or the way the rugged folds of the mountain kept them in shade.

And given the healing heat that still radiated from Ian, given the strain on his features and the obvious way his body still chewed through resources, she knew without hesitation that he pushed on her account—trying to get her off the range before night fell.

"I'll be fine," she told him. Sharper in tone than she'd meant to.

Not to mention a statement utterly without merit. She had no idea how she'd get through another night out here.

She sighed in capitulation. "I don't understand." This time her voice held the weariness of their situation. "We escaped Lerche in the evening, and made it to that little hidey-hole sometime in the middle of the night. Why would it take us so much longer to get out?"

Ian let his head drop back, his hands resting flat against his thighs; he released a weary gust of breath. "Because then, we weren't navigating. We were just *running*. Because the *running* took so much out of us. Because we've got to take a different route to get out of here or we'll end up right back in Lerche's territory—and that route has to be one that takes us into trailhead area and not over a cliff." He opened his eyes just enough to send her a meaningful look. "That explain it for you?"

"Yes," she said, numb at the hard edge beneath those words. Not the Ian of compassion.

Just, she thought, Ian when pushed past what he could actually do.

She slipped the backpack strap from one shoulder, then the other. Ian had taken his stumble on a south-facing curve, and the sun hit them full on, illuminating not just the fatigue over handsome features gone a little too sharp, but painting the hill in strong light and shadow.

Easy enough to find the gentle places on the terrain—the little hollow above them where rock and tree retreated, leaving an area of matted needle and leaf.

She struck out for it.

"What," Ian asked without opening his eyes, "are you doing?"

She tossed her backpack; it landed at the edge of the hollow. She tossed the jacket after it, glad enough to shed it during this time of warmth and in the wake of their unceasing activity. "Here's a spot," she said as if they'd come to some mutual decision.

"I told you I wouldn't argue. I meant it. This is my way, or no way."

"Fine," she said. "Leave me here, then. Maybe you can send someone to look when you get out."

He made a decidedly unfriendly sound. A growl. Something so deep and primal she thought he hadn't consciously decided to do it at all.

"Look," she said. "We're not going to make it before dark, are we?"

"We'll get closer. Close enough. I can see in the dark—well enough to get us the rest of the way. Didn't your Core ever teach you that?"

As if the Core would fail to disclose any small detail of the Sentinels' advantages over normal humankind when fear of the Sentinels lived at the heart of Core culture. *Fear of them. The need to stop them.*

Stop them from what? Ana suddenly wondered.

Because the Sentinels could no more allow their people to reveal their nature than the Core allowed their own to employ workings in any visible way. If any Sentinel misbehaved…

That's what Lyn does.

Sentinel tracker. A woman who tracked her own, bringing them to Sentinel justice.

This is so messed up.

"Ian," she said gently, "we won't make it out of here at all if we don't do it smarter than this."

For a long moment, he didn't move. Then he rolled his shoulders, one after the other, and pushed himself to his feet. She stood at the edge of her chosen spot and held out her hand, and when he made it up to her, she slipped around to tug the backpack off his shoulders, setting it beside hers.

"It's a bad idea," he said under his breath, dropping his coat beside hers as well, and then dropping down onto it sitting cross-legged.

"No doubt. But it's the best one we've got." She settled down beside him. "Close your eyes for a moment. I'll pull out one of the MREs and get it ready."

He rubbed a hand over his eyes. "Ana, if I close my eyes, they're going to stay closed for a while. We could end up spending the night right here."

"We'll be okay."

He shook his head, dropping his hand to look at her, and she stilled, not expecting his tortured look or the way his jaw worked. "Ian, what—?"

"*We're* not the only ones in trouble," he said. "You met Fernie. You *liked* her. And Lyn, and Ruger, and Shea? I'm the only one who can save them." His voice dropped. "If it's not too late."

"I'm sorry," she said. "Whatever the truth is about

the Core or about the Sentinels… Lerche is a monster. I can't believe I didn't see it before now. I just can't—" She bit her lip, hunting words. Overwhelmed by a surge of guilt.

"Don't," he said harshly. "We've been through this. He made very sure you didn't see it. And, Ana, I want to make this easier for you. I want to make it all *fucking go away*. But I don't have the energy for it, so, please… can we just not go there right now?"

To her surprise, Ana found these stark words more comforting than she could have imagined. Just matter-of-fact truth. Ian couldn't make this better.

In fact, *no one* could make the shreds of her life into some magically okay thing. Lerche had systematically created what she was and what she'd experienced, and now all she could do was break free of it to make her own decisions.

She shifted to her knees, bringing herself closer to him—close enough to touch his face and let her fingers linger there. He closed his eyes, and she wasn't sure if he couldn't quite bear her touch or if he simply needed it just that badly.

"Ian," she whispered. "You mean so much to me. In these few short days…you've changed my life into something I never could have imagined."

He swallowed hard, muscles working in his throat and jaw, eyes closed so hard she could all but feel his pain herself. She stroked across his cheek—the strong angle, the clean lines. She let her fingertips dust across dark lashes, ridiculously long lashes with the smudge of the big cat around the edges of his lids. She drew a whisper down the straight, strong line of his nose and touched his mouth—clearly defined, with a full lower lip that felt so very good against hers.

And was so very good at carrying off the faintest wry little smile he now offered her. "Colder than you could have imagined? More stupidly tired? More profoundly lost?"

Ana laughed, and it came out a throaty sound. *"Alive,"* she corrected him, and didn't bother to move her fingers before bringing her mouth down on his.

"Mmph," he said in surprise—but seemed to understand her need not to be kissed, but to do the kissing. His hands lay quiescent on his thighs as she explored his lips beneath hers, a sensation becoming familiar—just as was the sound of his quickening breath, the firmness of his response and the way he knew just how to woo her—one moment gentle, the next leaning into her kiss with a demanding clash that warmed her blood so much faster than any sunshine ever could.

Her hand found the hem of his shirt, slipping beneath it to touch smooth skin and inspire the responsive flutter of hard muscle. His groan sounded of frustration, and his hands lay quiet no more, instead reaching to her waist. Lifting her to straddle his lap just seemed to *happen*, and he left his hands there, thumbs curled around her hip bones and fingers splayed out just above the curve of her bottom. She shuddered at that sudden jolt of pleasure and he gasped against her mouth, his hold tightening in reflex.

In an instant he'd rolled her onto her jacket, his legs straightening to pin hers and his hands sliding up her sides to her arms, finding her fingers to interlace his own. "This," he growled, "is the stupidest damned time to—"

"Shut up," she gasped. "It's the perfect time, and you know it. Don't you dare start *thinking* about it—"

"*You* shut up," he said, and covered her mouth to make it so.

Or almost so, because she spoke right around their kiss. *"Fine,"* she said. "Take *this*." And with no hesitation at all, slipped her hand right down the front of his pants to find his erection.

Ian froze. "Cold," he said, his voice sounding strangled. "Cold, cold—"

But when she stroked him he stiffened into her, and she did it again, scratching lightly at velvet skin. "Not so cold?"

"Just—" he shuddered, his eyes squeezing shut "—just...*perfect*."

She rose up just enough to whisper in his ear. "Too many clothes, Ian."

He must have agreed. She quite abruptly found herself without a shirt, her pants unbuttoned and yanked off all but one ankle, his pants unbuttoned and out of the way. She reached for him again, owning him—fingertips and gentle pressure making way for a few firm strokes while she had him.

"Gah," he said on a gasp. "Wait... Ana... I don't have—"

Right. Condoms had been the last thing on anyone's mind as they fled Lerche's mansion.

"I'm safe," he said, on his elbows over her and trembling with the effort of control as her hand stilled but lingered. "Sentinels...we can...we learn to..."

Didn't matter. He'd be healthy—Sentinels were. "I'm protected, too," she managed. Because the Core required it, demanding the use of an implant, demanding regular health tests. Controlling even that.

"Your choice," he said, holding himself there by pure evident dint of will.

"I already made that choice," she told him. "Remember? In all ways, Ian."

"Ana," he breathed, and it sounded like something else. Something more important. *"Ana."* Whiskers brushed her skin as he buried his face against her neck, burying himself inside her. She arched up into him with a cry of welcome and a hot flare of pleasure, clutching as he retreated and thrust again—more deeply and then stilling there to absorb the feel of it. His teeth scraped her neck with a faint pinch that sent a delightful shock zinging along her skin; one hand roamed her body to find her breast beneath shirt and bra and gently roll her nipple.

She arched up into that, too, stunned by the fast-gathering heat of a climax and preternaturally aware of every inch of his touch. His breath on her neck, his lips and tongue soothing the spot he'd only just nipped, his fingers rough and perfect over her breast, the amazing sensation of her own body throbbing around his and his body throbbing within hers.

And though he somehow held himself still within her, trembling against the anticipation, she could do so no more. She twisted, writhing up against him, insisting... Her hands found the tight muscle of his beautifully rounded bottom, and she grabbed it, hard—pulling him in while she took him just a little bit deeper, reaching for that miraculous gathering of bright liquid imminence.

He cried out as he had before, a startled thing—a wild thing, set suddenly free and thrusting hard. A man, shouting in beautiful, vulnerable surrender. And again, and again, each shout bringing her nearer and closer and *oh. Please. Yes—!*

Ana spilled over into the hot shards of orgasm, her fingers digging into his backside, aware of nothing but the sensation he wrung from her, his final gasping thrusts and the guttural groan of his own release—not just a momentary pulse but a sensation that rocketed between them, building into something that was bigger than either of them and, in the end, leaving Ana with a sob stuck in her throat.

Ian slowly relaxed above her, his touch more languid as he stroked her beneath her shirt—gently on her tender breast, lingering on each rib, his thumb dipping into her belly button. His lashes brushed her chin as he raised his head, kissing that chin and then each corner of her mouth. "Ana! Are you crying?"

She nodded, a quick little surprised motion. "Yes," she said. "It's just so… It was…"

"Beautiful," he whispered, and kissed her again—briefly, before he laid his head on her chest, letting the weight of it settle slowly. She lifted her own head just enough to kiss the disarray of his silvered hair, and found his hand to interlace her fingers again. He briefly returned the touch with a squeeze of his own, and just that gently, relaxed into sleep. Still covering her, still keeping her warm.

Ana found his discarded jacket with her free hand, tossing it over his back with an awkward flick of her wrist and tugging it into place. Covering them both, and smiling into leftover tears as she let his presence lull her away into sleep beneath him.

Ian woke with a start, rolling away from Ana to land in a crouch—face lifted to the breeze, the night a sharp wash of blue-tinted detail around him and his hands flexing against the ground, phantom claws deployed.

The leopard awake.

Slowly, he relaxed—understanding that there was

no danger, no enemy on approach. It was only that the leopard, so repressed, so sickened, had come back to him in such a tidal surge of awareness.

Ana stirred within the gentle hollow of ground where they'd sheltered, still buried beneath his recently acquired jacket. They'd made love, they'd slept, they'd woken to disarray and satiated kisses, and they'd eaten…and then he'd acknowledged the inevitable.

It wouldn't have done his friends any good if he'd made it off the mountain in record time only to falter upon reaching the retreat. Especially if the Core was already there.

Waiting.

Not just for him. For Ana.

And he was far, far too close to that point of exhaustion.

So they'd slept again, one jacket beneath them and one above, Ana's gently heavy breathing lulling him back to sleep.

It had almost sounded like purring.

"Ian?" Her voice came sleepy from the hollow; material rustled as she pushed the jacket away from her face. "Ian—?"

"I'm here," he said, keeping his voice low only out of respect for the night. "Go back to sleep."

She made a disgruntled sound, and the rustling subsided. Ian stood, uncoiling to his full height. Aware of the leopard as he couldn't ever remember being.

Ana. She'd done what she did best, quieting him. Giving him the room to heal—and now, to feel the depth of what he'd always been. An Ian Scott that he'd never truly known, with his world too full of thought and motion and intent.

A quiet breeze slipped over his arms; he felt the chill of it for the first time since…

Since he'd first been affected by the kitchen amulet.

He stood a moment, still in the way only the leopard could be—in a way he'd never truly allowed of himself. Absorbing the understanding of how deeply—and how quickly—those amulets had affected him. Absorbing, too, the perfidy of such a subtle attack. He was the primary AmTech of this region, and if he hadn't felt the insidious nature of the damage being done, how would anyone?

Ana was right. Right to insist that they stop here, right to insist that they rest, that he heal. Because more important than the need to save those people he loved so fiercely was the need to convey the secret of the silent amulets as quickly and widely as possible. If he stupidly sacrificed himself along the way, that would never happen. No one would even know he'd solved the riddle—or that it was even possible.

Another breeze slipped over his arms, riffling his hair and evoking a shiver. The leopard pushed at him, whiskers bristling, the skin over his shoulders twitching. Ian glanced back at the small quiescent lump that was Ana under the jackets and then back out into the clarity of the night, stepping out into the silence of it—*bounding* out into the silence of it—and reaching for the leopard as he moved.

Coiled power, the graceful snap of a long tail, broad paws quiet against the earth, breeze a mere ruffle of fur, hunger growling in the emptiness of a body chewing through resources to heal.

Ian went hunting.

Lerche cursed the sling that bit into his neck, and he cursed the raking claws of the working still crawling through his system—one of those from the case Ian Scott had triggered *en masse.*

Lerche hadn't known him to be capable of any such thing. Hadn't known *any* of them to be capable of such a thing. And even if he'd known…

It wouldn't have occurred to him that any sane man would do it. Not when too many of the powerful workings were constructed to target the nearest Sentinel—unlike the workings that Scott had very clearly managed to direct away from himself and away from Ana. Across the household and onto Lerche and his men, so many of whom had been badly injured or died outright.

He hadn't had so many to waste. And now he hadn't heard back from the three posse members he'd sent into the mountain, readily following the silent amulet he'd had embedded in Ana before this operation.

She'd gone to bed without it. She'd woken with it. And she'd never known the difference.

Too bad the tiny silent blanks were so precious. Lerche could foresee a day when all his people carried such trackers, instead of just those who most needed to run silent.

But not until—*unless*—he got things under control before the regional *drozhar* ran out of patience. The entire Southwest had undoubtedly felt the ripple from the mass amulet release—including the Tucson Sentinels. Brevis reinforcements would already be on the way.

They'd be too late for those at the retreat. He was confident of the deadly web he'd woven there—silent amulets, triggered in unison to enclose the retreat and trap the occupants within its effects. If they weren't dead, they were dying. Brevis couldn't get here in time—because there was no *in time.* Until the working faded or the amulets were destroyed, any and all who entered that retreat would die, leaving the Sentinels only the need to clean up after them, bereft of evidence and hushing events to protect their own clandestine nature.

Just as Lerche now cleaned up after his own, whipping up the few men left to him. By the time the *drozhar* arrived, there'd be no one to contradict his story.

And it was a good story.

Ian Scott gone mad in the wake of Ana's assignment gone awry, Ana gone rogue and misusing amulets in an attempt to succeed in her own small assignment.

Of course Ian Scott had then come after Ana, tearing through the mansion with no regard to Core lives… and he had triggered the final amulet attack before fleeing into the hills, dragging Ana with him. There they'd both no doubt expired.

Things were well in hand. Lerche could be reasonably certain that Scott hadn't completed his work with the silent amulets, or he would have detected them on Ana long before Lerche ever had a chance to take him prisoner. Those results alone would justify his initial operation—the one he'd put on the record with the *drozhar*—and the Sentinels and Ana would take the blame for the rest.

Lerche resisted the urge to scratch his healing arm, and instead reached for his new phone—sliding it open and scrolling down the contacts to the men who ought to have returned from the mountain by now. They should certainly be within an area of reception.

"Answer, damn you," he muttered, glaring at the phone.

No one did.

Chapter 15

Ana saw Ian leave.

She saw him *change.*

And she froze with fear beneath the bundle of jackets, understanding for the very first time—truly understanding—what Ian *was.*

He was gorgeous. He was power and danger and primal energy.

He was *beast.*

Just as Lerche had always said. Just as she'd always believed, but as she'd not truly been able to comprehend.

Who *could*?

She'd made love with this man. She'd declared herself to him. She'd opened her heart to him.

And he was more dangerous than she ever could have imagined.

"I'm done now," she whispered into the night. "No more hard stuff, universe. It's somebody else's turn."

Intense gut-level fear, it seemed, was every bit as strong as any trust.

She pushed herself up from the ground, rising slowly to pull the jacket on and zip it up; the temperatures had fallen to their usual remarkable degree, and she had no intention of getting cold all over again.

After she found herself a bush, she hunted up hat and scarf from one of the backpacks, covering her ears and neck and then stuffing her hands in a pair of scavenged gloves. They flopped off her hands like clown fingers, and she laughed darkly into the night as she put both hands in one glove, salvaging warmth.

Waiting. Unable to sleep, knowing that he was out there. That the *leopard* was out there.

Snow leopard. A glimmer of pale spotted white as he prowled away, an amazing length of tail, small ears tucked tight to a beautiful feline head. Not the biggest of the cats, which suited him. He wasn't a brawny man, after all. He was all lean frame and muscle, broad shoulders and coiled movement.

Ana pulled the arms of the bottom coat up into her lap, making it into as much of a robe as she could, and huddled into the results.

Waiting. Watching for that glimmer of pale movement. Listening for the rustle of a big padded foot against the ground.

And therefore nearly missing him when he did return, walking upright and quite humanly in the darkness. His nearness startled her all over again and she sprang to her feet, tripping over the bottom coat and recovering herself.

"Thought you were asleep," he said, his voice low and conversational.

"I had to use a bush," she told him. "I...saw you leaving."

"Ah." His voice held understanding. She couldn't read his face.

She suspected he could very easily read hers. Sentinel night vision was a well-known thing—a combination of human and nocturnal physiology, with their earth powers thrown in. Clear, bright and detailed.

He didn't try to come any closer. "You gave me back the leopard, you know."

She didn't know. In fact, she didn't understand at all.

"I haven't been able to find myself since that first amulet started working on the retreat." He shook his head, a motion she could see in the rising moonlight. "To be fair, it's been a very long time since I could cut through the overlapping thoughts in my head to let the whole of the leopard through."

Ana struggled to absorb the meaning behind his words—hearing in his voice a reverence, a *relief*, that she found distinctly hard to comprehend. "It's that important to you?"

Ian laughed outright. "Is breathing important? Is *living*?"

She didn't quite know how to answer.

"Yes," he said, more quietly now—beginning to realize that her hesitation came not just from a failure to understand, but from her own reaction to the leopard. "It's that important. I'm sorry if I frightened you. I'll never hurt you, Ana. *Never.*"

She discovered she'd wrapped her arms around her stomach, holding herself tight. "When I first saw you on that trail with the cougar..."

He'd been beautiful. He'd been charging into a fight with a creature significantly larger than he was, and even in her fear of the power he held, she still remembered most vividly the bittersweet desire to have someone who cared enough for her to do the same.

But now he waited, and she made herself ask. "I wondered then...how much of yourself do you retain when you're leopard? How much of your humanity?"

His silence let her know the question came as something of a blow. His lingering distance told her the same. "What has the Core told you, Ana? That we're all beasts? That when we take the change we become the worst of both worlds? All the ugliness of humanity, all the ferocity of the animal? Killing machines?"

It took all her strength to stick to her truths. She wanted to say *no, never mind, I'm just being silly.* She wanted to find some appeasing response that would take the tension from his posture and make everything feel all right, even if it meant burying her fear.

She had learned well how to stay safe in her world.

But Ian had always been truthful with her. And he was teaching her that the only true way to be safe was to be honest with him—and with herself. So she said, "Yes. That's exactly what I learned."

Not from her family, in those early years when she'd learned what it did feel like to be loved. But after.

Ian's bitter, self-aware tone took her by surprise. "God, they suck."

And then he startled her again. "You need to figure it out, Ana. What you see against what you've been told. What you've experienced with me against the words of a culture that showed you how to live in disrespect and fear."

"I..." She started talking because it seemed necessary, and trailed away because she wasn't even sure what to say. Finally she managed, "I know. I just don't know *how*."

He took a step closer. A challenge of sorts—knowing he'd frightened her and now daring her to get past it as he finally answered her earlier question. "When I take the leopard, it makes me more than either of us. Everything that's me, free to glory in everything that's leopard. But the leopard doesn't control me. The leopard *is* me."

Ana took a step back. Not from fear—for this was Ian, the man who had held her and loved her and risked his life for her. Just because she needed…

Space.

Because at some point, that *one more thing* had simply become too much to process, in too little time.

He didn't pursue her. But he didn't back down, either. "We use who we are to keep this world safe from those who would harm it. We patrol wilderness areas, we find toxic dump sites, we work in zoos and parks. If we're not supposed to embrace who we are while we're at it?" He snorted. "Pardon me, but fuck that."

Embrace who we are.

It's what Lerche had tried to take from her, too. Pushing and squeezing and molding her to the understanding that what she was could never be enough. That she needed, somehow, to be somebody else.

"Whatever," Ian said as if it hadn't mattered at all. But it had, and she knew it. It mattered very much. And still she was all jumbled inside. Unable to offer him the responses he needed—not and be honest.

Ian cut her silence short by stepping up to pull the packs together. "Time to move out," he said, rummaging and discarding. "I think we can get this stuff into one pack, if we use the jacket pockets." He held out a handful of energy bars, and she belatedly stepped forward to take them, stuffing them into all the nooks and crannies of the jacket. He flattened the trash from the MREs and layered it into the bottom of the pack, offering her the final dinner along the way. "Here. You need it."

"So do you," she protested, finding herself with words again.

He gave her a glance that she couldn't read in the darkness, moonlight or no. "I've eaten."

The *leopard* had eaten, he meant. She swallowed hard and refused to think about it—and took the dinner, tearing it open to initiate the heating process and meanwhile tucking its little side packets into her pockets with the energy bars.

He zipped and buckled and hefted the pack. "It's good," he said. "We'll tie the jacket to it. I'm afraid you'll have to carry the second pack, too, but it's light."

"Why—" she started and stopped, looking for better words than *why do you have to be the leopard?*

"You can stay here if you want," he told her, reminding her of their earlier conversation. "Or go your own way."

"That's not what I meant." She drew on that new courage and stood her ground. "I can carry the packs, and I will. I'm only trying to understand."

He handed her the full pack. "Because the leopard can see better, hear better and move better. And if we run into trouble, I'm in a better position to do something about it."

"Okay," she said.

He gave her a sharp look that she felt even through the darkness. "And because I've missed it. I *want* it." He took a step closer, close enough so she could see his features and see the gleam in his eyes, and the yearning. "Because I *need* it. I'm not ashamed of that. Pretty much the opposite, in fact."

With that he turned her around to help her with the pack, and tied the jacket on it, and stepped away. Not just one step, but half a dozen—where he hesitated only long enough to say, "I won't let you get lost," before he spun into a silent blue-white explosion of energy and strobing light, and emerged from it as leopard.

Beautiful, graceful, *deadly* leopard.

Ian quartered the terrain before Ana, clearing it not only of a prowling bobcat but confirming the absence of human presence now that they neared the trail he'd been targeting. Never out of her sight long enough so that she felt alone, never so close as to frighten her.

When a small gathering of coyotes lowered their heads and trotted away with a collective sneer, he knew two things—that dawn was close, and the trail was closer. Coyotes packed up near the base of the range, skimming that intersection between humanity and the wild where rabbits, squirrels and small house pets kept them fed and entertained.

Ana greeted his return with less apprehension and more relief. He sat before her, long pluming tail wrapped around his feet, wishing he could explain how magnificent it was to prowl inside this other skin, soaking up scents and sounds that the human never noticed. How exhilarating to give way to the instinctive impulses of the leopard—from the leap that clapped broad paws over a mouse only to sit and twitch whiskers as it scurried away to the sudden dash across open ground, tail flipping along behind in the glory of muscles in play, bunch and leap and pounce and then *oh, did I do that?*

How *alive* it made him.

How important it was that this deep connection with his leopard had been restored.

By Ana.

But she wasn't ready to hear any of that, and he wasn't ready to be the human without letting the leopard shine through. He turned and padded away, leading her in such a deliberate manner that she understood they were close.

Just as well. Faint dawn and Sentinel sight painted deep shadows of fatigue beneath her eyes and hollows beneath her cheeks. He knew he'd look no better when he returned to the human—visibly gaunt in the wake of the extensive healing, worn by the pain and circumstances.

Not that he was complaining. Not even to himself. He didn't want to think too deeply on the state he'd been in, or what he'd have done without Ana's help.

The trail at this point was a narrow thing of marginal footing, but when they reached it, Ana released a huge sigh of relief. Ian turned to give her a cat grin, his rump perched ridiculously high on the slope and his paws braced below, jaw dropped just the slightest bit. But it only made her hesitate, one hand on a bracing tree.

When he moved out she waited for a decent distance between them before she followed.

As soon as he judged it light enough for her human sight to follow the emerging trail on her own, he slipped off to parallel it. The track widened; another trail merged into it and drew them around in a flattening loop toward the parking area. Ian drifted to shortcut the loop, stealing a few more moments with the leopard as the trees thinned and the bunch grass rose up, studded with juniper and hiding the oddball prickly pear.

Ana's unexpected voice drifted to him on a level parallel to his, out on the far part of the loop. Ian hesitated, ears swiveling, the rest of him frozen so as not to generate his own noise.

He couldn't hear the words...he didn't like the tone. Not just a greeting to an unlikely dawn hiker. Not a conversation with herself.

The rumble of a male voice cinched it. Demanding. Rude.

Ian swerved in that direction, trotting with purpose and long, loose strides. Not sprinting yet—the snow leopard didn't have a lot of sprint, and he'd save it. But pushing hard, with several hundred yards between them.

Until Ana cried out. *"Ian!"*

Then he ran, legs pumping, claws digging into earth—bounding over brush and dodging trees, ears flattened and tail counterbalancing even the most improbable leap.

He felt nothing of *Core*. Nothing of lurking amulets or the stinging taste of a working in progress. A crude, ping of wild energy returned no hint of a silent amulet.

Ana cried out again, this time in anger—in obvious struggle. She was brave enough, his Ana, and had struggled her way through an emotional and physical ordeal that would have left others a weeping mess. They'd *made* her strong, always holding victories and successes just out of her reach, creating a world for her in which *just keep trying* was the only option.

But she wasn't big enough, or strong enough, or trained enough, to overcome Core posse.

Ian bounded in without a hint of stealth, getting his first glimpse of them—Ana hampered by the oversize jacket and pack, not one but two men grabbing at her. Not yet trying to hurt her, not being the least gentle...

They must have waited here, taking a chance on the

location. This was the closest egress from the mountain, barring one that would return them to the mansion. It was familiar, the one from which they'd taken Ian the first time.

Where they'd gotten the men, Ian didn't know. But he'd screwed up. He'd thought them safe. He'd thought to steal a few more moments as the leopard.

He'd left Ana alone.

Now there was no stealth—not with Ana's struggles fueling his fury. If the men had no amulets, then they had conventional weapons, and Ian could only bear down on them hard and fast, kicking it up into that burst of a killing sprint. Taking them by surprise, simply because they'd never trained against such an opponent before.

They weren't as unprepared as all that. One of them shouted alarm; the other flung Ana away and snatched at his side—not quite fast enough with a gun as Ian leaped with claws extended, slapping the man in a quick series of swiping blows.

The gun went off, plucking a trail of fire along Ian's upper arm—and with it came an equally fiery rain of whipping blows across his back. He turned a snarl on the second man and his tactical baton, snagging the thing in one paw even as he came to rest on the man screaming beneath him.

The fallen man flailed, and Ian turned on him with the fiercest of snarls, all his teeth in the man's face—freezing him in gut-level terror.

Ana's scream came not in fear but in warning—no time to form words, just her own human cry to beware. Ian looked up to find that the second man had a gun, too, and now he had a shot, with his partner flat on the ground and out of the way.

Ana launched herself at him, arm raised, a blade glinting briefly in the barely risen sun. The man thought to shove her carelessly away and then jerked in surprise as she struck, whirling around to bat her down with a cruel blow.

By the time he turned back to Ian, he found himself face-to-face with an enraged snow leopard—one already inside the line of his gun, ears flat to his skull and teeth bared in the clearest of threats.

The man froze, instantly opening both hands so the gun sat only loosely in his palm, his finger off the trigger.

Ana scrambled back up to hands and knees, lurching beneath the pack and making her way to the other man—wrenching his gun away and backing off to the sweet spot where she was out of his reach but still close enough to call point-blank.

Under Ian's glare, his captive eased his own gun to the ground and stepped away. Ian batted the thing toward Ana.

She gathered it, too, breathless and wild-eyed, a smear of blood trickling from her nose and the split of her puffing lip. "This one looks pretty bad, Ian."

Ian didn't look away from his own captive. *Pretty bad* was likely an understatement. Sharp claws, soft neck. The man hadn't understood his fate before Ian had snarled him into compliance, but Ian thought he'd figure it out very soon.

This other man, though…

Ian gave him a hard eye, took a step in his direction. A stalking, deliberate step, head lowering.

"Hey," the man said. *"Hey."*

"Try sitting down," Ana suggested, a little starch coming back into her voice. Grim starch, as she, too, realized the likely fate of the man before her, but starch nonetheless. "In fact, try cuffing yourself with whatever you were going to use on me."

Irate nastiness bubbled out. "You watch yourself, bitch. When Lerche gets his hands on—"

Ian snarled. All teeth, all narrowed eyes, lowering over his shoulders. Taking another step.

"Okay, okay! Whatever!" The man sat as if his legs had gone out from beneath him, which might well have been the case. "Godammit, she stabbed me!"

Oh? Ian cast a glance over at Ana, a twitch of whisker. *Good for you.*

Her expression in return didn't give him any warm fuzzies. A grim thing, her mouth flat and her eyes looking trapped rather than relieved.

Ian stalked an unhappy, grumbling path around the surviving Core posse member, flicking his tail in the man's face as a reminder. The man cursed again, digging into his pockets—freezing just for a moment as he started to withdraw his hand and discovered himself under intense feline scrutiny. *"Handcuffs,"* he said, snarling the word. "Just like you said."

Ian sat. Watching. The man snapped the cuffs into place and held them up for inspection. "Okay? You happy now? You just going to let Levv die, or are you going to let me call someone?"

Ana's voice sounded remote. "Unless you're hiding an amulet with a miracle working on it, it's too late for your friend." She sat back on her bottom, legs loosely crossed and the gun in her hand as if she couldn't quite remember how to hold it.

Because, Ian knew, she'd been through *just. Too. Much.*

And he wasn't helping.

He moved to the edge of the trail, making sure the gunshot hadn't attracted the attention of an early morning hiker. The surviving man glared and Ana cast him a distracted glance, but they were alone in their little tableau, and Ian stepped into the human—straightening and reaching for that place within himself. The one that stood tall and sharp-eyed and still full of the leopard.

Full of concern for the woman who would never be anything but beloved, no matter what she could or couldn't cope with in the end. "Ana?"

"I'm okay," she said, and then laughed, a short sound with dark notes to it. "I mean, relatively speaking, right?"

Ian cursed—silently, sharply—and got to work. Gathering the gun, finding the knife that Ana had dropped, stuffing them into the backpack she'd also dropped. He checked the man's cuffs, ratcheting them down tight without concern for the man's sneer or the implied threat behind it.

It meant only that he and his buddy weren't the only ones looking for Ian and Ana, and it was information that Ian was glad to have. He stood and stepped away. "Who drove?"

The man's sneer only grew stronger, turning an ill-defined face into something ugly.

"Whatever," Ian said. "If I cut your jacket off to empty the pockets, you're going to get cold fast. If your pants come off, you'll be hanging in that breeze. Maybe you'll have a phone to call for help, maybe not."

The sneer shifted to narrowed eyes and a mean resentment, but the man's eyes cut to his partner.

Ian moved around to the other side of the dead man where he could keep an eye on the living, and patted the man's front pockets. "This is how it starts," he told

Ana, keeping his eyes on their captive. "He goes back to the Core and talks up the way I overpowered him with my animal nature. How his gun was of no use. How I slaughtered his partner." He risked a glance at her, catching her gaze only for an instant—big and brown and shattered. "I mean, my God! I stopped him from killing me! What is this world coming to?"

"Us," she said, no strength behind her voice. "You stopped him from killing *us*." But she scooted back slightly, leaving the gun behind. "But…look at his throat, Ian. Look at his *throat*."

Ian didn't need to. He hadn't used his teeth—hadn't bitten through spine or taken a suffocating hold on the man's throat. He simply hadn't put the man's safety above his own, risking himself to make sure he pulled those blows.

"I know what happened to his neck," he said, grunting as he rolled the man up to one hip for a better angle into his pocket. The keys came to hand fairly quickly, and he retrieved and reseated them firmly in his grip. "Was it less civilized to use claws in defense than it was for him to shoot me in the first place?"

That got her sharp attention. "Did he— Oh, Ian! Your arm!"

Just a flesh wound. Bleeding freely, hurting badly, through the bulk of his biceps and out again. "Yeah," he said. "But never mind. I'll heal, right? That's what makes it okay to hurt us and hurt us and *hurt* us, isn't it? Ask Lerche what he thinks about it, why don't you?"

She sucked in a breath and stared at him as if she'd never seen him before.

Maybe she hadn't. Maybe he'd protected her from the impact of Lerche's actions. From the impact of the Core on the Sentinels.

Maybe he wouldn't do it any longer.

He grabbed the back of the man's jacket and dragged him off the trail and into the trees—damned if that didn't hurt, too, or if a wash of light-headed sweat didn't flush across his brow and prickle down his back while he was at it. Too much accumulated insult at that, even if this one had made the leopard nothing but mad. Without the amulet working at him, without the clutter of extra chaos in his thoughts, that clear connection to his most basic self remained strong.

Damned strong.

Damned fine.

And nothing to apologize for.

He returned to find Ana standing off to the side, their captive still sitting sullenly in the middle of the trail. He wasn't into explanations; he hooked a hand under the man's arm and hauled upward, adding enough of a pinch in that tender spot to inspire compliance. From there he led the man to his partner and pushed him down into a sprawling sit. "Phone?"

The man gave him a wary look but only a momentary hesitation. Lessons learned. "Inside jacket pocket."

Ian tugged the jacket forward, unzipped and searched first one side and then the other—impersonal and efficient and finding the thing. But when the man grabbed for it, Ian held it just out of reach, just as efficiently thumbing the battery free. The man's protest died on his lips when Ian tossed the battery at his feet and then hurled the phone into the trees. "Have at it," he said, and left the man there.

Ana greeted him with a baffled stare. "What did you—?"

"He'll be a while finding the pieces of his phone," Ian said shortly. "It'll buy us some time." She stared into the trees, frowning, and he sighed. "No, Ana, I didn't kill him, though I have no idea how badly you might have hurt him with that not inconsiderable knife blade. But we need to get moving. I'm tired of bleeding, and I'd like to try to save my friends now."

She startled just a little, looking down at her own hands and the blood there. "I did stab him," she said, her voice low. "I don't think it went very deep."

"Doesn't matter if it did," Ian said. "Unless you want to buy into the Core mind games and call yourself the monster because you didn't want to die."

Her head snapped up. "That's not fair."

"Yeah," he told her. "It is. Come or stay, Ana. Your choice."

He really hoped she would come as he headed for the parking lot, scooping up the fallen pack on the way. He didn't think getting behind the wheel of a car was his best choice just now. Especially not as the stench of the car and its considerable amulet presence made its impact on his senses.

No wonder they'd been so clean. They'd divested themselves of workings before setting out. Smarter than the last two, or maybe they'd just learned their lesson.

Or just maybe they knew more of what they were about. It made him wish he'd lingered to question the survivor. If Lerche had called in reinforcements…if those reinforcements were of a better caliber posse…

Just what they needed, if the regional *drozhar* had gotten involved.

He reached the car, a ubiquitous pale SUV, and unlocked it with a click of the key fob. He yanked a back door open without much care and tossed the pack inside, only then hesitating to take stock of Ana.

"I'm coming," she said, from only a few steps away. "I'm seeing this through."

It held no promises, and it gave him little comfort. But it was something.

Chapter 16

"What do you mean," Lerche said, annunciating each word with precision, *"they got away?"*

Budian's voice didn't hold the respect it should have. "Not from me," he said. "I'm still keeping an eye on the retreat—not for long, though. Someone's got to go clean up after Stephan's mess in the mountain, and there aren't many of us left. In case you hadn't noticed."

Lerche stood too quickly from his massive desk, bumping the backs of his knees against the sturdy chair as light-headedness struck. But only briefly, and he was already on his way to the balcony, throwing the door open to scowl over the rolling foothills that fell away into the city. "If this posse had performed adequately, none of this would have happened!"

"Sure," Budian said without the convincing note he should have injected. "But things are looking good here. Not a peep from inside the retreat, and no sign that the amulet field has so much as a glitch. Plus, I hear that Tucson's on the way, so I figured you'd want to focus on wrapping things up here."

"Tucson?" Lerche said the word with a sharp alarm he hadn't meant to display. Not to Budian—not to anyone. "The *drozhar* himself?"

"Grapevine," Budian said as if it was completely acceptable for the man to have received such news before Lerche. "But about Stephan. He's cuffed out by the trail, and Levv is dead. Scott took their car, and you can bet he's on his way to the retreat. Not only that, Scott and Dikau must have taken down the first team—they wore our jackets and had our packs. Hell, Dikau stabbed Stephan with one of our issued weapons."

"Ana *stabbed* him?" No. *No.* Ana was *his*. His to command, his to use, his to *own*. Pathetic little bitch, her Sentinel contamination too light to be of any experimental use and too heavy to make her of use within the posse.

Ian Scott couldn't have her. The Sentinels couldn't have her. She was Lerche's to spare or to use or to put out of her misery. *His* misery. His fist clenched within the sling, his other hand tightening around the cell phone.

"You want me to deal with Stephan and Levv?" Budian said, left too long in silence. "I mean, I can stay here, but I figure you want that scene sterilized before anyone from Tucson—"

"Go," Lerche said, hearing his own voice as if from a distance—a veil of disbelief, and a veil of growing fury. Ana had betrayed him. She'd thought she could break free from him, and she should have already paid the price for that. Instead she dared to work against him—wounding his man, siding with the Sentinel Am-

Tech. Who even knew how many secrets she would betray along the way?

Not that she'd ever known anything of import to begin with. But even one word was too much. Her very *presence* was too much, and would confirm things the Sentinels might only suspect.

"Go," he repeated, more harshly this time. "Take care of Stephan, and clean the area. I'll deal with Ian Scott."

And Ana Dikau will be mine again.

As if Ana intended to allow Ian to drive when he was bleeding again. Didn't matter the confusion that lay between them, or the confusion that lurked so deeply within her.

Love the man. Trust the man.

Fear the leopard.

Fear everything about a man who could *become* leopard.

Even then, she knew better. He didn't become. He *was*.

And the rest of her world was upside down around him.

Still, she knew how to drive. So she plucked the keys from his hand and did just that, taking Ian into the city where his friends were at such risk.

Ian jerked, wincing, one hand going to his temple. "Annorah!" It sounded like both imprecation and relief, and Ana slowed, looking for and not finding a place to pull over as they wound through the foothills community and toward busier streets. Ian glanced at her. "It's all right. It's just...okay, a little hard to explain. A voice in my head." He turned his gaze inward—and Ana was certain he spoke out loud for her benefit. "Turn it down a little, huh?"

A voice in his head. Something Sentinel. Someone who could help?

Ian snorted. "She says it's always hard to break through to me and it always takes this volume, wants to know what changed."

Me, Ana thought. *I did that for him. Somehow. Just by loving him.*

She did love him. She just couldn't pretend she didn't also fear him.

Ian said, "It's a long story, Annorah. And yes, I'm talking out loud, and I'm relaying. I'm with Ana Dikau. That's another long story."

A pause, and he shifted, closing a hand over his arm—not the injury itself, but below it, as if he could rub the pain away from there. "She says she tried to reach me last night and couldn't. No surprise there. Southwest Brevis felt the amulet bomb I set off. They're sending help." She wasn't surprised when his jaw tightened on the last, and then he forgot to relay at all. "Nick's coming? Warn him off, Annorah—warn him off *right now*. The retreat is under a working—I don't *know*—just warn him off!"

In the silence to follow, Ana asked, "Is she…gone?"

Ian waited while she navigated a four-way stop. Closing in on the retreat, where Ana wasn't at all sure she wanted to be.

She'd liked those people. And she would never make assumptions about Lerche again—how far he would go. How many lines he would cross.

She already knew.

Ian rubbed his arm, his face pinched. "Yes. She'll warn him." He glanced at her. "Nick is our brevis consul."

"The Southwest commander," Ana said. "Right. I've heard of him. Nick Carter. He's a wolf."

"He belongs to the woman you met. Jet." He took on a wry expression. "I use the word *belongs* with some purpose. Point is, he knows she's in that house."

"She's the wolf," Ana said. "If Lerche used a Sentinel-specific working, maybe she's all right." She found herself hoping so. Jet had been frightening...but compassionate, and her eyes held an honesty that Ana had trusted.

Ian cursed short and hard, and this time Ana did pull over, making use of a generous shoulder. "Is she back? Is there a problem?" She glanced in the rear and side-view mirrors, looking for any sign of the Core.

"I didn't tell her how to find the silents," he said, self-recrimination written so clearly on his face that she couldn't help but reach out to him, her hand over his and holding tight.

"Call her back?" she suggested with no idea how it actually worked.

"Can't," he said, hitting the word short and hard. "Some people can. I'm not one of them. *Damn!*" He hit the door armrest with explosive force, startling her—but he hadn't moved his hand out from beneath hers, and she ran a thumb over his knuckles, the only comfort she could offer. "God, if only I'd gotten my head out of my butt earlier and gone *active* on the silents..."

"Hey," she said, a single sharp word that got his attention. "It's only been what...a little over a year since that night?" The night they'd all learned about the silent amulets, when Fabron Gausto had launched an attack of such perfidy that even within the Core, it was spoken of in hushed tones.

At least, among those who had worked at Ana's

level—those who had worried about the ramifications, perfectly aware of how deeply vulnerable Gausto's attack had made the rest of them.

"Something like that," Ian said. "We lost so many... and then I got messed up when I went to help Maks." He stopped, as if realizing she'd known nothing of it. "We got distracted by Eduard's work...and then the situation in the Sacramentos."

"Wait," she said, still catching up. "I don't know about those things, but...*wait.* You were *hurt*? And then someone else from the Core went after you?"

He gave her a look of such patience that he caught her attention completely. "Ana," he said, "they've never *stopped.* Not since Gausto kicked things into gear. Meanwhile there's someone else joining the party—someone who figured out we both exist and wants us both dead. And we're too busy with stuff like this to figure *them* out."

It was her turn for patience—but she had none. "My point is, you were hurt! And busy! And now you're all pissed at yourself because in the middle of all that you didn't turn your thinking inside out when it comes to these silents?"

He opened his mouth. Closed it. Muttered, "Pinging the things seems obvious enough *now.*"

"It's only obvious after you think of it." She crossed her arms, bumping the steering wheel. "Not when you're building on an entire history of never having to do it before."

"But I should have—"

"Ah!" She made it a scolding sound, freeing one hand to hold up a finger of punctuation. "Stop it. Get your head out of your butt *now.*"

His eyes looked startled, bright blue and clear in the

morning sun. His mouth didn't quite close on his unspoken words.

"I get it," she said. "It would have been better if you'd been able to detect the silents earlier, and it would have made things easier right now if you'd had the chance to give that information to Annorah, but honestly—do you think anyone but you can do anything with that information in the next fifteen minutes? In the next day?"

He frowned, but instead of irritation she saw uncertainty. Possibly no one had ever called him on his overblown expectations of his own genius before. Probably they'd never *scolded* him for it.

Eventually he said, "No. Probably not." He caught her hand, reaching across his body to do it with the arm that wasn't injured. The other still bled—they'd made no effort to bind it—but she saw the flow of it had much reduced, and couldn't help but wince at the memory of his bitter words. *I'll heal, right?*

He'd been right to think she'd been so indoctrinated in what the Sentinels could do that she no longer considered the extent of his pain, or what it took out of him. Out of any of them.

Ian stroked her hand, turning it over to trace the lines of her palm. Still, she thought, taking something from that contact between them. He said, "The thing is, Ana, I'm going to save my friends now—or to damned well try. Whatever that means. Lerche could be there. The amulet field could be more than I can handle. I don't have my gear, I barely have my brains, and my people are probably dying."

He hesitated on the next words, but she knew. Her response came out as a cry of dismay. "You're not counting on getting through it!"

He said with grim but careful words, "I'm not making assumptions."

Because Lerche would kill him if he got the chance. Ana didn't doubt it—not any longer. Not in her heart or her mind.

And Ian was tired. She saw that clearly enough.

Still, she found herself unaccountably annoyed. *"Fine,"* she said, and reached past him to flip the glove box open. "Write a note and leave it in the car. Or put it in your pocket."

"You can tell them," Ian said.

She froze. "What?"

"You," he said distinctly. "Can tell them."

She sat back. "You're assuming that I won't run like a rabbit. I don't want anything to do with your Sentinels, Ian. I don't want anything to do with the Core." She realized the truth of the words even as she spoke them. "I want my freedom, and I want to find out who I really am, and what I really want."

He went as still as a hunting cat. "And if I'm around when this is over? What then?"

"I'm getting the impression that *'this'* is never over," she told him darkly. "But I'll tell you what. You stick around, and you'll have a chance to find out."

"Hard bargain." The corner of his mouth twitched.

"I learn fast." She put the car in gear, checking the rear and side view. "Faster than Lerche will give me credit for."

"Idiot," Ian said of Lerche, muttering it. He rotated the wrist of his injured arm, flexing the hand. Keeping it moving, such as he could. "Let's go for it, then."

She pulled away from the curb and they drove in silence—into the city, into the little greenway area and the surprisingly undeveloped land that ran alongside it.

Driving with swift assertion and no idea what they'd do when they got there.

"Pull over," he said, abruptly enough so they skidded slightly in the dirt and gravel road in front of the retreat. They came to a stop beside the low adobe wall where she'd first met him, when she'd still believed this to be both nothing but a routine surveillance assignment and her big chance to advance in the Core.

On the other side of the wall, a large man lay where he'd fallen, awkward and unmoving at the base of the porch stairs. Ana didn't recognize him—and from the faint frown on Ian's face, neither did he.

But it was evidence enough that Lerche hadn't been bluffing about amulet workings. Or that they were just as effective as he'd claimed—possibly against them all. Humans included.

"Is he breathing?" she asked, unable to see it from the driver's seat.

"Can't tell." Ian flipped the door handle and hesitated with one foot out the door. "You should probably wait here. But it's up to you."

She undid her seat belt, her hand already at the door. "Wait here because it's safer, or because there's not much way I can help even if I want to?"

"A little of both." He disembarked into the narrow space between the SUV and the wall, and stuck his head back inside. "A *lot* of both."

"Then I'll wait," she said. For now.

But it didn't last long.

Three of them came at Ian as he moved toward the gate—not men she recognized, and to judge by his wariness, not men he knew, either. He stopped short, putting his back to the wall, his wounded arm held close. Ana slipped out of the vehicle without thinking about it, but hung behind the open door.

They didn't seem like Core—they wore jeans and cargo pants, T-shirts and button-ups under light jackets. Nothing black. Nothing silver. And their complexions varied from pale to dark brown, their eyes likewise.

But their expressions, to a man, weren't the least bit friendly.

"Don't know who you are," Ian said, standing with deceptive quiescence, "but you'll want to back off now."

"Don't know who *you* are," said the largest of them, big and burly—the darkest of them, and there was nothing of quiescence about him. "But you stink. Your car stinks. And the woman stinks."

"Then put some distance between us," Ian said, and something sparked in his eyes. A man reaching his limit.

Ana saw it, and she had no doubt the three men saw it, as well—and in their way, heeded it. Standing out of reach and on the balls of their feet, never mind that they all three outweighed him, standing taller and broader. She searched them for what she saw so easily in Ian—the sense of coiled strength, the hint of *other* in his movement and carriage.

Maybe it was there. But she didn't see it. So maybe these were Sentinels and maybe not—because according to Ian, a third faction had developed, an interloper group trying to dispatch both Core and Sentinel. Fully human and unfettered by the need to hide their most basic natures.

What they could get away with, they no doubt would.

She slid back into the car and rummaged for the nearest pack—and then rummaged within it, her hand closing around the crosshatched surface of a cool metal grip. But after she withdrew the pistol, she rested it beside her, one foot on the ground and the other on the running board, propped against the seat and waiting.

If anyone noticed, they gave no sign of it.

Ian was done waiting. He turned back to the yard without completely turning from the men, holding his hands out just a little, one higher than the other but the blood no longer dripping at all. *Searching.* As if he'd extended all his senses, and not just the invisible awareness that Ana had never quite fathomed. The uniquely Sentinel perception of the world.

"Hey," said the palest man, apparently also no stranger. "*Hey.* He's gonna—"

They moved as one—but only a single step. Ana straightened, both feet on the ground…a perfect line between her position and the three men, right through the triangle of space separating the curve of the metal door and the car body, the gun at her side.

They still failed to notice her. They stopped because Ian turned back on them, teeth slightly bared. Not in a way that looked dramatic or faked, but an entirely natural, completely effective threat.

If they had guns, they didn't reach for them.

The Core would have guns out already. The Sentinels, she thought, would respond as Ian had—and would respond *to* him.

That meant these men were from the third party. The unknown, inviting themselves into this conflict.

"People are dying in there," Ian said, his eyes dilated to darkness and revealing the *wild.* "You must know that. *Your friend* is dying." Not quite complete thoughts, distracted by the amulets as he was. "I can help them."

"You've done enough." The big man stood with fists clenched, muscles bunching, his restraint writ large across his body. "If it weren't for your kind—"

"Really?" Ian snapped. "You want to go there? Because I know who you are. And if it wasn't for your interference in the Sacramentos, this might not have happened at all!"

Yes. The third party. Ian believed it, too.

The big man laughed. "Nice," he said. "We wouldn't even exist if it wasn't for you and your counterparts."

"That's what our *counterparts* said two thousand years ago, and look where it's taken them."

Ana pressed a hand over her mouth at the truth of his remark. It smelled of gun oil and powder, sharp scents that only reminded her how the weapon had already been used this day.

By her own people.

The ones who'd begun just as Ian said, but who now seemed able to justify far more than monitoring the Sentinels and stopping their bad behavior. Who now simply persecuted them.

As these men would inflict themselves on her. On Ian, as he strove to save lives.

Ian bit off a curse. "I don't have time for this. Either come and get me or leave me alone." He turned back to the yard. Searching, as she'd known he would, for the working that threatened his friends. Or that had already killed them all.

Of course, the interlopers didn't leave him alone.

But they didn't attack all at once, either, and even Ana knew that to be a mistake. The middle man, the one with Middle East coloring and second largest in size, broke first.

She jerked the gun up, realizing then how little use it was. She could never bring herself to shoot a man in cold blood, and she wasn't good enough to hit them without hitting Ian. Not cold enough to do it, even knowing Ian would most likely survive.

He'd been hurt enough at the hands of her own.

But Ian didn't need her help. He was ready—he was waiting. And injured or not, he was so fast that Ana barely followed what happened as he moved—ducking under the man's attack, rolling in behind to box his ears, kicking his knee away and landing on his chest, just barely pulling a mortal blow to the neck.

As leopard, that blow had torn out the side of a man's throat. As human, even pulled, it left the man gasping for air, a bruise rising around critical blood flow.

Ian crouched beside the man, ruffled but with a stillness that Ana had come to understand presaged a preternatural alertness. *Ready to move.*

"Ana," he said, not looking at her, "tuck the gun away and see if there are extra cuffs in that car. And an ice pack in the first aid kit. These men will wait quietly for the moment, if they want their friend seen to."

Ana straightened, startled; the men seemed to see her only for the first time.

Ian had known about the gun all along, for all that he hadn't even seemed to notice. And he'd made sure the men knew about the gun, too, now that he'd asked her to come out in the open.

She tucked the weapon into her back waistband and did as he asked, quickly scaring up a set of restraint cables and the vehicle's first aid kit. She gave the two men a wary glance on the way by, going all the way around the SUV so she could approach Ian from along the wall.

"Ice his neck," Ian said, moving away once she got there, taking the restraints with him. "And sit on him."

Ana did just that, taking Ian literally as she was meant to. He whipped the restraints into place, threading them through the man's belt to keep his hands pinned there, and stood aside, looking at the men from beneath his lowered brow—a gaze that only underscored what Ian was. What he could do.

What he *would* do.

He shifted his shoulder, the single evidence of discomfort from his arm, and spoke to them in inexorable tones. "Now leave me alone, so I can try to save some lives. Or else come at me now and get it over with. Because if I have to come at you, I'm going to do it as fast as I can, and at least one of you is never getting up again."

Ana believed him. She thought the men believed him, too. They exchanged a look, took a step back…

A single step.

Early morning along a scarce-used road, and they stood in a standoff. One man dying in the yard, the Sentinels within and Ian at the end of his patience. No longer willing to coddle them along, or spare them from what he intended.

Ana drew a sharp breath as his gaze went inward, recognizing the nascent flicker of energy and light that came with that focus. She glanced along the road in alarm, but quickly realized that of course Ian had already checked and knew the area was clear.

For the moment.

By then the energy had blossomed into full light, crackling strobes that lashed and tangled, snapping out to touch Ana. She flinched and cried out—but only for that first instant.

For that touch had been soft. It had been a mere whisper of light and presence, and it left her arm tingling with an unexpected pleasure as Ian emerged.

Leopard.

The men bit off curses and stepped back—not so much flight as strategic retreat, repositioning to support each other and reaching for the weapons they'd not yet employed.

Ana lifted her gun, sure enough of her aim at this range so she didn't need to fake her confidence. "You'll want to drop those," she said, and of all the choices she'd made recently, of all the confusion she'd faced with them, this one left her no qualms. Protecting Ian from those who would do him harm simply because they felt entitled to interfere.

Not so different from the way Lerche had behaved. Or from the other things the Core at large had done, things they never revealed to those such as Ana.

The men hesitated on dropping their guns, of course. Enough so that Ian lowered his head, crouching slightly.

One leap and he'd be on them.

"Over here, by the wall," Ana told them. "And then you sit down." When they still hesitated, she felt her patience snap. "Quit being such babies. You came, you stuck your noses in and it isn't working out. Deal with it! We don't care if you walk away in the end—we only want to be left alone."

Not so different from the sentiments Ian had expressed about the Core.

A car turned onto the lane, moving without haste, its tires crunching slowly over the scattered gravel.

"Ian," Ana said. But of course he'd noticed it. A swift blur of movement and he crouched low to the ground near the gate, his tail still, his body flattened behind the clump of towering hollyhocks.

The men moved, too, angling themselves off the bumper of the SUV and using their considerable size to block any casual view of Ana and the man she sat on. *Of course*, she realized. They didn't want outside interference any more than the Core or Sentinels did. They wanted to enact their vigilante excesses without the inconvenience of legal oversight.

The car curved slowly out of sight, obscured by the high wall of the adjoining property.

The men darted forward at Ana, moving before Ian did.

Or thinking they had.

He was a streak of pale beauty and flowing tail, knocking Ana aside and bounding to intervene. His paws flashed and Ana cried out, having seen more violence in this single day than she'd seen in her entire life. One man went down beneath the thrusting impact of his attack, grunting hard and fighting back—as if there was anything to fight. Ian had already doubled back on himself to leap at the man who hesitated on the trigger of his gun, unable to fire without hitting his buddy.

Down they went, and this time the victim fought back, slamming his gun against the side of Ian's head. *Hurting him.*

"Stop it!" Ana screamed, not knowing if she spoke to Ian or to the men he'd attacked. *"Stop it!"*

She hadn't meant for the gun to go off. She screamed when it did—startled at the sound and the recoil, horrified that she could have pulled the trigger without meaning to…relieved as dirt chipped up in response. *Only the road…*

The men froze. Ian froze, too—but just for the merest instant before he bounded away, suddenly back beside the wall with his whiskers lifted in a silent snarl and no weakness to be seen.

Ana leaped up to stomp on the fallen gunman's hand with both feet, stumbling back when he shouted in pain and then dashing forward just long enough to wrench the weapon away from fingers that no longer quite held it.

The man was too busy realizing himself still alive to fight over the piece. And Ana was too staggered to search for the other gun. For Ian had pounced, and he'd taken them down, but he'd left no blood in his wake. She could still feel the terror where his fur had brushed her on the way past, but…

No blood. No *claws*.

More civilized than they were. Than *all* of them. Maybe even more civilized than Ana herself—having the power, wielding it and walking away.

Ana had pulled the trigger.

A strained new voice broke their silence. "Ian!"

For all the effort behind that voice, it barely carried out of the yard—but it still got everyone's instant attention.

Shea sat on his knees in the doorway of the retreat, slumped against the door frame, scowling hard. "For fuck's sake," he said. "Get away from the fucking yard. There's a silent—"

Ana ran up to the wall—but didn't touch it. Didn't get nearly close enough for that. "Are you all right? What about the others?"

Shea laughed, a harsh sound. "Fuck, no, we're not all right. Never saw it coming. Lyn's down hard… Jet, I dunno… Ruger's trying. Got shields up then, but… too late. Can't hold them much longer. No idea about this poor fuck." He gestured at the prone figure in the yard. Then he tipped his head and looked directly at Ana across the distance, his gaze a shock of accusation. "Did you do this?"

Ana recoiled. "No!"

Shea slumped a little farther, straightening with obvious effort. "Just stay away," he said, sounding weary. "We never saw it coming. Fucking silents...can't be found. Maybe Lyn, but she's..." He glanced over his shoulder and didn't finish the thought. Didn't have to.

Not nearly far enough away, the snow leopard growled.

No, not growled. Just a sound in his throat. Inquiring.

Ana stood suddenly straighter. "We can find them!" she said. "Ian can do it! He's got them figured out!"

Shea lifted the head that had started to droop. "Has he, now? Irony, that. Because all his isolation gear is in the house, isn't it?"

Ana had no idea what that meant, in particular. But she knew that Ian had had hope and intent, and she clung to that. "We'll find them," she told Shea. "You just hang on. All of you!"

Shea didn't respond, slumped where he was, and Ana realized he'd passed out. She bit her lip, looking back over her shoulder to the two men just now climbing to their feet. They looked stunned, their faces red from the blows they'd taken, a few scratches trickling blood.

She readjusted her grip on the gun she'd never dropped. "Just leave us alone," she said. "We're trying to save them. To save your friend, too, if we can."

The one man cradled his hand. The other had relocated the loose gun, but held it low...and then he raised both hands slightly in capitulation. He slowly returned the gun to the flat holster inside his waistband, nodding at her clenched grip on her own weapon. "Nothing as dangerous as a gun in the hands of someone with a trigger finger like yours."

That, she thought, was likely true.

"But watch yourself," the other man said. "Because we're sure as hell going to be keeping track."

But Ian had already moved on, pacing to the corner of the yard with a stalking grace even as the wounded leg gave way slightly beneath him. He crouched to let another car pass by and lingered there, his ears canted back in focus.

After a moment he just barely turned the corner, hesitating there, and then returned to his original spot, reaching a large paw to the adobe wall and extruding claws to leave the most deliberate of marks.

Triangulation. Just as he would have done with the amulet in her shoulder, if they hadn't found it through dead reckoning.

Then he paced on down the wall, paralleling the extended driveway. It split to enter the retreat property while the other branch continued to the undeveloped property beyond; he stayed with the retreat fence line, finishing the section of latilla fencing and moving onward to the idiosyncratic corner of tall adobe. Ana followed at a distance, pausing when he did and moving on as he did, and altogether too painfully aware that the interlopers trailed her once they'd dragged their stunned friend behind the SUV where he wouldn't draw attention. Their low conversation revealed that the man was coming back to himself—that they felt he would be back in the game soon enough.

Also not reassuring.

But then, here she was following in the wake of a man no longer human, a beast the likes of which she'd always been warned against. She'd defied her direct superior, she'd contributed to the death of her fellow Core members, and Nick Carter was on his way. So she was about to find herself a captive of either the Southwest Brevis Consul himself, or the unknown organization that wanted to do away with them all. Unless she escaped, in which case the Core would no doubt hunt her down.

Reassuring wasn't even an option.

Chapter 17

Ian padded unevenly along the fence line. He had the taste of this particular working, now—knew it to be destructive and indiscriminate, a powerful thing that would simply suck the life out of anything within its bounds. He narrowed his focus, searching swiftly—sending energy out, waiting for the response, moving onward to triangulate.

He'd found two amulets so far, both at the eastern corners of the enclosed property. He very much expected to find two more at the western corners, once he'd circumvented the adjoining property along that side. And though his heart beat hard and fast with fear for the Sentinels trapped inside, he felt the thrill of the moment, too. At the potential unfolding before him.

Because anyone skilled at sending and receiving subtle energies could be trained to perform this kind of search. It wouldn't take Ian's skill; it wouldn't take Lyn's talent. It wouldn't even take an AmTech team.

Got you, he thought at the Core. *Got you good and hard.* The silent amulet code was broken; the amulets themselves would no longer be the ever-looming threat they'd become.

It was a short-lived thrill. Finding today's amulets didn't come close to disabling them. The greater work was yet to be done.

And it was a thrill diminished by Ana's expression as he'd charged past to defend her on the road—her unthinking terror at the brush of his fur.

Not to mention a thrill diminished by the presence of the two men still following behind along with Ana, making no attempt to interfere. *Yet.* Ian wasn't sure if they'd been convinced, scared or simply bided their time.

He skirted the back of the enclosed area, moving swiftly now in spite of his limp—the third amulet already targeted and pinging back its sly stench at his ongoing outreach. To the south, behind the house, lay a patch of undeveloped land, grown up in junipers and tall high prairie grasses—here, the two men waited, keeping their distance and still keeping their eyes on Ian. One of them snapped a phone closed and slipped it away; Ian could only hope that if it was a call for reinforcements, they'd be some time in getting here.

Two outbuildings snugged up against the high section of adobe wall at the corner, and then the wall fell away to nothing more than a token rail fence. At the juncture of the adobe and rail, dark metal gleamed.

The third corner. Ian knew where he'd find the final amulet—off in the clumpy weeds in the other back corner of the property, just inside this same rail fence.

It told him everything he needed to know.

He might not be able to disengage the working, and

he might not have his isolation equipment, but with a boundary-enclosed working like this one, the fastest solution was simply to bring all the amulets together and let them run down together.

Simple. He growled softly to himself. Not so simple at all, when there was no safe way to touch the things or to move them. Without nullifying tools, the amulet would conduct through any buffer—metal faster than wood, wood faster than rubber.

He crouched outside the fence, tail flicking. A shovel from the shed might do it, if he moved quickly. Start at the far corner, scoop up the diminutive amulet, run counterclockwise from around the corners and dump all the amulets with the one in the front west corner, leaving them until they could be dealt with. They might even run out quickly. The Core couldn't afford to leave an undiscriminating working of this magnitude lying around.

Ana moved up beside him, looking over the fence with him—surprising him with her nearness. Ian slid a paw under the lowest rail, pointing it at the amulet. It took all his control to resist cat impulse—the slap of a stunning paw, the flick of small prey into the weeds—

A car on gravel. Someone comes. His tidy ears snapped forward—and then flat. A car on the lane was nothing; a car coming up the long drive was very much something. *Nick, I told you to hang back.*

But it wasn't Nick.

It was a gleaming high-end SUV, a thing with more luxury than utility. And black, here where the strong sun made such things a constant folly. Not a Sentinel vehicle at all.

Ana made an uneasy sound. "Ian…"

The SUV came on with an inconsiderate speed, spitting gravel against the latilla fence and slewing slightly around the bend. Even through the darkened windows, Ian recognized the occupants—Budian behind the wheel and Lerche in the passenger seat.

No time to become the human and grab a shovel; no time to gather amulets. Ian faced the vehicle with his ears slanted back and his tail flicking into cold anger, crouching just enough to make his intentions plain—he could and would take them down at the first sign of threat.

No matter that the Core would simply use such an incident to decry his lack of humanity.

Lerche disembarked with stiff discomfort, his arm in a snug sling. He had no amulets, silent or otherwise. A quick check revealed that he—and Budian and the car—were entirely clean.

Lerche had learned that much, it seemed.

It meant only they'd have other weapons to hand. Budian hadn't yet done more than open his door, and it was to him that Ian looked for trouble.

Lerche held out his good hand to Ana. "Come, my dear. Time for you to return home."

Ana didn't move. "You didn't come here for me. I don't matter that much."

"It's true, I'm also here to clean up this mess before the *drozhar* arrives." Lerche let his hand drop. "But you're also wrong again, I'm afraid. It matters very much to me what happens to you. And how."

Ana's voice came stronger. "Only because if someone's going to hurt me—to *kill* me—you think it should be you."

Lerche smiled. The smug cruelty behind it made Ian want to slap the expression right off his face, claws extended and sharp. He quivered with the effort of holding his place, whiskers bristling and a growl growing in his throat.

Lerche said, "You are exactly correct, my dear—you personally matter to me not at all. But no one else has the right to touch what's mine. You should have considered that before you allowed yourself to care for this Sentinel. You sealed his fate with your actions."

Ana made a noise that might have been taken from Ian's leopard. "I don't *care* for him," she said, moving closer than Ian had ever expected of her.

Not while he was leopard. *Beast.*

Ana rested a startling hand behind one leopard ear, her fingers sinking into deep, plush fur. "I don't care for him," she repeated. "I *love* him."

The peace of her touch flowed through him, open in a way he hadn't yet felt. More than just calming, but full of *Ana.* Full of everything that Ian needed in that moment.

He moved, putting himself between Lerche and Ana—perfectly aware of her trembling, and even more aware of the fact that she leaned into him instead of away from him.

Lerche's face darkened. "Maybe you think you do," he said. With his restless motion came the scent of gun oil. "Had we more time, I would show you the error of those ways. But the *drozhar* is coming, and I expect the Tucson Sentinels are, too."

Budian said something from inside the car, too muffled for even Ian's keen ears to catch. Lerche looked sharply over his shoulder. "Ah," he said. "Already here, I see. Well, we should get on with it, then. Before the beasts work up their nerve."

"They're not Sentinel." Ana's voice had an angry edge pushing behind its tremulous note. "Did you and the others think you could keep pushing and attacking and hurting people without drawing attention? Because if you did, you were wrong. You were wrong about everything, and you were really, *really* wrong about me! I'm not yours, I'm *mine.* And if I want to give everything of myself to Ian, I'll do it."

"By all means," Lerche said, straightening the edge of his sling, hand lingering there—and then reaching within. "Just as I do what you've forced me to do."

Such a perfect place to secure a gun, that sling.

Ian gave Lerche only enough time to dip his hand into the sling before he leaped—a single reaching bound, a hard impact—

Ian jerked as the gun discharged inside the sling. Ian sprang away, crouching with lashing tail and flattened ears, while Budian scuffled with someone on the other side of the vehicle.

Lerche looked down at himself, the gun in his hand now. The sling obscured his torso, but the tang of blood in the air and the stunned look on Lerche's face said enough. He'd been hit, and hit badly. And he knew it.

When he raised his eyes, he pinned his gaze on Ana. "That's a shame," he said, his voice strained. "But you're still mine."

Ana stood straight and tall—not very tall at that, and not very large, but with a fresh certainty in her voice. "No," she said. "I'm not."

A new car turned into the driveway, large tires on the gravel—and another, not making quite as much noise. Budian, now caught up between the two lingering interlopers, nonetheless had line of sight along the curve of the drive. "The *drozhar,*" he said, his voice pitched low to carry. "And more of *their* people."

Nick, dammit! I told you to stay away—

Not that he'd truly expected it to happen.

But he hadn't expected the mad look that crossed Lerche's face, the sudden hard gleam in his eye as a surge of blood soaked through his suit.

He hadn't expected the man to charge forward—at *Ana.*

Ian leaped for him, too late—catching the back of his shoe, tearing out the back leg of Lerche's trousers. And Lerche bowled into Ana, knocking her against the rail fence, flipping her over it to land hard on the dried grass of packed ground.

Inside the amulet perimeter.

"No one moves!" bellowed one of the interlopers, a man who no doubt now had Budian's gun. Nick's voice responded with calm authority, words unintelligible past the roar in Ian's head, the sudden chaos of fear and understanding and complete and utter absence of *Ana* in his senses. His awareness narrowed down to that one single view—her attempts to scramble out from beneath Lerche, her cry of fear as Lerche's body weighed her down and the amulet working sank into her, weakening her just that fast.

"Ian!" she cried, hardly more than a hoarse, whispering shout, "I can't—"

The amulet. It gleamed newly exposed beneath the tangle of the fence.

No shovel, no tech gear, no options.

Ian pounced, scooping the thing up with a flick of his paw—feeling the instant drain of direct contact, his paw burning with a cold fire that ran along all the small bones to his wrist, hooks already setting into his forearm. The amulet settled between his toe pads and his heel pad and he closed his paw around it, tail lashing terribly as his whiskers drew back in a silent, terrible snarl.

He meant to carry it to the other corner and instantly knew he couldn't. He flipped his paw, clumsy now, and the amulet tumbled through sunlight toward the other back corner—redrawing the boundary and freeing Ana as it disappeared into the dry grass.

Not too late. Please, not too late!

But the house still lay within the field, there where Shea had worked so hard to shield his friends and Ruger had done his best to fortify them. *Not too late! Please, not too late!*

Ian pounced on the amulet, defying the heaviness of his legs and giving the thing an expert flick into the far corner—redrawing the amulet boundary once more, this time to cut diagonally through the house. *No way to tell where they are in that house...*

He fell to a brief crouch, panting heavily and drawing on every bit of what he was. Drawing on what Ana had taught him about quieting his thoughts to send out the finest, purest pulse of energy.

It bounced back at him from right beside the first one—and once he'd found that again, he quickly saw its gleam, an uneven chunk of slightly darker metal.

Leaden legs took him there, his pounce still quicksilver fast but taking the last of such speed from him. He scooped up both amulets in one swipe—tumbling back into the human as he rolled into the rough adobe of the far wall. Only then did he hear Nick's astonished commands to *stop the hell what you're doing!* and Ana's weaker cry of dismay— "*Ian, no!* Ian!"

And yet behind those protests lay the anguish of what Ian already knew.

Without this, his friends would die.

If they hadn't already.

He staggered upright and along the wall, his gaze

focused on the spot where the interior courtyard met the wall—as far as he could go, and far enough so the amulet field would cut only across the very front corner of the house. The man in the front yard might yet lay within that brutally damaging field, but Shea would be free of it.

The ground met Ian's face with bruising force; he couldn't remember falling. Back to his feet, his vision tunneled to include only the courtyard's wrought-iron fence…falling…back to his feet again with one unfeeling foot clomping down in front of the other, his arm turned to stone and a shaft of volcanic cold making its way down the long bones of his arm to his shoulder.

"Ian." Nick's voice came just behind him—full of understanding and full of inexorable command. "It's far enough. *Enough*, Ian."

Another step and he'd fall against the wrought-iron bars, wavering so uncertainly before him. Ian held out his hand and stared stupidly at it, willing it to open.

Dead dull flesh, nothing of his own.

Nick moved in beside him, reaching for the hand—Ian turned on him, snarling him off. Impotent threat if Nick chose to ignore it.

"Ian!" Nick snapped. "You know better. *I can stop it!*"

Because Nick could. Nick, among them all, had the knack of focusing down on an amulet to burn it out in a flash. But it was a knack the Core knew nothing of and could never know of.

Supposing the working didn't leave Nick instantly incapable of any such thing.

Ian had no words. He had only the snarl, the lift of his free hand in warning, fingers lifted to reflect the dagger-tipped spread of the paw beneath.

"Then *get rid of it*!" Alpha fury underlined the snarl in Nick's own voice.

Volcanic cold, creeping through his shoulder, along his collarbone and tracing his ribs, reaching for his spine...

Ian turned his threatening fingers on his own hand, prying at deadened, clutching flesh. Something snapped and he didn't feel it, though Nick made a grinding sound of horrified dismay. Another snap and Ian clumsily turned his hand, the first spark of pain radiating down his spine as he shook his wrist to dislodge the amulets from his grasp.

A single dull pebble hit the ground, bouncing into the mowed scruff.

Ana's voice cut through the roar of amulet-dulled senses—weak but coming closer, full of horror. *"Ian!"*

"No!" Nick grunted with impact, and then snapped a curse over the ensuing sounds of struggle. "Dammit, don't—!"

But Ana's hand landed on his back—ever so briefly, a stunning infusion of light and emotion and love before Nick wrenched her away.

Ian sucked in a mighty breath and somehow managed to drop the last amulet from the crease of his palm. But a final lingering shard of fire lanced along his spine, arching him back and twisting him from agony down into darkness, leaving him only the final echo of Ana's scream.

Ana blinked her eyes open to bright New Mexico sky. The sun tingled against her face and stubby dead grass poking through the back of her shirt, and she rolled over just enough to push up on one arm.

"Ana, I presume." The man crouching before gestured impatiently to those outside her view, commanding them to come on.

He wore such an intensity about himself, such obvious *other*, that Ana gasped and flinched away from him—from his pale green eyes and black hair rimmed with hoarfrosted silver and from the very palpable effort to restrain all of it to human expectations.

He didn't seem to notice her recoil. "You fainted. Be still. There's a lot going on, and if I have to manage *you*, someone else is likely to die. Maybe even Ian."

Ana could only gape at him—and realize instantly that his hard, no-nonsense words were ones she could trust. *Nick Carter. Brevis consul.*

And no wonder.

"Mariska, the house!" Nick said, a command snapped across the yard to those who had come with him. "Report! Maks, get this place shielded—and no more of our visitors leave!"

Meaning someone had already gone. Ana lifted her head to discern who remained, but there were too many figures in motion, and she wasn't nearly steady enough to sort it all out.

She looked for Ian instead.

Nick's attention snapped back to her. "I told you—"

"I'm not going anywhere!" But she was tired of taking orders from those who hadn't earned the right to give them, and she was tired of being afraid. And Ian…

Sprawled beside her, his body limp but still reflecting that final wrenching cry before he'd collapsed. It hurt so much to look at his mangled hand, a thing of gray flesh and unnatural angles. Ana slung a defiant look in Nick Carter's direction and crawled the few feet to reach Ian, her own limbs dull and heavy in the wake of even brief exposure to the amulets.

Ian had *held* them. *Carried* them.

She rested a hand on his shoulder, finding it cold. Rested her forehead beside his hand, trembling there. Reaching out to him in the way she'd learned and finding no sense of a presence in return, no impression that he heard her. "Ian," she said, shaking him ever so slightly, and then more insistently. "Come out of there and follow me!"

A woman's voice called from the house. "Alive! Nick, they're alive—all of them! But they're weak as hell—Joe, get your ass in here!"

Nick jabbed a short gesture at the house. "Do it," he said, voice raised for the distance. "Stabilize them and get back out here."

"Healer?" Ana said, watching in dismay as a big man in a flannel shirt and jeans broke away from the cars and ran to the house, hopping over the fence to reach the gate the woman Mariska had unlocked. "But Ian—"

"Not our healer," Nick said shortly. "Someone who can give them back some of the energies they lost." He lifted his chin to indicate the approach of someone from behind, and Ana twisted to find a slender woman with large eyes and an uncertain demeanor, a gear bag slung over one shoulder. "Katie, see what you can do for Ian until Joe gets back out here."

As Katie went to work, Mariska jogged up to them—short and sturdy and athletic, her deep complexion full of brown tones and her eyes rimmed with darker coloration, her hair darkest black and pulled back into a short French braid. "Jet's as good as any of them," she said, her mouth thin with strain. As she looked back to the house, her silhouette showed the slight rounding of early pregnancy. "Ruger is pretty rugged, and so is Shea. They tried so hard to protect everyone. Fernie… I really don't know. She and the others had been through a lot before the Core set off this particular bomb."

"Fernie!" Ana said in dismay.

Mariska looked at her with a ferocity that sent Ana flinching away. Another field Sentinel, this one, and furious to boot. "Yes," the woman snapped. "*Imagine.* We're people, just like you. Ruger is mine, and if anything happens to him, I will never stop coming for you. *Never.*"

"Mariska," Nick said, but his tight voice spoke volumes, and he caught Ana's gaze with those pale green eyes. "We'll figure out Ana's story before we condemn her."

"And if Jet—"

"She won't!" Nick snapped. "Lyn is in there, too—Joe will find a way to give back what they've lost until Katie can figure out—"

But Katie interrupted him in turn, her voice grimmest grim. "I'm nowhere near Ruger's league with this stuff," she said. "I don't know if I can reverse whatever this working did. I don't even know *what* it did."

Words fell from Ana's mouth. "Then let me help."

Nick regarded her with narrowed eyes. "How?"

Ana lifted her gaze to the clump of figures milling by the cars. If Budian had been correct, one of those men was the region's most recent *drozhar*. Budian would know what the working was…and the *drozhar* could command him to talk.

"I know how they think," she said. "I know how to talk to them. I can learn what we need. Just don't—" she faltered, looking down on Ian; it seemed to her that even in these last moments, his color had worsened, her sense of him diminishing. "Please. Don't let him die."

Katie had unzipped the gear bag, digging efficiently

into pockets to pull out vials and shake them vigorously; already she unscrewed the top of one to withdraw its full eyedropper. "It's not my intent," she said. "But I need a clue, and I need it fast."

"Mariska," Nick said. "Go with her. Don't let them intimidate her." As if he somehow already understood that they would.

Mariska bared her teeth. "No fears."

But the Ana who could be manipulated by the need to belong to these people no longer existed. She'd already lost everything she'd hoped to have with them… and she'd already gained so, so much more in return. She would get the information they needed, and she'd get it fast.

She gave Ian's shoulder a final squeeze and climbed unsteadily to her feet, grateful for Mariska's helping hand. "Oh," she said, remembering her promise. "Ian… he told me to make sure you knew. He figured out how to find the silents. I know how he does it. If it comes to that… I can explain."

Nick stood to look down on her. "If they find out you just told me that—"

"Oh, yes," Ana said. "They'll kill me. But then… what's new? I'll get what we need to know—I can do it." The *drozhar* would have to learn about Lerche—his activities, how he'd compromised them, how the Core could position themselves to blame the man and minimize his damage. Budian could tell him nothing without damning himself—but Ana could. She had exactly what she needed to get what the Sentinels required. "And then you help Ian. Help the others."

"You get it, and I will," Katie promised fiercely—but she, too, glanced over her shoulder at the detained *drozhar* and his evident temper.

"They can't hurt me anymore," Ana said—and then laughed a little with the true understanding of it—of her freedom to hand. "And they can't have me anymore. Besides, I choose my own people." She looked down at Ian, crouching to cup his face one last time before facing all her fears at once. *Defeating them.* Ian Scott, dark lashes shadowing his cheek, silvered hair in charming disarray, lean strength captured by injury but the *other*…

The *other* still lingered there, making him everything that he was. *Snow leopard. Human. Lover.*

Hers.

Epilogue

Ian beat a quick drum tattoo against the standing height worktable in his home lab—one of a series of such tables, with a single token chair tucked away beneath stacked gear. Steinman rolled out over the speakers, all drama and operatic rock, as Ian bounced between scowling at an amulet case design and his ongoing text chat, where two of his AmTechs struggled with a streamlined approach to teach the new silents detection method across the whole of Southwest Brevis.

Or at least, to those who had even the faintest ability to manage it.

Start with bouncing off something loud, he typed.

Although in actuality, the message read Strt w smthng looud, because even fingers raised on a keyboard couldn't type well when encased with plaster. Or whatever they'd used in this particular cast.

It turned out that bones broken in the thrall of that

particular deadly working didn't heal any faster than anyone else's. Slower, in fact.

But he was alive.

Ana was alive.

Fernie was alive, and Ian's friends were alive, if all just now recovered these weeks later. Katie had been filling in for Ruger until recently, augmented by Joe Ryan. The man's deft skill with undefined earth energies allowed him to replace—slowly, carefully—what the working had stolen.

Joe had had plenty of incentive. Along with Ruger, Joe's partner Lyn had been nearly consumed by the working.

But now Lyn was back at work, Ruger was splitting his hours between brevis and preparing for fatherhood, Shea was out shielding the unwary, and Jet was off visiting her former pack. Only the very human interloper who'd stumbled into the working was just as dead as everyone had thought him to be.

His three partners had left quite smartly during the immediate aftermath of the convergence of the three factions. It had been Nick's decision, Ian gathered, to let them go. There'd been enough to deal with already, between the injured, their shortage of manpower...and the Core's regional prince, the *drozhar*, to manage.

The text pinged back at him. Start with something loud, what?

Gahhh. Ian typed, intro thm to prss dammt procss w big honkn loud aml dammt am.;/ fck!

Let them chew on that for a while. He was done typing. Such as it had been. He returned his attention to the work case design, and most importantly, to the swatches of buffering material on one workbench. Experiments to do, oh, yes. He turned up the music.

A draft of moving air signaled invasion of his AmTech turf.

Ana. She stood in the door, still dressed for what passed as winter in Tucson, her arms crossed and a wincing amusement on her face.

Ian scooped up the sound system remote and hit the mute button. "Hey," he said. "Soundproofing!"

"The house still vibrates after a certain point," she said drily, tugging off her gloves and unzipping her jacket.

Hmm. Maybe so.

"Anyway, I wanted you to know I was home." She only entered the workroom by a few feet, always respectful of this space.

Not that she didn't have good reason. The activity here was, on some days, the equivalent of defusing bombs in the basement.

The text screen bleated a plaintive request for clarity. Ian dropped out of the chat with a click of the mouse and put his back to the worktable, propping his casted hand on the forearm of the other. It was as close as he could get to crossing his own arms. "How'd it go?"

She waved a dismissive hand. "The Core is…the Core. They're trying to pretend they're not appalled that Southwest's new liaison is a woman."

"One with tainted blood at that," Ian said, his expression a dramatic nonverbal of *Oh! The horror!* "So basically, still stalling."

"It's okay," Ana said. "They're also still talking."

"Nick knew what he had with you," Ian told her. "He's like that."

A new liaison. A new *perspective.*

That perspective was the reason Nick hadn't hesitated to move Ian to this home workspace once Ana had walked into his brevis lab and said, "No wonder!" And she'd turned on Nick and said, "How can you expect him to think in this space? It's full of everything and everyone! He's already got enough going on in that head of his."

Nick had sent a stunned look to Ian—still in a wheelchair at that point, still under close care at brevis where doctors combined conventional skills with Sentinel needs and healing—and Ian had only shrugged. He'd learned to trust Ana's eyes. Especially when it came to the things to which he'd long inured himself. He was a snow leopard with an overactive mind and never enough quiet, and it hadn't truly occurred to him that things could work any other way.

"You people have time to secure and equip that gaping workroom in his basement before he gets out of your private little hospital," she'd said, hands on hips. "Why don't you?"

So they had, and she'd moved in to make sure it was done right—and Ian's echoing bachelor pad slowly showed increasing signs of actual inhabitation. A few more pieces of furniture, a small collection of cooking utensils, actual throw pillows on the couch…

She'd made herself at home. She'd made it into *their* home, and more so every day. Not with any great declaration, because they'd already done that, each in their own way. But because she belonged there.

"That's an interesting smile," she told him. Daylight LED lighting revealed every bit of her in blossoming health—a little more curve to her hips, less strain in her face. And no bruises at all.

"Just thinking," he said, though he knew he wouldn't get away without explaining, and there—she'd already cocked a brow at him. "About changes."

He hadn't meant for that alarm to cross her face. "You're feeling okay?"

"Fine," he said. "Totally fine." And then, because they both knew better, he added, "Okay, still taking naps. But it's getting better. And there's nothing wrong with a good nap."

"Why, no," she said, straightening. She slipped off the jacket, tucking it over her arm, and went straight for her top blouse button. Ian found himself coming to all kinds of attention.

One button. Two. "Nothing wrong with a good nap at all," Ana said, glancing at him with an innocence that Ian didn't trust. Not for one moment. "In fact, I think I might just take one."

"Ana," he said, giving it a bit of the leopard.

Ana looked at him over her shoulder as she turned away, heading for the stairs that bypassed the main house and led directly to the second-story bedroom. "I thought you might want to follow along, see where it goes."

Ian turned off the collection of monitors with a flip of a switch and the light banks with the flip of another, putting him not very far behind Ana as she ascended the stairs. "Ohhh, yes," he murmured. "Entirely my choice."

And Ana laughed softly, and led him into the rest of their lives.

* * * * *

REQUEST YOUR FREE BOOKS!
2 FREE NOVELS PLUS 2 FREE GIFTS!

HARLEQUIN®

INTRIGUE

BREATHTAKING ROMANTIC SUSPENSE

YES! Please send me 2 FREE Harlequin® Intrigue novels and my 2 FREE gifts (gifts are worth about $10). After receiving them, if I don't wish to receive any more books, I can return the shipping statement marked "cancel." If I don't cancel, I will receive 6 brand-new novels every month and be billed just $4.74 per book in the U.S. or $5.49 per book in Canada. That's a savings of at least 12% off the cover price! It's quite a bargain! Shipping and handling is just 50¢ per book in the U.S. and 75¢ per book in Canada.* I understand that accepting the 2 free books and gifts places me under no obligation to buy anything. I can always return a shipment and cancel at any time. Even if I never buy another book, the two free books and gifts are mine to keep forever. 182/382 HDN GH3D

Name (PLEASE PRINT)

Address Apt. #

City State/Prov. Zip/Postal Code

Signature (if under 18, a parent or guardian must sign)

Mail to the **Reader Service:**

IN U.S.A.: P.O. Box 1867, Buffalo, NY 14240-1867

IN CANADA: P.O. Box 609, Fort Erie, Ontario L2A 5X3

Are you a subscriber to Harlequin® Intrigue books and want to receive the larger-print edition?

Call 1-800-873-8635 or visit www.ReaderService.com.

* Terms and prices subject to change without notice. Prices do not include applicable taxes. Sales tax applicable in N.Y. Canadian residents will be charged applicable taxes. Offer not valid in Quebec. This offer is limited to one order per household. Not valid for current subscribers to Harlequin Intrigue books. All orders subject to credit approval. Credit or debit balances in a customer's account(s) may be offset by any other outstanding balance owed by or to the customer. Please allow 4 to 6 weeks for delivery. Offer available while quantities last.

Your Privacy—The Reader Service is committed to protecting your privacy. Our Privacy Policy is available online at www.ReaderService.com or upon request from the Reader Service.

We make a portion of our mailing list available to reputable third parties that offer products we believe may interest you. If you prefer that we not exchange your name with third parties, or if you wish to clarify or modify your communication preferences, please visit us at www.ReaderService.com/consumerschoice or write to us at Reader Service Preference Service, P.O. Box 9062, Buffalo, NY 14240-9062. Include your complete name and address.

HI15

READERSERVICE.COM

Manage your account online!

- Review your order history
- Manage your payments
- Update your address

We've designed the Reader Service website just for you.

Enjoy all the features!

- Discover new series available to you, and read excerpts from any series.
- Respond to mailings and special monthly offers.
- Connect with favorite authors at the blog.
- Browse the Bonus Bucks catalog and online-only exculsives.
- Share your feedback.

Visit us at:

ReaderService.com

RS15